Inspiring Stories
for Young
Latter-day Saints

Inspiring Stories
for Young
Latter-day Saints

Compiled by Leon R. Hartshorn

Published by Deseret Book Co.
Salt Lake City, Utah
1975

Lithographed by

DESERET PRESS

in the United States of America

Contents

The Taming of Thunder

OTTO LEPPERT

When George Washington was eleven years old, his father died quite suddenly and unexpectedly.

Young George had to look after his younger brothers and his sister, Betty. Besides his studies, he spent much of his time on the Mount Vernon plantation hunting, fishing, and taking part in such active sports as swimming, wrestling, and foot and horse racing. His happiest times were when he could take his rifle and his dogs, mount his horse, and go hunting. George seemed to have a special fondness for pets of every description, and a visitor would always find a number of pet animals around the stable.

One day, when George was sixteen, his friend Billy Bustle, who was envious of his skill with horses after George had beaten him in a horse race, dared George to ride a wild stallion owned by Sam Wheeler, a horse dealer in Alexandria.

Billy said, "You think you are so smart that you can master any horse, but I challenge you to ride this unbroken animal. I have heard that he has thrown a dozen riders and now every man fears even to try and mount him."

"I accept your challenge," replied George. "I have confidence that I can tame any horse, no matter how spirited. You and I will ride over to Alexandria this afternoon, and I'll put my skill with horses to the test."

"Good," exclaimed Billy, "but I think you will meet your match this time, if what I have heard about this stallion is true."

Upon arriving at the outskirts of Alexandria, the two boys soon spotted Sam Wheeler's horse ranch. After George told him of his plan to ride the unbroken steed, Sam led the boys to the outer corral. On the way he cautioned George about the horse, saying, "I must remind you that this is a very spirited animal. He has never been ridden, and every man who has attempted to mount him has regretted it. However, he is not a mean horse. He is intelligent and has never kicked or trampled any man who has been thrown. In fact, you can approach him and perhaps even touch him, but as soon as you start to mount, he will rear and buck so violently that you will fly off the saddle. I warn you that you could be injured. Because of his wildness I have vowed to give him to anyone who can successfully ride him."

By this time they had reached the corral, and the horse stood before them. George could see that this was no ordinary animal, but a powerful, blue-blooded steed, more than sixteen hands high, with a glossy, reddish-brown coat, long mane, well-shaped neck, and large breadth of bone. His eyes were large, black, and expressive, and he looked imposing and unconquerable as he switched his tail, stamped his hoofs, and snorted in defiance as the men came near him. In all, he made a majestic-looking figure, with his fine combination of beauty and strength.

George exclaimed, "What a magnificent steed! If you will have your men saddle him, I'll mount and we'll soon see who is master."

Sam had his stablemen lead the horse into a small enclosure where he could not buck or rear. After a struggle they managed to put on a saddle and tighten the saddle girth.

George quickly lowered himself onto the animal's back and firmly grasped the reins. As soon as the enclosure gate was opened, the stallion dashed into the corral, bounding high into the air, crashing down swiftly, bucking wildly, and wheeling around in circles. George felt he would be thrown. He did not think he could continue to hold on at this furious pace. He knew his horsemanship was being tested as the powerful beast tried every way to dislodge him.

Gradually, the swift and violent tempo of the battle diminished as the horse tired. He reared, laid back his ears and showed his teeth, and breathed deeply with inflated nostrils. Then, letting out a scornful neigh, he began to paw the ground, puzzled because he was unable to throw off the rider.

At this point George called for the corral gates to be opened. With a great plunge and a flashing burst of speed, the stallion dashed out into the meadow, galloping swiftly with long, sure strides. George held the reins tightly as the wind whistled past and the landscape rushed by.

The amazed little group watched the horse and rider disappear into the distance while Sam remarked, "I sure hope George can stay in the saddle. He and the stallion make a good pair."

Some time later, when Sam was on the verge of sending some of his men out to look for George, who he feared had been thrown, they glimpsed a horse and rider approaching at a trot. Then George and the stallion came into clear view with the rider in full control.

Sam greeted George enthusiastically. "Congratulations, young man! You are now the owner of a full-blooded stallion."

George replied, "I cannot accept him, because I was dismounted on the way to Mount Vernon. I did manage to hold onto the reins, though, and I believe that he actually allowed me to remount!"

"No matter," said Sam, "you did subdue him, and he is now rightfully yours. How did you manage it?"

"He is a strong animal, with courage, intelligence, and great endurance," replied George. "I had to be firm and convince him that I was his master, and at the same time I had to make him realize that he had nothing to fear from me. I think I'll name him 'Thunder' after the booming sound of his hoofs on the road. I can assure you that he will receive good care. I'm sure that Thunder and I will become the best of friends."

The men were astonished to see the great change in the stallion that now stood quietly at George's side as he dismounted, playfully nipping his sleeve as if to say, "That was fun. Let's do it again!"

Children's Friend, February 1970.

A Strange Journey

THELMA J. HARRISON

It was a July night in 1963. Don Marshall, a Brigham Young University student who was touring Europe, sat in his hotel room in Innsbruck, Austria, planning the remainder of his trip. The time had come when he must plan definitely where he was going and when.

As Don planned, he decided his first stop would be Vienna. The second day he would travel into Yugoslavia and stay in Belgrade. The third night he would spend at the "Student House" in Skopje (pronounced Scopia). He planned the rest of his trip in this way.

However, before going to bed, Don knelt in prayer. His summer had been a wonderful one, and though he was traveling alone, he felt the Lord had ever been with him to guide him and make his travels more pleasant and meaningful.

As Don prayed, he told his Heavenly Father that though he had made a schedule of his own, he still wanted to travel under his Heavenly Father's direction and do the things he would have him do.

Early the next morning Don left Innsbruck, but strangely, he did not drive toward Vienna as he had planned. Instead he traveled down the Alps toward Venice, Italy. Why

Don drove to Venice he did not know. He had planned to visit Venice three weeks later. The trip was out of his way, taking precious time and costing extra money. Still he did not turn back. Somehow the direction in which he was going seemed right.

Late the night of Don's second day of travel, he arrived in Venice. He stayed only overnight; then he headed straight for Vienna to follow his original schedule. He arrived in Vienna late that night after sixteen hours of driving through rugged mountains. Wearily, he tumbled into bed.

The next morning, refreshed, he sat listening to the radio. In German, a language Don understood, he heard a sad and alarming report. During the night, the city of Skopje had been destroyed by a violent earthquake. Don reached for his schedule. Tears filled his eyes. If it hadn't been for his strange journey to Venice, he would have been staying in Skopje when the earthquake struck.

Three days later Don visited Skopje. He walked through the ruins of what had been the third largest city of Yugoslavia. Where was the "Student House"? Nowhere among the remaining buildings could he find it.

Later, Don met another student traveler. Don inquired, "What happened to the 'Student House' in Skopje?"

The traveler replied, "It was completely destroyed."

Children's Friend, July 1962.

Something to Drink

LUCILE C. READING

The boy tossed and turned with fever. His mother, Mrs. Smith, had tried in every way she knew to make him more comfortable, but George Albert hurt all over and was almost too weak to raise his head. He remembered how his mother had told him that once there had been two other children in the family but both of them had died. He wondered if he were going to die too. Somehow he knew that his mother was wondering the very same thing.

There were few doctors at that time in Salt Lake City, where George Albert lived, but his mother was able to get one to come to the house to tell her what was wrong with her boy and how to help him. The doctor said the boy had typhoid fever, which was a hard disease to cure in those days. He said George Albert was very ill and that even after he began to get better, he would have to stay in bed for at least three weeks. The doctor told Mrs. Smith that in the meantime, her son was to have no solid food but that he needed to drink a large quantity of liquids. The doctor suggested that she brew some coffee to give to the sick boy every little while.

George Albert had been taught that in the Word of Wis-

7

dom given by the Lord to Joseph Smith, all Latter-day Saints were advised not to use coffee. George Albert said he would drink a lot of water instead of coffee and he asked his mother to send for Brother Hawks, a ward teacher who called at their home each month.

Brother Hawks worked at the foundry, but as soon as he could get away he hurried over to the Smith home. Mrs. Smith told him of the doctor's suggestion about coffee. She told him that George Albert said he did not want to drink any coffee, but he knew that if Brother Hawks would give him a blessing, he would get well.

Brother Hawks looked down at the feverish boy who tossed uncomfortably on his bed. Then he placed his hands on the child's head and gave him a blessing, promising him that he would be well again very soon.

Early the next morning George Albert opened his eyes. He stirred in the bed, which felt cool and comfortable to him. He called his mother to tell her he felt fine and to ask if he could get up. A few days later when the doctor called at the Smith home to see his patient, he found him outside playing.

George Albert Smith died on his 81st birthday, April 4, 1951. He was the eighth President of The Church of Jesus Christ of Latter-day Saints. He often told the children of the Church the story of his recovery from typhoid fever. And always he added, "I was grateful to the Lord for my recovery. I am sure that he healed me."

Children's Friend, April 1966.

"I Shall Give Her a New Name"

BERNADINE BEATIE

'd feel safer about leaving if Beth were older, and much safer if she were a boy!" Father's chair made a small scraping noise as he pushed back from the supper table.

Beth understood. A rancher needed a son, especially in this wild frontier country of 1873. A boy going on fourteen could do almost as many things as a man.

"We'll be all right, Father." Mother rose and started clearing the table.

"Beth killed that old rattlesnake quicker 'n lightning!" Jim Bob piped up in his high six-year-old voice. "She's most as brave as you, Papa."

"She is that!" Mother smiled reassuringly at Beth. "I wouldn't trade her for any boy her age in the whole world."

Father caught at Beth's hair, hanging down her back in two fat reddish braids, and gave one braid a playful tug. "She'll do, I reckon, at least until Jim Bob grows up."

Tomorrow, Father was leaving to join the cattle drive headed for Abilene. Three years of drought had stripped their land of its rich prairie grasses, and day after day Beth had worried with her father, watching the thin, starved cattle pick listlessly at scrubby brush. Finally her father and the neighboring ranchers had decided to keep only foundation herds and drive the rest of their cattle to the Kansas railhead for shipment to eastern markets.

"The Indians have been peaceful enough, but I still hate to leave you three alone," Father said. "If there's any sign of trouble, you must ride to the Davis ranch."

"We will. Now you must quit worrying about us!" Mother smiled brightly.

The next morning, Beth stood at the gate with Mother and Jim Bob, watching Father and one of the Davis boys skillfully head the cattle toward Roundrock, where they were to join the drive.

"Ai-ai!" Father's voice rose above the bellowing of the hungry cattle. The swirling dust almost hid his figure, but Beth saw him raise his arm in farewell and heard his words, "Take care of your mother, Beth, and of Jim Bob!"

"I will! I will, Father!" Beth cried. A great happiness spread through her heart. Father's last words had been for her. He was depending on her to take care of Jim Bob and her mother!

Father had said he would be back at the end of three months, and the long, hot summer days passed slowly. There was not enough breeze to turn the windmill, so each day Beth and Jim Bob pumped water for the cattle when they straggled in from their hungry search for food.

One morning, after Father had been gone for almost two months, one of the Davis boys rode over. Several Indians had been sighted, he said, but he didn't think it was a war party. Still, he cautioned Beth and Jim Bob to lock up the cattle each night and to be on the lookout.

Beth awakened at dawn the next morning. She jumped up hardly believing her ears, for the sound of blessed, life-giving rain drummed on the roof.

Beth ran to her mother's room. Mother was tossing restlessly. "Mother," Beth whispered. She placed a hand on her mother's face and found it very warm. Mother was sick. What should she do?

Beth glanced out the window. Her breath caught in her

throat and her heart seemed to stop beating for a moment. Three Indian braves were squatting just out of rifle range, on a small rise in front of the house. They were motionless, staring silently at the house. Beth ducked back into the shadows of the room. Had they seen her? Did they know Father was away? She turned frightened eyes toward her mother.

"I know, Beth," her mother whispered weakly. "They have been there most of the night. You must take Jim Bob and slip out the back way. Go to the Davis ranch."

"We can't leave you, Mother," Beth cried. "Besides, they may be friendly."

"They're Comanches and they're wearing warpaint! I saw them clearly in a flash of lightning. They came quite close to my window. They are only waiting for daylight. You must take Jim Bob—you must go !" Mother pleaded.

"All right, Mother," Beth spoke soothingly. Father would not want her to leave Mother alone. Somehow she must get help! A plan formed in her mind. It might not work, but it was better than nothing.

Beth dropped a quick kiss on her mother's forehead and hurried to Jim Bob's room. When she shook him awake, told him of the Indians, and whispered her plan, Jim Bob nodded in frightened agreement.

"Are you sure you can find your way to the Davis ranch?" she asked.

"Yes. I'll hurry, too!" Jim Bob insisted stoutly.

Breathlessly, Beth watched Jim Bob crawl across the backyard to the barn. She sighed with relief when he came out again, leading Old Lightning and then moving as silently as the gray dawn, disappearing in the early morning darkness.

Mother was asleep. Beth tiptoed to the clothes chest in the corner of the room. She took out her father's long black coat and pulled it over her nightgown, then crammed her red braids beneath an old wide-brimmed hat. Her fingers trembled when they closed about an old rifle, unfireable because of a broken lever.

Beth opened the front door just a crack. The Indians sat motionless, staring at the house. Beth took a deep breath and stepped out on the porch. The lower part of her body was hidden by blocks of adobe that edged the porch to a height of about two feet. Swallowing the fear in her throat, Beth drew herself up as tall as possible, placed the rifle over her shoulder, and marched slowly across the porch. She turned and retraced her steps. Out of the corner of her eye, she watched the Indians. They remained as still as statues.

The longer she could delay an attack, the more time Jim Bob would have to bring help. Just then, Beth heard the sound of horses.

Two more Indians had ridden up and joined the others on the hill! The Indians were quarreling. Then one of the newly arrived Indians leveled a rifle at the squatting braves, while his companion slipped from his horse and bound the arms of the seated Indians.

The tall Indian, who seemed to be in command, handed his rifle to his friend and rode slowly toward Beth. He raised his hand in the sign of peace.

Beth's knees shook as she walked to the steps, placed the rifle at her feet, and raised a hand in greeting. When the Indian rode into the yard, Beth was startled to see how old and tired he looked. Yet, his face was kind and there was a twinkle way back in his dark eyes.

He looked at Beth's disheveled little figure. One of her braids had fallen down from beneath her father's hat, and her nightgown hung beneath the oversized coat, making her look even younger and smaller than she was.

The Indian spoke. "I am Ish-a-tai, chief of the Comanches. These three young braves are troublemakers; they have a sickness in their hearts!" A smile creased his face. "Now, I can cure that sickness forever!" Ish-a-tai raised his hand and motioned for the other Indians to join him.

The Indian with the rifle prodded the three bound braves to their feet and followed them down the hill and into the yard. Then the Indian who held the rifle threw back his head and roared with laughter.

Ish-a-tai spoke, and his words were like little pebbles falling sharply on rock. "If you leave the reservation in search of trouble again, I shall tell of your shame! I shall tell of how you trembled before a small brave woman-child with a broken rifle!"

Ish-a-tai turned to Beth. "You have saved your people and mine much sorrow and grief. Had you gone away, my braves would have stolen your cattle and they would have brought bloodshed and grief to my people."

"I—I couldn't leave. My mother is ill," Beth said.

"I will help." Ish-a-tai turned and walked into the house. Beth followed.

"It is the fever," Ish-a-tai said. "Bring hot water."

When Beth returned with the water, Ish-a-tai crumbled dry leaves and herbs into a cup. He placed the cup to her mother's lips and spoke soothingly. Mother opened her eyes and drank. In a few minutes her face was damp and cool, and she slept peacefully.

Then Beth heard the sound of running horses and many voices shouting and calling.

"Beth!" Jim Bob's voice called above the confusion.

Beth ran to the door and right into the arms of her father. Mother opened her eyes, smiled, and fell asleep again.

Then Father explained his early return. Cattle buyers had ridden out from Abilene to meet the drive. Father had received a good offer, sold his herd, and rushed home. He had just arrived at the Davis ranch when Jim Bob had ridden up. Father turned to Ish-a-tai. "I thank you for protecting my wife and my daughter," he said warmly.

Ish-a-tai's old eyes twinkled. "I shall give her a new name, an Indian name. Beth Braveheart!" He smiled at Father. "It is good to have such a daughter. She is almost as good as a son."

Father placed a hand on Beth's shoulders. "We wouldn't trade her for any son her age in the whole world." He smiled proudly down into Beth's eyes.

Beth blinked back a rush of tears. It would not do for Ish-a-tai to see tears in the eyes of Beth Braveheart!

Children's Friend, August 1963.

"I Knew You'd Come"

AUTHOR UNKNOWN

Listen to the story of the soldier who asked his officer if he might go out into the "No-Man's Land" between the trenches to bring in one of his comrades who lay grievously wounded.

"You can go," said the officer, "but it's not worth it. Your friend is probably killed, and you will throw your own life away." But the man went. Somehow, he managed to get to his friend, hoist him onto his shoulder, and bring him back to the trenches. The two of them tumbled together to the bottom of a trench. The officer looked very tenderly on the would-be rescuer, and then he said, "I told you it wouldn't be worth it. Your friend is dead, and you are wounded."

"It was worth it though, sir."

"How do you mean 'worth it'? I tell you, your friend is dead."

"Yes, sir," the boy answered, "but it was worth it, because when I got to him he said, 'I knew you'd come.'"

General Boards of the Primary Association and Sunday School (comp.), *A Story to Tell* (Deseret Book Co., 1971).

14

"He Honest Man"

JACOB HAMBLIN, JR.

When I was about twelve years old our family lived in Kanab, Utah. A band of Piute Indians were camped a few miles away, across the wash. My father, Jacob Hamblin, the Indian missionary, said to me, "Son, I want you to go to the Indian camp this afternoon and trade that little bay pony for some blankets, which we will need this winter."

When the midday meal was over I climbed astride old Billy the horse and, leading the little bay pony, rode across the flat toward the Indian camp.

When I rode in, the chief helped me off the horse and asked, "You Jacob's boy. What you want?"

When I told him my errand, he looked at the trade pony and grunted his assent. He led me to his wigwam, where there was a pile of hand-woven Indian blankets. He pulled out a number of them. Determined to show my father that I was a good trader, I asked for another blanket. The chief looked at me out of the corner of his eye and added another blanket to my pile. Then I asked for another and another and still another. By now the chief was grinning broadly, but he continued to add as many blankets as I demanded.

Satisfied that I had made a really good trade, I closed the

15

deal. The chief piled the blankets on the back of old Billy and lifted me up.

Father met me in the yard and looked at the blankets. Then he made two piles of about equal size. One pile he placed on the horse and put me back on, saying, "Go back and give these to the chief. You got enough blankets for two ponies."

As I approached the camp, I could see the old chief. When I rode up, he laughed and said, "I know Jacob send you back. He honest man. He my father as well as your father."

Several years later when Jacob was alone with a band of angry hostile Indians, the fact that he had always been honest with them saved his life.

A Story to Tell (Deseret Book Co., 1971).

Lightning Came Down the Chimney

HAROLD B. LEE

One day, my grandmother, my mother, and two or three of the younger children were seated before an open door, watching the great display of nature's fireworks as a severe thunderstorm raged near the mountain where our home was located. A flash of lightning followed by an immediate loud clap of thunder indicated that the lightning had struck very close.

I was standing in the doorway when, suddenly and without warning, my mother gave me a vigorous push that sent me sprawling on my back out of the doorway. At that instant, a bolt of lightning came down the chimney of the kitchen stove, raced through the open doorway, and split a huge gash from top to bottom in a large tree immediately in front of the house. If I had remained in the door opening, I wouldn't be writing this story today.

My mother could never explain her split-second decision. All I know is that my life was spared because of her impulsive, intuitive action.

Years later, when I saw the deep scar on that large tree at the old family home, I could only say, from a grateful heart, Thank the Lord for that precious gift possessed in abundant measure by my own mother and by many other faithful mothers, through whom heaven can be very near in time of need.

During my young boyhood, there were many occasions when mother's instructive and intuitive understanding prompted her to know that help was needed. Once on a stormy night she directed my father to go and search for me, only to find that my horse had stumbled and thrown me into a pool of half-frozen mud. My mother had known that help was needed.

Someone has coined a statement that has great significance: "God could not be everywhere, and therefore he made mothers."

Within every child born into the world there is a heavenly gift. The Lord has revealed that this is the Light of Christ, or the Light of Truth. Even in early childhood, this gift gives to every person the ability to tell the difference between what is right and of the Lord and what is wrong and of the world. Sometimes we call this our conscience, or the voice of the Spirit of God within us.

Following baptism and as a blessing from the elders of the Church, we are given another gift—the gift of the Holy Ghost. As explained by the Master, this is to teach us that we may know the truth of all things, to bring all things to our remembrance, and to even show us things to come.

When one becomes a father or a mother, it is especially important that he or she prepares to receive, through these wonderful gifts from the Lord, the great gift of understanding necessary to rear children and make certain they are taught properly as commanded by the Lord. These heaven-sent instructions or warnings parents receive for their families might be called intuition or the voice of the Lord coming into their minds to safeguard their homes. Parents have the responsibility of teaching and training in correct principles. Then when children are old enough and have the stability and responsibility to make mature judgments and right decisions, they will have received proper teaching from wise parents in the homes from which they have come.

From my experience, it would seem that faithful mothers have a special gift that we often refer to as mother's intuition. Perhaps, with the great blessings of motherhood, our Heavenly Father has endowed them with this quality, since fathers, busy in priesthood callings and earning a livelihood, never draw quite as close to heavenly beings in matters that relate to the more intimate details of bringing up children in the home. It might be described in this way: Father is the head, but Mother is the heart, of the family home.

The Friend, November 1971.

The Hidden Furs

FRED VAN DYKE

Angie sat on a braided rug in front of the hearth, rereading a worn primer. Her father walked in with a small box of clean furs and dropped them beside the fireplace.

"I'll sort the furs when I come in from milking," he told Angie. "Tomorrow, I'll take the furs to the general store at Mills Landing. There, I'll trade them for the items your mother needs. On the way home, I'll stop at Tom Jenkins' place and buy a milking cow."

Angie knew how badly they needed another cow. Her mother had been waiting for the fur money to buy flour, sugar, spices, and canned goods for the winter months.

Angie also thought about the leatherbound book of poems that she had seen a few months before on the shelf at the general store. That day in the store she had shown her mother the book and told her how much she would like to have it.

"It is lovely," her mother had commented, "but your father has to buy boots today. We won't have money to buy it."

Angie couldn't forget the book. She wanted to have the poems to read in the evening by lamplight. In the spring she

20

could read through the day while she sat and tended the smokehouse fire. She imagined sitting out under the willow tree on summer evenings and reading. Someday she hoped to be a schoolteacher; then she could read the poems to her students.

Angie pictured the book as she heard her father carrying the milk pails down the slope toward the barn. Her mother stood beside the cookstove, frying meat for supper.

The hearth logs crackled loudly as the fire burned vigorously. The heat became so intense that Angie decided to go up to the loft and read from the fading daylight that came in from the small window above her bed. She had just settled herself comfortably when she heard horses galloping into the yard. Startled, she turned and looked through the window. Two rough-looking men, dressed in deerskin jackets and carrying rifles, dismounted. There was not time to warn her mother.

Terrified, Angie started to hide under her bed. Then she thought of the furs. If the men stole the furs, there would be no money for the cow or for all the things her mother needed.

Angie flew down the ladder, her primer clutched in her hand. She landed beside the furs. Quickly, she sat down on the furs and spread her skirt out until there wasn't a fur in sight. With shaky hands, she opened her book and pretended to read. She had no more than opened the book when the two unshaven men pushed open the door. Holding their shotguns, they stepped into the kitchen.

Mother stepped back from the stove, her face drained of all color. Remaining speechless, she saw what Angie had done.

"You two, don't move," the first man warned. "We don't aim to hurt you. We saw your husband down at the river no more than two days ago. We'll search for those furs he had."

Angie was too frightened to speak. But it would have been hopeless for either to have called out. Father was out in the barn and would be unable to hear with the door closed.

Seeing nothing in the first room, the shorter man in dirty

boots scrambled up the ladder to the loft. Angie heard him overturning things above her in the loft. The bigger man ransacked the adjoining bedroom.

"The furs are not in here," the first man announced. "We'll search the smokehouse and barn." The intruders stomped out of the house without closing the door.

"Don't move until you're certain they're gone," Angie's mother warned, as she shut the door. "They won't find the furs outside. I don't imagine they'll give your father any trouble. Besides, he'll handle the situation if they go to the barn."

Angie listened without moving. Then she heard the men's horses galloping off toward the east.

Immediately, her father burst inside, looking angry and worried. Seeing that his wife and daughter were all right, he said, "I'm thankful you're unharmed! Did they get the furs?"

"The furs are safe," Mother informed him, "thanks to Angie!" Then she told him how Angie had hidden the furs.

Father looked down at Angie. "You have a lot of courage, daughter, and you acted fast. I'm proud of you. We won't be bothered again. Those two will be riding off in search of bigger profits. Tomorrow when I take the furs to Mills Landing, I'd like to take you with me. I'll buy—what was it you wanted the last time we were in the store?"

"A book of poems," Angie said, "but you need the money for the cow and Mother's things."

"Well," Father commented, "if you hadn't saved our furs, we wouldn't have any money at all. We'll buy the book."

"Tomorrow evening," Mother added, "Angie can read us some poems from her new book."

"I will," Angie said, her eyes shining.

Children's Friend, January 1969.

Apaches

C.D.

About the year 1885, Brother Z. B. Decker was living with his family on a ranch about twenty-five miles from any settlement. He kept a small herd of sheep that his twelve-year-old son, Louis, watched during the day; at night they were left in a bunch on the hill, where they could be seen from the house.

One day Inez asked if she might go with her brother to watch the sheep. Since Louis always took his lunch and stayed all day, Sister Decker hesitated, but as he expressed a desire to have his little sister with him, their mother at last consented.

The sheep moved from their camping ground at sunrise, and the children started after them. Inez carried the well-filled lunchbasket that their mother had prepared, and Louis carried his big gun, which he always took with him.

While the sheep were grazing the children sat under a tree and read from a book they had brought with them and played jacks and other games; and when the sheep moved, they followed them. Thus the forenoon passed before they realized it. They were very much interested in a story Louis was reading when he happened to think about his sheep and looked up to see where they were. "I can't see one of the sheep," he said, springing to his feet. Then, looking at the sun, he exclaimed, "Why, it is nearly noon! We must have been here a long time. I wonder where the sheep have gone."

Inez was just going to speak when a terrible yell was heard that made the children turn pale.

"It's Indians," exclaimed Louis, "and they will be driving the sheep."

Then, noticing his sister's white face, he tried to convince her that there was no danger if they were brave. Putting his arm around her he said gently, "Don't be afraid, Inez, they won't hurt us if we can make them think we are not afraid of them."

His words encouraged her, but she could tell that he was frightened, for his voice trembled; she also knew his fears were mostly for her safety.

As he was telling her that he would put her in a safe place and would then go to see where the Indians were driving the sheep, six Apaches on horseback came in sight from the direction in which the sheep had gone. There was no chance to hide now, and as the Indians were coming straight toward them, they could do nothing but stand and face the foe.

Louis stood with his gun, which was as tall as he, in his hand, and his timid little sister stood as near him as she dared to, trying not to appear to be frightened.

The Indians shouted to each other as they hurried their horses along toward the frightened children, whose courage almost gave way when one Indian who seemed to be the chief called to two others behind him and they stopped to load their guns.

Just then a happy thought came to Inez, and she whispered to her brother, "Let us ask the Lord to keep them from hurting us." Louis nodded assent, and the two whispered a prayer for safety.

By this time the chief had stopped his horse in front of them. He spoke English so that they could understand him. He asked in a gruff tone if they were not afraid, where their home was, and if it was their herd of sheep he had seen.

Louis answered all the questions as bravely as he could. Then the chief jumped off his horse, walked up to the boy, and asked him for his gun.

"No, you can't have it," said Louis with as much courage as he could muster. The Indian was going to take the gun by force, but the boy's determination surprised him, and he decided to let the boy keep the gun. This was a great relief to the children, for they knew that the Apaches took a special delight in shooting people with their own guns.

Then the chief tried to get Louis to give him a sheep. Louis told him he could have one if he would pay for it, but the chief said he would not do that, and in an irritated manner he turned to his braves, who talked with him a moment.

Turning again to the children, the chief asked for their lunch. Louis took the basket from his sister and handed it to him. He divided the contents among his companions, leaving a small portion for the children.

As soon as the Indians had eaten their portion, the old chief sprang into his saddle and they all galloped off. The children did not speak a word till the Indians were out of sight. Then Louis turned to Inez, who stood almost paralyzed, and said, "Now, sister, didn't I tell you they wouldn't hurt us? But I'm glad they have gone, aren't you?"

She could only say, "Our prayers were answered." Then she began to cry. When she had dried her tears, her brother took her by the hand and led her in the direction the sheep had gone. When they reached home that night they related their experience and told of their simple prayer for safety. To their parents, it was a most miraculous escape.

Juvenile Instructor, March 15, 1902.

Tell Me About Columbus

MARGERY CANNON

Adventurous boys today often think about flying through space to explore the moon or Mars. But five hundred years ago, boys didn't think about exploring space; they dreamed of sailing the ocean in search of new lands.

Christopher Columbus was an adventurous lad, born about five hundred years ago in Genoa, Italy. In the mornings he helped his father, who was a weaver. But in the afternoon, when he had finished preparing the wool for weaving, Christopher would hurry down to the waterfront. There he watched ships being built and talked to sailors about their adventures.

Even at home he thought about ships.

"Someday I will have one of my own. Then I can sail away and explore the world," he said.

This worried his younger brother, Bartholomew, who had heard people call the ocean the "Sea of Darkness."

"Sailors are gobbled up by monsters or burned alive in boiling hot water," he cautioned Christopher.

People then didn't know much about the ocean or the shape of the earth. Some even believed the world was flat like a pancake, and that ships that sailed very far away would lose their way in the darkness and fall over the edge, never to be seen again.

But Christopher Columbus did not believe this was so. Many sea captains and learned men had said the world wasn't flat, but round; they knew there were no such things as monsters and dragons waiting to swallow ships. Christopher was not afraid, and he planned to become a sailor.

Sometimes fishermen would take Christopher on short fishing trips at night. This made him even more eager for a life at sea.

Then one day, when he was about fourteen years old, he went on his first real voyage. It wasn't a long one, but it was the beginning of his life as a seaman. He continued to help his father in the weaving shop, but whenever possible he went on sailing trips along the coast of Italy.

On these trips he learned everything he could about ships and maps and astronomy because of his dream to sail to distant lands. When he turned twenty-two, he became a full-time sailor.

Columbus once wrote: "From my youth onward I was a seaman, and have continued until this day. Wherever ships have been, I have been. I have spoken and treated with learned men, priests, and laymen, Latins, Greeks, Jews, and Moors, and with many men of other faiths. The Lord has well disposed to my desire, and He bestowed upon me courage and understanding. Knowledge of seafaring he gave me in abundance; of astrology as much as was needed, and of geometry and astronomy likewise. Further, he gave me joy and cunning in drawing maps and thereon cities, mountains, rivers, islands and harbors, each one in its place."

Columbus married a captain's daughter, and they had a son named Diego. When Columbus's wife died, he married again and had a second son, whom he named Ferdinand. Like his father, Ferdinand also loved ships. When he was between twelve and eighteen, Ferdinand went on several voyages with Columbus.

He later wrote a book about his famous father. This is the way he described him:

"The Admiral was a well-built man of more than medium

stature, long visaged with cheeks somewhat high, but neither fat nor thin. He had an aquiline nose and his eyes were light in color; his complexion too was light, but kindling to a vivid red. In youth his hair was blond, but when he came to his thirtieth year it all turned white. In eating and drinking and the adornment of his person, he was always content and modest. Among strangers his conversation was affable, and with members of his household very pleasant, but with a modest and pleasing dignity."

Christopher Columbus was a religious man. In his journals he tells about his regular private prayers several times a day.

There were also religious ceremonies held on board ship for the sailors. These services were performed by the youngest seamen.

Columbus heard about Marco Polo and his travels. He began to think more and more about exploring new lands as Marco Polo had done. At that time, the only way to reach China and the other strange new lands Marco Polo had seen two hundred years before was to sail around the coast of Africa. There was much talk of finding a shorter way. Columbus studied his maps. He knew the world was round. Surely he could sail west, all the way around the world, until he reached the Indies in the Far East. He talked about his plan and said, "I have seen and truly studied all books, cosmographies, histories, chronicles, and philosophies, and other arts for which our Lord with provident hand unlocked my mind."

It was several years, however, before Columbus could find someone who would help him with his plans. Queen Isabella of Spain finally agreed.

On August 3, 1942, Columbus left the port of Palos, Spain, with three small wooden ships—*Nina, Pinta,* and *Santa Maria.*

Columbus felt the importance of his voyage. He said, "The Lord sent me upon the seas, and gave me fire for the deed. Those who heard of my enterprise called it foolish, mocked me and laughed. But who can doubt but that the Holy Ghost inspired me?"

Ferdinand quotes his father as also saying: "God gave me the faith and afterwards the courage so that I was quite willing to undertake the journey."

Children's Friend, October 1970.

A Special Birthday Present

LUCILE C. READING

It was a warm autumn day in Salt Lake City, and the neighborhood children were all enjoying the last few days before the beginning of school. Ruth Ann and her friend had spent the morning under a big shade tree playing with their dolls.

At lunch that noon, Ruth Ann asked her mother, "Why didn't you tell me that today is President David O. McKay's birthday? He is our very own neighbor, and I'd have given him a present."

"I'm sorry, Ruth Ann," her mother answered. "I thought you had heard us talking about him being seventy-nine years old today." Then she smiled as she added, "But I wouldn't worry about a present for him. He'll receive so many that he probably wouldn't even know it if you did give him one."

Ruth Ann ate her lunch in thoughtful silence. A few minutes later Mother looked out the window in time to see Ruth Ann and Sandy talking earnestly about something. But it was nearly two weeks later before she thought again of the incident. That was the evening the phone rang and a woman's voice asked, "Do you have a daughter named Ruth Ann? I have a letter for her and want to be sure it reaches the right little girl."

30

The very next day the mailman brought an envelope with two letters inside it. One letter was for Sandy and the other was for Ruth Ann. Ruth Ann, who was only eight and couldn't read it by herself, listened with growing excitement as her mother began:

> Dear Miss Barker and Miss Davis:
>
> When Sister McKay and I returned from Los Angeles last evening we found awaiting us some flowers and a box of peaches with a note "from Ruth Ann Barker and Sandra Davis—Happy Birthday." Whether you sent the flowers or the peaches, we do not know, so we are thanking you both. . . .

As Mother continued to read the letter to Ruth Ann, the little girl's eyes grew big and bright in delighted wonderment to think that a great and busy man would take the time to write to two little girls who had remembered his birthday.

The letter was signed, "David O. McKay, President of the Church of Jesus Christ of Latter-day Saints." It was dated September 22, 1952.

Children's Friend, September 1966.

Three Indian Braves

ARVIS LAVERNE ROGERS

I was born at Kanosh, Utah, June 17, 1878. When I was four years old my father was called to leave his home and help settle in Arizona.

As I was growing up I learned to cook and sew and keep house and do the things girls should do. My mother was an excellent teacher, and when I grew older I used to work out for people.

It was while I was working with my aunt and uncle, who ran a boarding house at the mines, that I met George Samuel Rogers. He drove to the mines with loads of hay and watermelons. He would make the trip about every two weeks. This was in 1895. After I moved back home I started going with him and we were married at my home by Collins R. Hakes, my grandfather, on January 8, 1896.

In August 1897 we traveled to St. George by team and wagon. It was a hard trip and took us seven weeks. On the way home we found the water was so high in the river we had to camp for a week, waiting for the water to go down so we could ferry the wagon across. We came through Flagstaff and camped about five miles out in the pine trees. We had had our evening meal and were prepared for bed.

32

While we were kneeling in prayer we heard this terrible whooping and yelling and thundering of horses' hooves. The temptation was just too great, and I couldn't resist taking a peek. I turned my head just enough so I could look out the corner of my eye. My heart beat about three times faster than it should, for three Indian braves, all painted, were riding in on us just as hard as they could ride.

How he did it I will never know, but George, not even hesitating to take a peek, just kept right on praying and asking Heavenly Father to protect us from these Indians. They rode right to the wagons before they reined up. They were so close we could almost feel the breath of the horses as they stopped. The Indians looked in and saw George praying; then they gave a whoop, whirled their horses around and left. We could hear them yelling as they rode away.

Needless to say, we had a great deal to be thankful for that night. We were later told that Indians are very superstitious about people praying, and that was probably why they left without bothering us at all. We knew that the Lord had answered our prayers as he had done so many times before.

Roberta Flake Clayton, comp., *Pioneer Women of Arizona* (Mesa, Arizona, 1969).

Prayer Rock

RUTH WALKER

Prior to the close of the century, pioneers were called from their newly made homes in Utah to colonize the Big Horn Basin in Wyoming. With heavy hearts they contemplated making new homes in this wild, dry land of sagebrush and badlands. A canal must be built to carry water to the parched land.

Directly in line with the surveyed ditch, a huge rock towered high in the air. There was a crevice in that part of the rock which stood above the ground. How far this crevice continued no one could tell, but the rock must be moved.

The general manager, Byron Sessions, said that with the help of all the available young boys of about fourteen years of age, the rock could be moved by the time the ditch was dug that far. The extra horses and slipscrapers were handled by these boys. They scraped and hauled the dirt away from around the base of this huge rock, exposing more and more of its surface.

One night Brother Sessions could not sleep. He worried for fear some of the boys might be crushed should this mighty rock fall while they were at work. At dawn he kneeled by the rock and prayed earnestly for wisdom and for protection for the boys.

He returned to camp and ate breakfast; then he and the boys returned to work as usual. About ten o'clock he was impressed to call all the teams away from the work. The last team was scarcely away before the rock began to move. The crevice opened and the rock fell apart, leaving a channel for the canal to pass through. Not a soul was injured. The pioneers very humbly and gratefully thanked Heavenly Father for his protecting care.

This rock has ever since been known as Prayer Rock.

Children's Friend, July 1941.

An Indian Never Forgets

MARY PRATT PARRISH

It was a lazy day in August. The sun was hot, and Tommy and Elija were lying on the ground near the creek, enjoying the shade of a big cottonwood tree. They had been assigned to watch the thirty head of cattle, which were grazing a half mile upstream.

"Herding cattle might be important," said Tommy, "but it isn't very exciting."

Just then the cattle started to low. The boys heard them moving around as if they were frightened. "Something is bothering them," said Elija. "Let's see what it is."

In a moment the two boys were running toward the cattle, but they stopped short when they saw a small band of Indians coming toward them. They had no way of knowing whether or not they were friendly, but Tommy knew that the Omaha Indians had given the Mormon pioneers permission to camp on their land for the winter and to use their water and their timber.

When the boys came within talking distance, a young Indian stepped forward and spoke to them in halting English. "Last night our enemies, the Iowas, attacked our camp. All of our men except Chief Big Head and I were on a hunting trip. The Iowas took our horses and all of our food. They wounded many women and children. Chief Big Head they left for dead. He will die if he does not get help."

Tommy looked down on the willow bed that the Indians had made for their chief. What he saw made him want to close his eyes.

"I'll go for help," he said.

"I'll go with you," said Elija.

The young Indian put his arm across Elija's chest to keep him from going. "You stay here till boy gets back."

Tommy knew that Elija's safety depended on his speedy return, so he ran almost all of the two miles to Winter Quarters.

He went at once to the home of his bishop and told him what had happened. "The Indians really need help," he concluded, "and they're keeping Elija with them to make sure I bring it back."

Bishop Morley listened quietly; then he put his arm around the boy to comfort him while he thought about what to do. "We must find Brigham Young," he decided. "He might be down at the ferry. You take my horse and ride down there as fast as you can. In the meantime I will look around here."

The ferry was twelve miles away, and it took Tommy an hour to get there. When he arrived, he found Brigham Young and told him his story.

"We will help the Indians, of course," Brigham Young said, "but our first concern is for Elija. You must get back to him as soon as possible. Take your wagon and ask Bishop Morley to take his. These two wagons should be enough to bring the badly wounded to Winter Quarters. I'll meet you at my house."

Bishop Morley was waiting for Tommy. They took the two wagons and went to get Elija and the Indians.

When they came to the camp, Elija ran up and began talking to Tommy. "At first they were afraid I would run away," said Elija, "but when I took off my shirt and wet it in the creek so I could cool the forehead of Chief Big Head, they knew I could be trusted."

"I'm so glad you are all right," Tommy said.

Bishop Morley and the young Indian helped Chief Big Head into Tommy's wagon, and the boys started back to Winter Quarters. The other Indians who were badly wounded were put into the Morley wagon. The rest of the Indians walked beside it.

The sun was almost setting when the wagons arrived at the home of Brigham Young. He soon determined that the Indian chief would need special care. He turned to Tommy and said, "Please go and ask your mother if she could take Chief Big Head into her home and nurse him back to health."

Tommy was off in a flash. He returned in a few minutes with his mother, who said, "Of course, I'll take care of him."

Brigham Young smiled and said, "You won't be sorry. An Indian never forgets a kindness."

The weeks that followed were anxious ones for Tommy and his mother. Chief Big Head was very sick and needed constant care. Either Tommy or his mother stayed day and night by his side. Then one day, without any warning, the Indian got out of bed. "Chief Big Head well," he declared. "I must go to my people." That night he left Winter Quarters and took with him all of the other Indians.

Some time after this, Tommy was so sick with black canker that his mother was afraid he was not going to get well. Unexpectedly, Chief Big Head came to their door and handed Tommy's mother some horseradish. "Grind this," he said, "and make tea for boy. It will make him well." Without even waiting to be thanked, the Indian turned and left.

The horseradish did help Tommy. Afterwards, many who had black canker, a form of scurvy, were given horseradish tea as medicine, and it helped to save their lives too.

"Chief Big Head didn't forget, did he, Mother," Tommy said one day.

His mother answered, "No, Tommy, and neither will we."

The Friend, September 1971.

He Was an Unusual Boy

MATTHEW COWLEY

A few weeks ago I was called to the County Hospital in Salt Lake City by a mother. I didn't know her. She said her boy was dying from polio and asked if I would come down and give him a blessing. I picked up a young bishop whom I generally take with me, for I think his faith is greater than mine, and I always like him along. We went down there and found the young lad in an iron lung, unconscious, his face rather a blackish color, with a tube in his throat. He had been flown in from an outlying community. The mother said to me, "This is an unusual boy—not because he's my child, but he is an unusual boy." I think he was eight or nine years of age.

After the hospital attendants put coverings on us, we went into the room and blessed the boy. It was one of those occasions when I knew as I laid my hands upon him that he was an unusual boy, and he had faith. Having faith in his faith, I blessed him to get well and promised him he would. I didn't hear any more about him until last Sunday. I was on my way to Murray to conference, so I dropped in at the County Hospital and asked if I might see the lad. The nurse said, "Certainly. Walk right down the hall." As I walked down the hall, out came the boy running to meet me. He ran up and asked, "Are you Brother Cowley?"

And I said, "Yes."

He said, "I want to thank you for that prayer." He added, "I was unconscious then, wasn't I?"

I replied, "You certainly were."

He said, "That's the reason I don't recognize you." Then he said, "Come in my room. I want to talk to you."

We went in the room. He still had a tube in his throat, and I said, "How long are you going to have that tube there?"

He said, "Two weeks. Two more weeks, and then I'll be all well. How about another blessing?"

I said, "Certainly," and blessed him again.

I was in a hurry, for I wanted to get out to my conference, but the lad stopped me and asked, "Hey, how about my partner in the next bed?" There was a young fellow about sixteen or seventeen.

I said, "What do you mean?"

He said, "Don't go without blessing him. He's my partner."

I said, "All right." Then I asked the boy, "Would you like a blessing?"

He said, "Yes, sir. I'm a teacher in the Aaronic Priesthood in my ward." I blessed him, and then my little friend went and brought another fellow in. Here was another partner. And I blessed him.

Now, except ye believe as a child, you can't receive these blessings.

Brigham Young University *Speeches of the Year*, February 18, 1953.

The Test

DOROTHY PIERCE LEHMAN

David pedaled furiously. Why did he stay to pitch that last game? On collection night of all times, when it would take twice as long to do his paper route!

He'd never get out to Perch Lake in time for the Scout meet if he took time to make all his collections.

As sorry as his mother was, she could not keep from saying, "If you had come directly home from school, you might have made it in time. If you hurry you still might be able to get there in time for the tests."

David put the papers into his bicycle basket and sadly swung into his seat. He pedaled gloomily along until a page of the Scout handbook flashed into his mind.

"8. A Scout is always cheerful. He smiles whenever he can. His obedience to orders is prompt and cheery. He never shirks or grumbles at hardships."

He started to whistle.

I'm not fooling anyone—not even myself, he thought, and he broke off his whistling abruptly.

He'd do his duty but being cheerful was just a little too much to ask—with his chance of passing the advancement test as good as gone.

The test was on first aid. He practically knew the handbook word for word. He'd practiced on his father. He had next picked his sister, Judy, for his victim.

A lot of good it had done to work so hard to become letter perfect! He'd be an old man with a long gray beard before he would get to be an Eagle Scout!

He turned in at Mrs. McNary's gate. Instead of an airy, practiced fling of paper to the porches tonight, he'd have to stop and ring doorbells for people who would take their time to answer—and some would not be home at all.

He caught sight of Mrs. McNary in her little garden plot.

"Oh, David, I'll come right in," she said. "I put your money out for you in the kitchen."

Good! David thought. If everyone would be as prompt, he might get out to the lake in time for the tests.

"Oh, David, could you carry these tomatoes in?" She had a big basket of green tomatoes. "I know they are green, but they will make good pickles. There's going to be a frost tonight, and they won't ripen after that."

David picked up the basket of tomatoes. A reputation for being obliging did have its drawbacks.

"Oh, David," Mrs. McNary stopped again. "Do you know whether your mother puts cinnamon in her tomato pickles? I seem to have lost my recipe."

David had to confess that his training had not included making green tomato pickles.

The next stop was Mrs. Stannard's. He'd make quick work of that; she was not the talkative type.

Mrs. Stannard came to the door promptly and offered David a five-dollar bill!

"I don't have change, Mrs. Stannard," he told her. "Just let it go until next week."

"No," said Mrs. Stannard. "I don't like to have unpaid bills. I'll get the change." And she was off across the lawn to her neighbors' home, leaving David to wait.

He was luckier on the next five stops. And then he came to the Lawrence home.

As she came to the door, Mrs. Lawrence was good-natured as always.

"Oh, David, could you wait a minute until I take my cookies out of the oven? I don't want them to scorch."

Mrs. Lawrence took the cookies out of the oven and off the pan, and put another batch in the oven. Finally she came with the money and three warm cookies wrapped in wax paper. "Thank you," David said.

He gave up trying to hurry. He just made his stops with dogged patience. He didn't even fuss when he had to stop to fix his loose bicycle chain.

Finally, there were only two more collections—the Sayners and the Brinks. The Brinks were the young couple with the cute baby who lived in an apartment in the Sayners' big house.

Little Susan was the baby. She always had a big smile for David. David liked pretty and friendly Mrs. Sayner.

The scene in the Sayners' front hall made David forget all about his fussing. Mrs. Sayner had run out to meet Mrs. Brink, who was dashing down the stairs with Susan in her arms.

"She fell out of her high chair," sobbed Mrs. Brink, "and I can't get her to breathe!"

The baby lay blue-lipped in her mother's arms.

"Let me try," said Mrs. Sayner. "No, keep trying while I call Dr. Bennett."

A page of the *Scout Handbook* flashed before David's eyes. "Save the seconds and you have a better chance of saving a life. Go to work instantly where you are."

Little Susan showed no signs of breathing—the precious seconds were going fast!

"Mrs. Brink," said David, "maybe I can make her breathe."

"Oh, David," said Mrs. Brink, seeing him for the first time, "can you?"

David's head was clear and cool. He laid the baby face up on the living room floor and raised her chin up. He pinched her nose closed and then leaned over and blew gently into her mouth. He waited a moment for the air to return and then blew again.

Mrs. Brink watched with a prayer in her eyes.

Mrs. Sayner was back, saying, "Dr. Bennett is coming as fast as he can."

Suddenly a faint breath fluttered past Susan's little blue lips—another—and then a cry that was music to her mother's ears.

David stood up and let Susan's mother pick her up. "Oh, David! David!" Mrs. Sayner hugged him. "What could we have done without you?"

For once David didn't mind being fussed over—that was just women's ways!

"Well, I guess I'd better be going," he said.

Just then Dr. Bennett came hurrying up the porch steps. Mrs. Sayner and Mrs. Brink gave him an account of what had happened, and Dr. Bennett seemed to understand. He examined Susan carefully, but he could find no injuries.

"She lost her breath from the fall and fright," he said, "but you were mighty lucky that this young man happened along."

"Oh, I just remembered our Scout lesson."

David rode home along quiet shaded streets feeling strangely peaceful and elated at the same time. He didn't even worry about what the troop was doing.

He gave his mother an account of what had happened while he was eating his late supper.

"Oh, David!" she said with misty eyes, "and to think I was feeling sorry that you had to miss your Scout meet!"

The next morning when David was counting his collection money, the telephone rang.

"For you, David!" called Judy. "I think it's Mr. Jordan."

She stayed close by and heard David say, "Well, I just tried to remember the way I had practiced. Oh, thank you, Mr. Jordan! I surely appreciate that! Good-bye."

"What was it, David?" Judy asked.

"Dr. Bennett told Mr. Jordan about Susan, and he'll pass me without taking the test. Isn't that great?"

Children's Friend, March 1966.

"I Know That My Father Will Go"

ELIZABETH CLARIDGE McCUNE

No place on earth seemed so precious to me at fifteen years of age as dear old Nephi, Utah. How eagerly we looked forward to the periodical visits of President Brigham Young and his company! Everything was done that could be thought of for their comfort and entertainment, and with all, it was a labor of love.

One of these visits I shall never forget.

We went out with our Sabbath Schools and all the other organizations, with bands of music and flags and banners and flowers, to meet and greet our beloved leader and his company. On this occasion the people were lined up on each side of the street waiting for the carriages to pass. Among them were twenty-five young ladies dressed in white, who had strewn evergreens and wild flowers along the path. Brother Brigham, Brothers Kimball and Wells,* with the entire company, got out of their carriages and walked over the flowery road. When Brother Kimball passed me he said

---

*The First Presidency of the Church—Brigham Young, Heber C. Kimball, and Daniel H. Wells.

45

to the group of girls around me, "You five girls right here will live to be mothers in Israel."

The company having been taken to our home, the dinner was served. How we girls flew around to make everything nice for the stylish city folks! As soon as they were seated at dinner, we slipped upstairs and tried on all the ladies' hats. That was a real treat. I venture to say that could the ladies have seen us next Sunday they would have been struck with the similarity of styles in Nephi and Salt Lake City millinery.

We all attended the afternoon meeting, the girls in white having reserved seats in front. The sermons were grand, and we were happy until President Young said that he had a few names to read of men who were to be called and voted in as missionaries to go and settle up the "Muddy."

This almost stilled the beating of the hearts of all present. Many of our friends had been called to go to settle the Dixie country, but the "Muddy," so many miles farther south and so much worse! Oh! Oh! I did not hear another name except Samuel Claridge. Then how I sobbed and cried, regardless of the fact that the tears were spoiling the new white dress.

The father of the girl who sat next to me was also called. Said my companion, "Why, what are you crying about? It doesn't make me cry. I know my father won't go."

"Well, there is the difference," said I. "I know that my father will go and that nothing could prevent him, and I should not own him as a father if he would not go when he is called." Then I broke down sobbing again.

Everything occurred to prevent my father from getting off. Just as he was nearly ready to start, one of his horses got poisoned. He had to buy another horse. A week later one of his big mules was found choked to death in his barn. Some of our friends said, "Brother Claridge, this shows you are not to go." My father answered, "It shows me that the adversary is trying to prevent me from going, but I shall go if I walk!"

Susa Young Gates, *Memorial to Elizabeth Claridge McCune* (Salt Lake City, 1924).

The Coat

LUCILE C. READING

Heber shivered in his thin coat as the cold November wind whipped around him. All he really wanted for his birthday was a warm overcoat, but he knew that asking for one would upset his mother. He remembered how she had cried the Christmas before because she didn't have enough money to buy him even a stick of candy.

Nine days after Heber was born, his father had died and his mother had moved him from the fine house where he had been born to a small one where they lived for many years. The roof leaked and sometimes they went to bed early because there was no coal for heat. Sometimes they went to bed hungry, for the fried bread hadn't been sufficient supper and there was no money for anything else.

There were days and nights when Heber's mother would sew and sew even though she was really too tired to finish a dress for a customer. Then Heber would go under the sewing machine and push the pedal up and down so that his mother's tired legs might have a rest. As they worked together in the lamplight, she would tell him stories and they would plan together for the time they would have plenty of coal, food, and all the clothes one could wear. Neither of them dreamed that one day Heber J. Grant would be the seventh President of The Church of Jesus Christ of Latter-day Saints.

November 22 dawned clear and cold. "Happy birthday, Heber," called his mother as she handed him the most beautiful coat Heber had ever seen. It was made of material his mother had been sewing, and it fit him perfectly. He hugged it to himself and could hardly wait to go out in the cold day and feel its warmth about him.

A few weeks later as Heber was hurrying on an errand he saw a boy just his size who was crying with cold. The boy was wearing a thin sweater, and Heber shivered, even though he had on his new overcoat.

As Heber hurried by, the crying boy looked at his coat with such longing that almost before he knew what he was doing, Heber had stopped, taken off the coat, and insisted that the boy wear it.

That very afternoon his mother saw Heber wearing his old coat instead of the new one. "Heber," she called, "what have you done with your lovely new overcoat?"

For just a moment he wondered how he could tell her he had given it away. He wondered what she would say. He hoped she wouldn't cry. "Oh, Mother," he finally explained, "I saw a boy who needed it lots worse that I did, so I just gave it to him."

"Couldn't you have given him your old one?" she asked.

Heber longed to have her understand, and yet he despaired of her doing so. And then he looked up anxiously into her face. Her eyes were misty with tears, and he threw his arms around her as she answered her own question, "Of course, you couldn't, Heber; of course, you couldn't."

Children's Friend, November 1966.

The Morning Chore

LUCILE C. READING

It was so dark that the sleepy seven-year-old boy could hardly find his way down the path to the barn. He had planned for days how he could get out of bed, dress, creep quietly down the stairs, take the milking bucket from the pantry shelf, and leave the house without waking anyone.

He had to feel his way in the dark barn to find the peg where the milking stool hung. His heart was beating fast as he placed the stool by the cow and sat down on it. The cow didn't even raise her head from the manger where she was munching hay, but a swish of her tail indicated she knew he was there.

The boy had seen his sister, Mary, milk the cow many times. He found it wasn't as easy as he thought it would be to get the cow's udder washed and then to draw out the warm, foamy milk from it. Before long his fingers and wrists ached. He had to stop often to rest them. He thought about going to the house to ask for help but decided against it. He was determined to finish the job alone.

The boy was so intent on milking that he did not realize how long it had taken, and he was surprised to find that daylight had come and smoke was curling up from the chimney when he finally left the barn and started for the house. As he entered the kitchen, Mother looked up from the stove where she was preparing breakfast and asked, "Why, Joseph, what have you been doing so early in the morning?"

He held up the filled milk bucket in answer, and felt a warm rush of joy at his mother's smile of approval. "Well," she said, "since it seems you are big enough, milking each morning will be your job." She paused and then questioned, "But why is it you were so anxious to milk that cow?"

Joseph lifted an earnest face to his mother as he answered, "I just want to help while Father is on his mission. And you see, Mamie (the name he called his beloved sister Mary) has so many other things to do, I thought if I could take care of the morning milk, she wouldn't have to worry about that!"

It was a shining moment for Joseph Fielding Smith (who later became the tenth President of The Church of Jesus Christ of Latter-day Saints) when his mother put her arms around him and held him close as she said, "How pleased your father will be when I write and tell him that he has a fine young *man* to take care of milking the cow while he is away!"

Children's Friend, April 1970.

Straw for the Manger

KATHRYN E. FRANKS

The boys and girls in Miss Bell's class at Belmont School gathered in the school auditorium to prepare for the yearly Christmas program.

Pete, the tallest boy in the class, was up on the stage nailing wood together for the manger scene.

Sara, a pretty girl with long hair, and Molly, with short hair and dimples, had been fitted for the angel costumes. Now they were busy pinning the flimsy white material together for their mothers to stitch.

The other children were lined up in the back of the room waiting to be called into the music room for chorus practice.

Lisa hadn't been assigned anything yet. She stood alone, among the empty seats. *If I weren't so tall,* she mused, *or if I had long, blond hair, I'd like to do something besides stay backstage and pin on costumes, or stand in the doorway and welcome parents.*

She was new in the class, and living on the outskirts of town in a trailer with her grandmother and father. It was only natural, she felt, that she wasn't very well acquainted.

Standing alone among the rows of empty seats, Lisa waited anxiously for Miss Bell to come back into the room. She

51

tried to busy her hands, although there was nothing really for her to do. She had started stacking some songbooks when Pete, upstage with the manger scene, called out, "We haven't any straw. How can we make a manger scene without straw?"

Some were busy talking and did not hear. Others looked up with little concern, then turned back to their work.

Pete stepped to the front of the stage and called louder this time. "Hey, all of you! If any of you have any straw, I'll pick it up after I finish my paper route."

Why didn't someone speak up? Lisa wondered. Sara lived in a big house on the edge of town. She owned her own riding horse. She would have straw.

"Well—?" Pete waited impatiently for an answer.

We have straw under the trailer, Lisa's conscience reminded her. How could she offer, though, if the other girls hadn't. She shuddered at the thought of being conspicuous, but she could not take her eyes from the unfinished manger scene.

"I have straw, Pete," she said, "if you'll come get it."

The girls looked quickly at Lisa, then turned back to their work.

"Good," Pete answered. "I know where you live. It will probably be dark before I get there."

The room was embarrassingly quiet. Lisa picked up her books and hurried out the rear door without waiting for Miss Bell to come from the music room and excuse her for the day.

A cold wind blew from the north as Lisa hugged her thin coat around her and hurried across town. She walked along the outskirts untill she reached the trailer park. The trailers were back a distance from the road, protected in front by a grove of trees.

After Lisa explained to her grandmother what she planned to do, she went outside to look under the trailer. She ran back. "The straw is greasy and oily! What shall I do?"

She looked out the window at the field that stretched southward to the Norris farm.

"I'll have to cross the fields to the Norris farm," she told her grandmother. "Mrs. Norris will give me some fresh straw."

Grandmother was old, but she understood that things are important if they are promised. "Go," she said, "but be back before supper time—before it gets dark."

Lisa climbed under the barbed wire fence and ran down the slope to the gully. There she pushed through thistle and tall grasses and then scurried upward to the second fence. In the distance the bare trees of the Norris orchard looked small and far away. It hadn't seemed this far before, Lisa thought, as she panted up the last hill to the orchard. The rough, wooded gate opened into the orchard. Here Lisa followed a narrow path to the backyard.

Mrs. Norris welcomed Lisa and asked her about her grandmother. "As soon as I put this bread in the oven, we'll go to the barn and fill a clean gunnysack with straw." The good smell of fresh bread made Lisa hungry.

Daylight had started to fade by the time Lisa stepped out the door. Snow clouds slid over the first evening star.

At the second fence Lisa decided that if she cut across the cornfield, she would cut the distance to the trailer in half.

In the half-darkness she stumbled over the corn stubble with every few steps. As she hurried through the thickets, she tripped and fell, hitting her chin against a sharp stone. Half crawling, she pulled the sack until she regained her balance.

Lisa sobbed out as the sharp weeds tore her stocking and cut her hands. The taller cornstocks snagged at her coat, slowing her down as she tried to run.

Then as she reached the slope that stretched uphill to the last barbed wire fence, she spotted the tiny light from the trailer window. Like a distant star, it guided her forward.

Lisa barely had time to change her clothes before Pete came for the straw. "Thanks, Lisa," he said. She told him nothing of her trip to the nearby farm.

"Would you have time to arrange the straw around the manger for me tomorrow after school?" Pete asked. "I have a longer paper route now. I never get in before supper time."

"I'll do it—I'll be glad to."

After school the next day, Lisa, with her dark sweater around her shoulders, tip-toed quietly on the stage in the auditorium.

She was on her knees carefully spreading the straw when Miss Bell came into the auditorium. As she came through the door, she paused, stopped, then slowly she took a few steps forward. "Lisa!" she called excitedly, "you are just right! You are the person I want to play Mary." She walked toward the stage. "I asked Mrs. Laurel, our music teacher, to select a taller girl for the part. She misunderstood, and I just now found out that we have no one for the part."

Miss Bell stepped upon the stage. She took the sweater from Lisa's shoulders, and placed it, like a shawl, around her face. "Your features are just right. You will be wonderful."

Slowly Lisa lifted her face, her eyes wide in wonderment.

"Miss Bell," she answered softly, her fingers moving the wisps of straw, "I would love to—more than any other part."

Miss Bell did not see the tears that fell and lost themselves in the straw.

Miss Bell told Lisa, "You will kneel beside the manger with the colored lights soft upon you. Pete, who is playing Joseph, will stand beside you. Keep your fingers lightly on the manger while the choir and the angels sing in the background. You will keep motionless while the shepherds gather slowly around the crib."

Miss Bell hurried out of the room after giving Lisa instructions to be ready for rehearsal the next day. A joyful little song burst through Lisa's happiness and followed her across town to the trailer, where she rushed inside to tell Grandmother her wonderful news.

Children's Friend, December 1965.

The Lost Gold Piece

JOHN A. WIDTSOE

There were not many after-school jobs in Logan when I was a boy, but I found one that took only two or three hours a day. One day my employer told me I had done very well, and he gave me a five-dollar gold piece for my several weeks of work.

Five dollars! That was money! I was jubilant! I would give half of it to my mother, buy a new book, and save the remainder. Into the pocket of my trousers went the bright new gold piece, and off I ran to tell my mother of my good luck.

On the way home, I put my hand in the pocket to feel and caress the money. It was not there! I felt all through the pocket again. The gold piece was not there! Instead, I found a hole in the pocket through which the coin had slipped. It was terrible! I was so sorry that I sat down by the ditch bank and cried.

Then I slowly walked back the way I had come, looking every step for that gold piece. The sidewalk on Logan Main Street was made of planks. I looked in every crack for my lost fortune. Not a sign of it! Then I walked back over the same road, stopping, looking everywhere. No little shiny gold coin was there to lighten my heart! Again I walked slowly back and forth over the road I had been following when the precious coin was lost. But it was not to be found! It was lost for good.

Then I remembered that the Lord knew where that gold piece was, and that if he would help me, and wanted me to find it, it could not be lost for long.

So I got down on my knees behind a big tree and told the Lord all about my trouble, and asked him, if he thought it was the best thing for me, to help me find it. When I got up I felt so much better. I felt sure the Lord had heard my prayer.

Dusk was gathering. One could not see anything on the ground very clearly, especially a small piece of gold. But I walked right on, not so slowly this time, for I knew the Lord was helping. About halfway up the second block, there in the grass lay my lost five-dollar gold piece. It gleamed in the darkness, as if to say, "Come and take me; I want to make you happy." I almost shouted with joy. How glad my mother would be, and how I would enjoy that book I had planned to buy. I leaned up against the fence and said, "Thank you, O Lord, for finding my money for me."

Since that time I have known that the Lord hears prayers. And, since that day, I have been careful to have no holes in my pockets.

Children's Friend, September 1947.

How Grandfather's Family Was Saved

VERN DUFFIN

My grandmother told this incident to me. It happened in the days of Nauvoo, at the time of bitter persecution of the Saints.

Grandma's father, John Lowe Butler, was one of the bodyguards for the Prophet Joseph Smith during the perilous times. One evening on the streets of Nauvoo, the Prophet said to him, "Brother John, is your family still on the farm?"

"Yes," John replied.

The Prophet said, "Go at once and bring them to Nauvoo; you must have them here before morning."

Grandfather hurriedly arranged for a team and wagon, and he lost no time in getting to his farm. He told his wife, Caroline F. Skien, what the Prophet had said. She quickly took her little children from their beds, and while she dressed them, he loaded some bedding and clothing and a few things in a wagon box, and they were soon on their way to Nauvoo. They went to the home of some friends who welcomed them and made them comfortable.

The next morning at dawn, a neighbor of Grandfather

Butler was awakened by the barking of his dogs. He looked out of the window and saw a mob of about fifty men riding wildly toward the Butlers' home. The mob set fire to the house and burned it down, while they yelled like madmen.

Grandfather and his family were saved by obedience to the voice of the Prophet Joseph Smith.

Children's Friend, July 1941.

Georg's Special Smile

SHERRIE JOHNSON

We've decided Georg can't play with us anymore," Johnny said to his friends as he stood up straight.

"Why not?" David asked.

"Come on, you know!" Johnny answered.

"No, I don't. Georg might be different from us, but that's no reason to keep him from playing," David defended.

"Different? Georg is more than different. He's stupid."

"He can't understand, but he's not stupid!" David exclaimed.

"If you ask me, not understanding is what stupid is," one of the other boys joined in.

Eleven-year-old David looked helplessly at his cousin. Georg's innocent face was one big smile as he watched David, who wanted to run and hide and never have to look at that smile again. But that was impossible.

Georg's parents had died, and Georg had come all the way from his home in Denmark to live with David. David looked again at Johnny and his other friends. Their faces glared from a circle around him, waiting for an answer.

"All right, I'll take Georg home," David sighed.

Angry with himself for not knowing what to do, and

angry with Georg, David took hold of his cousin's arm and started toward home.

"No, David," Georg said as he stood still. "Ball."

"Georg, you don't understand," David said, feeling very helpless. "The guys won't let you play with them anymore."

Georg's smile faded and his eyebrows pushed together very puzzled. Then just as suddenly he smiled again. "Yah, Davy."

"Georg, they don't—" David started to explain, and then he realized that Georg wouldn't understand anyway. "Oh, never mind. Come on!"

David walked a little faster, thinking hard about what had happened. *Why did Georg have to come live with me? Why don't I have an ordinary cousin like everyone else? One who can speak English!*

Soon they were home. Georg went to play in the family room and David went to his room and stretched out on his bed to think some more.

"Are you sick?" Mother asked as she came into David's room to put away some clothes.

"No," David answered. "I'm just thinking about something."

"You certainly must be thinking hard. Can I help you?" Mother asked as she sat on the bed.

"I don't know." David stared at the ceiling. "Mom, why is Georg the way he is?"

Mother looked surprised, "What do you mean?"

"You know. He's well, he's different," David replied.

"How do you mean different? He's the same size as you. As a matter of fact, he's wearing your clothes. Georg likes the same things you do—chocolate bars and pancakes. And he gets happy or sad over the same things you do."

"But, Mom, he's—" David stopped, not sure of how to say what he meant.

"Did something happen today?" Mother asked.

"Yes. The guys wouldn't let Georg play because they said he isn't smart enough."

"Georg is very smart. He doesn't speak the same language we do, but he's learning fast. Georg has other traits that make him very special, though, and you don't need to speak the same language to understand those."

David looked puzzled. "But my friends don't want Georg around, and I don't blame them. He just doesn't understand when we try to tell him how to do something. What am I supposed to do?"

"I can't tell you," Mother advised. "That is something you have to decide for yourself."

Mother smiled as she stood up. "There are two things you should remember, though. First, Georg loves you very much. Second, Georg may not be able to understand yet, but he is a child of God just like you and your other friends, and Heavenly Father loves him just as He loves you."

Suddenly Georg ran into the room. "Come, Davy!" he cried breathlessly.

Mother winked at David as she left the room.

"Come, Davy," Georg urged.

"Oh, all right," David said, not really wanting to go. "I'll come."

Georg took hold of David's arm as he guided him to the couch. Then he opened a book and started to read. "Vay," he sounded out a word carefully, smiling that happy smile David knew so well.

"Vay?" David repeated.

"Vay." Georg's smile grew bigger and bigger.

David looked at the book. "We! The word is we."

Georg looked disappointed, but then he smiled again. "Vee," he said.

David shook his head back and forth. "No, we," he said, as he turned away from his cousin and went back to his room.

Why? Why? Why? he kept thinking as he flopped on the bed. *If Georg could only understand, we could have so much fun together!*

David had been on his bed only a moment when he heard a soft knock at the door. The door opened slowly, and Georg's blue eyes peered cautiously around the door.

"Davy?" he asked softly.

David didn't answer. He didn't even look at Georg, who

walked over to the bed and sat down. Georg spoke slowly, but it was no use. David couldn't understand. The words just didn't mean anything to him.

David looked at Georg. He doesn't understand what I say, but I don't understand him either. For the first time David began to wonder what Georg must think of him. Maybe Georg thinks I'm stupid because I don't understand him.

David looked at Georg again. He was still talking as if he were desperately trying to explain something. All at once David knew exactly what Georg was trying to say. He wanted to be friends. He was telling David how much he liked him. David didn't need to understand Danish, for he could see it in Georg's face.

Georg had finished talking now, and he sat waiting for an answer. David felt ashamed. Then he smiled and Georg smiled back. Both boys understood without words!

"Dinner is ready," Mother called.

David motioned to Georg, and they both hurried from the room.

As David passed his mother in the hall, he stopped. "I was wrong, Mom. It isn't Georg who doesn't understand— it's me. And, you know, Georg may not understand English, but he sure understands friendship. And he's teaching me. Georg really is a special friend."

Mother smiled. "You know, you're pretty special yourself," she replied.

Georg was already at the table. His face was all aglow with his special smile that beamed, "Hi, friend!"

"You know, Mom," David chuckled, "maybe Georg could teach me Danish!"

The Friend, March 1973.

Standing Up for the Right

LLEWELYN R. McKAY

As a boy, David O. McKay enjoyed playing baseball on the town square. It wasn't long before he was chosen to play second base on the team that had been organized to compete with other teams of nearby towns.

On a Fourth of July, the Huntsville group (David's team) was playing with a visiting team and the grandstand was full of spectators. The game had been tied for several innings and everyone was excited. One of the Huntsville players had stumbled and sprained his ankle, so David was called on as a pinch-hitter to take his place at bat. David hit the first pitch—but it was a foul ball. Then the umpire called the next two throws "ball one!" and "ball two!" The following pitch he called "strike two!" The visiting team's pitcher, a large, burly fellow, came up to young David and told him that he was "out."

"The umpire called 'strike two'," said David.

"I don't care what the umpire said; I say that you're out. Now take a seat over there on the grass or I'll whang you one with this baseball bat!" Then the bully picked up a bat and came menacingly toward David.

A hush came over the spectators as they watched this

63

little drama. Would David, who was much smaller than his opponent, do as he was told, or would he hold his ground?

David knew that he was within his right, as did everyone else.

"You have miscounted the strikes," said David calmly. "The umpire has the final decision. Go back to your pitcher's box."

The pitcher took a long look at David's determined expression, turned around, and sauntered back to his place.

The next throw was a straight, swift ball directly over the plate. David connected for a "two bagger." The next man hit a single, which brought David to home plate for the winning score.

David was a very determined lad when he knew he was right, and he could not be bullied into giving in, although the odds were against him.

The Children's Friend, September 1969.

Just One More Step

GEORGE ALBERT SMITH

(The following occurred during President Smith's labors in the Southern States Mission.)

Late one evening in a pitch-dark night, Elder Stout and I were traveling along a high precipice. Our little walk was narrow; on one side was the wall of the mountain—on the other side, the deep, deep river. We had no light and there were no stars and no moon to guide us.

We had been traveling all day, and we knew that hospitality would be extended to us if we could reach the McKelvin home, which was on the other side of a high valley. We had to cross this mountain in order to reach the home of Mr. McKelvin. Our mode of travel was of necessity very halting. We walked almost with a shuffle, feeling each foot of ground as we advanced, with one hand extended toward the wall of the mountain.

Elder Stout was ahead of me, and as I walked along I felt the hard surface of the trail under my feet. In doing so, I left the wall of the mountain, which had acted as a guide and a steadying force. After I had taken a few steps away I felt impressed that something was wrong and I must stop immediately. I called to Elder Stout and he answered me. The direction from which his voice came indicated I was on the wrong trail, so I backed up until I reached the wall of the mountain and again proceeded forward.

Elder Stout was just a few steps in front of me, and as I reached him we came to a fence piling. In the dark we carefully explored it with our hands and feet to see whether it would be safe for us to climb over. We decided that it would be secure and made the effort. While I was on the top of this big pile of logs, my little suitcase popped open and the contents were scattered around. In the dark I felt around for them and was quite convinced I had recovered practically everything.

We arrived safely at our destination about eleven o'clock at night. I soon discovered I had lost my comb and brush, and the next morning we returned to the scene of my accident. I recovered my property, and while I was there, my curiosity was stimulated and aroused to see what had happened the night before when I had lost my way in the dark. As missionaries, we wore hobnails in the bottom of our shoes to make them last longer, so I could easily follow our tracks in the soft dirt. I retraced my steps to the point where my tracks led to the edge of a steep precipice. Just one more step and I would have fallen over into the river and been drowned.

I felt very ill when I realized how close I had come to death. I was also very grateful to my Heavenly Father for protecting me. I have always felt that if we are doing the Lord's work and ask him for his help and protection, he will guide and take care of us.

A Story to Tell (Deseret Book Co., 1945).

Don't Lie to an Indian

J. H. PAUL

An early settler near Tooele, Utah, was Tom Hale. Long before the white inhabitants amounted to much in the way of numbers, his ranch and cabin were widely known. Both Indians and whites acknowledged his prowess, and he was especially famed among his red neighbors. His record as a hunter and a wrestler was heralded afar by the native tribes.

The Indians liked Hale and had given him the name "Strong Arm" because of his terrific grip in the wrestling contests. They liked him also because he had always dealt fairly with them, never taking advantage over even the least of them. In his numerous trades and deals with either new or old acquaintances, he always played fair, so they bartered freely with him for the various articles they needed.

Hale, moreover, had a saying that was also widely known, a sort of motto that was verified anew by each transaction the red men had with him: "Never lie to an Indian." In the simple life he lived, this rule held good for all people of either race, and neither friend nor foe had reason to complain that at any time he had sought to deceive them.

One summer day, as Tom Hale stood musing at the door of his cabin, his eye was attracted by a cloud of dust arising from the road out on the desert that lay westward of his home. The cloud came nearer; it was not a whirlwind, and, the day being calm, not a breath was stirring. Hale paused, for the sight was unusual; and as the little white billows of the desert rolled forward, he made out two human forms running swiftly toward him. Soon from out of the white mist sped a powerful Indian followed by a young Indian mother carrying her babe in a papoose basket tied to her head and shoulders.

As the two rushed panting up to Hale, the red man exclaimed, "Hide us quickly, Strong Arm. I am Arrowpine, the Ute Chief; the Shoshones are after us. They will kill me and carry into slavery my young wife."

Hale had met Arrowpine and had liked the man; they had hunted together and were friends. He thrust the pair into his cabin and pulled back a rug carpet from a hatchway in the floor; the Indians dropped into the cellar out of sight. Hale replaced the door and the carpet just as a shout from his young son Sol announced another, greater cloud of dust approaching out on the desert road.

Standing outside of the cabin, Hale watched the clouds of dust roll near; soon out of them came galloping a band of Shoshones mounted on Indian cayuses. They were fully armed, their faces streaked with red paint, their bows in hand and arrows ready, their faces eager and determined. Riding up to Hale and saluting the white man, whom he knew, the leader asked, "Have you seen two Indians, a chief and his squaw, come this way?"

For a moment Hale looked puzzled, and he stroked his chin; he had never lied to an Indian and hated to do so even in this emergency. As he turned and lifted his eyes to a hill on his left, a little cloud of dust arose there. With a shout as they saw the dust, the Indians wheeled their horses to the right and dashed toward the hill, thinking that Hale had intended to give them a hint to go in that direction. As soon as they were well up the hill, Hale removed the carpet and door from the hiding place of the Indian couple, who eagerly climbed out.

"We are here on a visit to Northern Utes," Arrowpine

explained, "and were out by ourselves picking chokecherries when the Shoshones discovered us. They hate the
Southern Utes and would like to get me for torture, because
I have often defied them in battle. My young wife would
meet a horrible fate if we should fall into their hands."

"Could you find your way back to the friendly tribe,"
Hale asked, "if one of us should lead you by a secret trail to
the northern road?"

"Yes," answered Arrowpine. "We know the way from
there and could elude the Shoshones."

"Who will go as their guide?" inquired Hale, looking
around at his neighbors, who had come in upon hearing that
Indians in war paint were about. None of them, however,
was willing to undertake so dangerous an errand. Hale's
question remained unanswered till his young son, Sol, then
about nine years of age, spoke out, saying, "I'll go, Father;
I know every step of the way and can be back in a few
hours."

Instantly Sol's mother protested that he was too young to
risk his life on such a journey, with the chance of falling into
the hands of the raging Shoshones; but after some hesitation
Hale said, "Mother, let him go. He will be as safe as anyone;
and it will be hours before the Shoshones get back, even if
they should return this way."

Food for the journey was quickly prepared for the Indians, and off toward the northern hills at a smooth trot went
Sol, closely followed by Arrowpine and his young wife with
the Indian baby on her back in the basket woven of sumac
branches. The entire company, watching them, breathed
with relief as the little party finally disappeared among the
cedars.

The anxious hours dragged slowly; but at nightfall, a faint
shout was heard from the cedars on the distant hillside. The
call came nearer, accompanied by the steady beating of
feet—the Indian dog-trot; and out of the twilight into the
arms of his waiting mother emerged the lad, exhausted but
otherwise not one bit worse for his perilous adventure.

Seven years had passed from the time of this incident. Sol
Hale, now sixteen, had become skilled in frontier life and

outdoor experiences, which had included several visits to
Indian tribes. Arrowpine was again in the North, engaged in
training a select body of his younger braves, as blunder by
inexperienced travelers going to California had resulted in
the death of one of Arrowpine's younger braves, and not
even the influence of their wise chief had been able to keep
them from taking revenge on the whites.

When Arrowpine had found that he could not restrain his
men, he had placed himself at their head, with the desire to
lessen their depredations. Word of the onslaught sent the
people for miles around to the Hale ranch for safety. On
came the Utes, sweeping up all the horses, cattle, and sheep
they could come across. Hastily the livestock were driven to
the Hale ranch, where a large enclosure with water from a
spring afforded easy facilities for guarding them.

With the stock thus folded, all seemed well, and the people could await with confidence the approach of the ma-
rauding Utes. Then Tom Hale suddenly remembered some
choice animals in a distant pasture over the mountain—stock
that had been overlooked and forgotten while the others
were being driven in. It would not do to leave them out, so
Hale called for a volunteer to go and bring them. At first no
one spoke. Then Sol Hale spoke up, declaring himself willing
to go. It was decided, over his mother's remonstrances, to let
him try it; and away he went afoot upon the precarious task
of bringing in the distant livestock before the Indians could
reach them.

When he had crossed the mountain and reached the pasture, he found it already raided. The Indians had been there
and had driven off the animals, though which way they had
gone was uncertain. Yet he judged, from certain signs he had
been trained to recognize, that the Indians were even then
getting between him and the ranch house, so he took to the
cedars to make a long circuit back. To keep under cover,
however, he had to make so wide a detour that darkness
came on and he was still many miles from home. He was
hungry, and it was growing cold.

As he threaded his way, stooping, hiding, crawling at
times, he came upon a calf, which he recognized as one of

the Hale animals. He knew that it would presently seek its mother, so, urging it forward a little, he followed its zigzag meandering in the darkness till, in answer to its bleat, came the welcome "Moo-oo" of its mother, telling them which way to go. As the calf knelt on one side beside the cow for its milk, Sol knelt on the other, milking into his mouth till hunger and thirst were satisfied with the warm, welcome fluid. Then the cow lay down with the calf beside her. Some claim that Sol wedged himself between them to keep warm. At all events, he fell sound asleep on a bed of leaves.

Just before daylight the boy awoke, impressed with the feeling that he was in great danger. As he stood up and tried to see in the darkness, he fancied that shadowy forms of tents loomed not very far away. When his eyes became accustomed to the darkness, he made out a few tents, besides many human forms stretched out upon the earth. It was the Ute camp, and he had been sleeping within 300 yards of it. There it was, slowly becoming visible right before his eyes.

He knew the ways of Indians and was well aware of the fact that he could not get away. That they had not found him already was due merely to circumstance that animals were all about, so that the guards had paid little attention to this one, which they must have heard and seen. He decided to do as trained scouts everywhere have done under such circumstances: he would go straight into the encampment.

As he walked toward the big tent, Indians lying on the ground sprang up and seized him. They threw him to the earth, then bound his hands and feet. Hearing the commotion, a chief came out of the tent. It was Arrowpine, whom the youth recognized. The chief spoke sternly.

"What are you doing here and why did you come into my camp?" he asked in anger. "Are you a spy?"

"I came here," answered the youth, "to find my father's animals, which your men have driven away."

"Who is your father?" demanded the chief, "and who are you?"

"My father is Tom Hale; I am Sol Hale and no spy, but a friend of the red man," the boy responded.

"Are you Strong Arm's son?" asked the chief, peering

doubtfully through the dim light at the prostrate form beside him. "Don't lie to me."

"I do not lie; neither did my father ever deceive you or your people," declared the boy in strong tones.

"Stand him up," the chief commanded; and they stood him erect before Arrowpine, who eyed him keenly. But the boy had changed so much in seven years that the Indian leader failed to recognize him. "Can you prove to me," the chief asked, "that you are Strong Arm's son?"

"Seven years ago, when you were hidden in my father's house to get away from the Shoshones, I led you and your wife with her baby boy through the cedars and along the secret trail to the northern road; and I had to run all the way back, for the Shoshones might have captured me."

In answer to other questions by the chief, Sol gave significant details of the journey—details that only those who made it could accurately relate: how they had stopped only once at a tiny spring to drink and rest a few minutes before running on again; what the chief had said as they parted that day; the token that the chief had given him as a mark of his gratitude—a grizzly's tooth, which the boy had strung upon his leather-woven watch chain, and which he now asked the chief to look at.

The chief had closely watched the youth during this testimony, his features changing and his face lighting up as he remembered the race through the cedars; and now, in the clearer light of the dawn, he recognized in the youth the boy who had stood by him in his hour of need.

"Unbind him," the chief commanded his men; and they untied the rawhide thongs they had wound about him. Sol rubbed his wrist and ankles, then faced the chief.

"Would you know your father's animals if you saw them?" asked Arrowpine, this time in a friendly and considerate voice.

"I could pick them out anywhere," young Hale answered.

"Then follow me," said the chief, striking off toward a large enclosure where the animals secured during the raid were being guarded by watchers.

The chief spoke to his men, who straightway proceeded to drive the animals one by one past a makeshift gate where the chief and young Hale stood. When one of his father's stock would pass, Sol would say, "That's ours," and the guards would turn it out of the enclosure. One after another he picked out his father's animals till he felt that he had nearly all of them.

Just then a handsome mare came trotting up to the gate, her eyes shining, nostrils blown, head erect, and tail held high, as she pranced and plunged, showing that the blood of her Arabian ancestry had lost none of its fire by her transfer from the deserts of Asia to those of America. She did not belong to the Hales; she had been imported for breeding purposes by a near friend and neighbor.

As young Hale saw her come forward, he began to think of the loss the whole community would suffer if he did not claim her and take her home to his father's friend, and a battle as fierce as those waged on fields of carnage began to rage in his brain. The horse was not his father's, to be sure; but these Indian thieves had no right to her, so why should he not deceive them and recover her for the people, especially, he argued to himself, since the Indians would probably make little good use of her and by abuse and neglect would soon destroy her extraordinary value. On the other hand there arose in his mind the words of his father—"Never lie to an Indian"—and after brief hesitation, with the Indians eying him closely, he shook his head, saying, "She is not ours."

The chief immediately called for a guard to escort young Hale and his stock back to the vicinity of the Hale ranch. A murmur of disapproval, amounting almost to mutiny, rose in words and gestures of increasing excitement from the assembled braves. They had understood little of the English conversation between Arrowpine and young Hale, and they now perceived they were to be cheated of both their intended human victim and many of the animals they had rounded up in the raid.

In words of fervor and eloquence, Arrowpine now addressed his men, relating how the life of their chief and his wife and young son had been saved by this son of their famous friend, the well-known Strong Arm.

The braves, after talking it over, accepted the chief's decision. A select guard forthwith escorted young Hale and the livestock back to the vicinity of the ranch. As Sol drove in the stock, he found a large company in a high state of nervous tension awaiting news of him. By this time they believed him to be killed or captured.

There had been little sleep at the ranch through the night. Sol's mother had paced the floor of her room; his father with scouting parties had scoured the country in all directions in search of him, but they had not been numerous enough to invade the Indian camp.

That morning the Indians moved off with their plunder.

Improvement Era, February 1930.

A Long Night

IRIS SYNDERGAARD

Her early breakfast finished, Hilda stood beside the cabin. She watched Father drive the wagon around the big bend by the river. She could not see Mother, who lay in back of the wagon because she was too ill to sit with Father.

When the wagon was out of sight, Hilda said, "You go play, Matthew. You too, Jane,"

Hilda felt very lonely but very proud of her ten years. Father had told her she must take care of her little sister and brother and their cow, Bessie. Father would have to drive most of the day to get Mother into town, where she could be taken care of by the doctor.

The day passed. In the morning the children played on the great red rock above the cabin. After lunch they made stick houses in the damp sand beside the swift river.

Hilda fixed beans with cold johnnycake for supper. At bedtime the three children knelt down for family prayers.

Jane stood up. "Do we have to sleep in the loft, Hilda?" she asked. "Can't we sleep down here?"

"Yes," Hilda said. "There is room in the big bed for all of us."

She banked the fire to burn slowly through the night, and

75

then she snuggled into the soft, warm bed beside Jane.

Hilda knew she had been asleep a long time when she wakened suddenly. She lay still. A sound had wakened her. "It must be Matthew," she said to herself. "He snores when he sleeps on his back."

But Matthew lay quietly on his side. Hilda decided she had imagined the noise. She pulled the warm quilt up and closed her eyes.

In the dark night, the sound came again. Her skin prickled with fear, because Hilda knew what it was. She had heard the roar of a hunting mountain lion before—but never so near.

"Our house is tight," she told herself. "No lion can get in." Suddenly Hilda thought of Bessie. Only yesterday she had heard Father tell Mother the cow was not safe in the lean-to. It was too open. Hilda knew it could never keep a prowling lion out.

The lion will not come down to the river. It will stay high on the mountain among the trees, Hilda thought to herself.

For some time all was still. Then, nearer, the lion roared again. Matthew stirred in sleep. Jane sat up.

"I hear a noise, Hilda," she said. "Is someone outside?"

"No, Jane," Hilda answered quickly. She was glad Jane was awake. Maybe with both of them listening they could tell how close the lion was to their cabin.

The next time the lion roared, it was very close. Hilda was sure it must now be on top of the big red rock above the cabin. She wondered why it would come so near. Father said wild animals were afraid of people.

It was their cow the lion was after.

Hilda knew what she must do. Without stopping to put on her shoes, she ran to the door.

"Jane," she said as she unfastened the leather thong that held the door tight, "stand right here. Open the door wide when you hear me call. I must get Bessie."

Outside, a quarter-moon hung low in the west. By its dim light, Hilda ran along the path to the lean-to. She could hear Bessie stamping in her stall. When Hilda unlatched the low gate, the cow snorted with fright. Hilda quickly took a rope and tied it around the animal's neck. "There, Bessie," she murmured, as she led the cow onto the path.

Hilda looked at the black shadows under the rocks beside the lean-to. She was afraid she would see the crouched figure of the mountain lion. Bessie was also very frightened. She pulled against the rope with all her strength. Hilda knew the cow must not break away and run into the night. She would not get far before the lion would catch her.

"Jane," Hilda called, tugging at the rope. "Come and help me."

The small figure of her sister ran from the cabin. "Shove the cow from behind," Hilda panted.

Together they pushed the terrified cow to the cabin and got her inside. Hilda banged the door shut and fastened it.

"Jane, put more wood on the fire. Matthew, help me push the dresser in front of the door."

Hilda tied the cow to the bedstead. She sat beside Jane and Matthew in the middle of the big bed. The children sang songs and tried to remember stories as the minutes crept by. Often they sat very still to listen.

Hilda knew the lion was pacing around and around their cabin. She knew it stopped circling sometimes to sniff at the door. The younger children also knew it.

Once Jane whispered, "Can it come in the door?"

"No," Hilda said firmly.

"Can it break the window?" Matthew's voice squeaked.

Hilda answered "No" again, but not so firmly. The panes of glass looked very thin.

"Let's all say our prayers again," she said. "Heavenly Father will keep us safe."

Hours later, over the great red rock, the sky finally grew pale as the new day began. It wasn't very long until they heard a familiar, welcome sound—the clop-clop of Father's horses.

Later, after Father told them Mother's infection had been treated and she would be home soon, Father asked Hilda if she was sure the lion had really come down to the cabin.

Hilda took her father's hand. She led him toward the

spring that ran behind the cabin. She pointed at the damp mud. Father said nothing, but he nodded his head. Beside the stream were enormous footprints left by a mountain lion.

Children's Friend, April 1969.

A Special Dog

LUCILE C. READING

The boy's name might have been Donnie, and he wished with all his heart that he could have a dog. He often watched his playmates running and playing with their pets.

His father had carefully explained how difficult it would be for the boy to have a dog, but he promised that if they ever found just the right one, they would try and buy it. The longing for a pet grew with the boy. He was sure even his father couldn't understand how hard it was to wait for a special dog.

One day Donnie saw a man putting up a sign that said "Puppies for Sale," and he asked about them. The man who owned the dogs liked Donnie at once. He seemed to feel there was something special about the boy, although he couldn't tell just what it was.

"Want to see the dogs?" he asked, and when Donnie nodded, the man whistled, and a mother dog ran out of her kennel. She was followed by five frisky little puppies and then another one that lagged behind the rest.

"What's wrong with him?" asked the boy, pointing to the dog that could not keep up with the rest. The man explained that the puppy had something wrong with his hip.

"That's the very one I want," cried the boy, his eyes following each faulty movement of the puppy with growing excitement. "And I know my father will let me have *this* dog."

The man shook his head. "No, son," he suggested. "Why don't you think about one of these frisky pups? That dog will never be able to run as you'd want him to do."

"I don't run so well myself," Donnie explained as he pulled up his trousers and pointed to a heavy brace on one of his legs. "This dog needs somebody who understands him. He's the special one I've been waiting for."

Children's Friend, March 1963.

"Get Up and Move Your Carriage"

WILFORD WOODRUFF

In 1848, after my return to Winter Quarters from our pioneer journey, I was appointed by the Presidency of the Church to take my family and go to Boston, to gather up the remnant of the Saints and lead them to the valleys of the mountains.

While on my way east I put my carriage into the yard of one of the brethren in Indiana, and Brother Orson Hyde set his wagon by the side of mine, and not more than two feet from it.

Dominicus Carter, of Provo, and my wife and four children were with me. My wife, one child, and I went to bed in the carriage, the rest sleeping in the house. I had been in bed but a short time, when a voice said to me, "Get up and move your carriage."

It was not thunder, lightning nor an earthquake, but the still, small voice of the Spirit of God—the Holy Ghost.

I told my wife I must get up and move my carriage. She asked, "What for?"

I told her I did not know, except that the Spirit had told me to do it.

I got up and moved my carriage several rods, and set it

by the side of the house. As I was returning to bed, the same Spirit said to me, "Go and move your mules from that oak tree," which was about one hundred yards north of our carriage. I moved them to a young hickory grove and tied them up. Then I went to bed.

In thirty minutes a whirlwind caught the tree to which my mules had been fastened, broke it off near the ground, and carried it one hundred yards, sweeping away two fences in its course, and laid it prostrate through that yard where my carriage stood, and the top limbs hit my carriage as it was.

In the morning I measured the trunk of the tree that fell where my carriage had stood, and I found it to be five feet in circumference. It came within a foot of Brother Hyde's wagon but did not touch it.

Thus, by obeying the revelation of the Spirit of God to me, I saved my life and the lives of my wife and child, as well as my animals.

In the morning I went on my way rejoicing.

Retold in George C. Lambert, *Gems of Reminiscence* (Salt Lake City, 1915).

"Stand By for Torpedo!"

WENDELL J. ASHTON

"**P**ray always, that you may come off conqueror."

During World War II the postman dropped me a letter from a missionary companion of mine, John Boud. Some seven years before, we had worked together in the offices of the European and British missions in London. John Boud, now a lieutenant senior grade, was stationed at San Diego, California, and had the honor of being the first Latter-day Saint chaplain in the United States Navy, so far as is known.

Lieutenant Boud's letter carried the usual good cheer that his correspondence always exuded, but he related a war story that was particularly stimulating.

Each Wednesday, Chaplain Boud held a service at the Marine base for Latter-day Saint boys. Many of these services took the form of testimony meetings. He related the experience of one Mormon boy who had been in the Navy about a year when a destroyer was blasted from under him. The Mormon had been kidded, perhaps even ridiculed a bit, during the wanderings of the destroyer because he always turned down the drinks and passed off the smokes. Some of this slur was tossed at him in the typical taunts of hardened tars.

Then one day the ship's captain bellowed out: "Stand by for torpedo!" All hands rushed to the fore of the ship. Some of the more frantic sailors dropped to their knees, calling in loud voices for the Lord to spare them. Walking about in the crisis, the boy from Idaho noticed among those with outstretched arms calling to the heavens for mercy the same fellows who had blasphemed him.

Then the explosion came. The torpedo hit like a terrific bolt of thunder and lightning. The Mormon was hurled into the ocean. Later he was rescued.

When the survivors of the sunken vessel gathered together to recount their experience, one of the first questions was directed at the sailor who never drank or smoked. "Why, tell us," one of the seamen asked, "didn't you fall to your knees like the rest of us and pray?"

Then came the Mormon boy's classic reply: "Because—I had been doing some praying long before our lives were in danger."

A Story to Tell (Deseret Book Co., 1971).

Lost Cow, Found Cow

HENRY D. MOYLE

When I was a young boy, my father entrusted the family cow to my care, both at our home in Salt Lake City as well as at our summer home in the mountains, in Big Cottonwood Canyon. My first trip from the city to the mountains with the cow was made on the back of my Indian pony. . . . It can be hard work leading a cow by a rope attached to her halter with the other end wrapped around the horn of the saddle. It took most of the day to get the cow just from Salt Lake City to the mouth of the canyon.

Around noon I stopped at a farm located on Highland Drive below Sugar House. I milked the cow to make traveling easier for her and fed the pony and the cow. The fresh warm milk tasted good with the sandwiches Mother had put in my saddlebag.

We began to climb the canyon road, and continued our journey uneventfully until early evening, when the cow suddenly balked. I lost hold of the rope and the cow took off up the hill in the thick scrub oak brush. I left my pony on the canyon road and went to find the cow. I climbed through the brush, but I could not find her, and it was getting darker all the time. When I felt I had done all I could to help myself,

85

I knelt down to pray. I knew then that the Lord hears and answers our prayers when we do our part. I felt good when I stood up. I was not afraid any more. I walked a short distance up the hill and came upon an old irrigation ditch. A short distance up the ditch I saw my cow hidden by the bank.

After thanking the Lord for answering my prayer, I drove the cow ahead of me in the ditch until we came out into a clearing. I tied the cow to a bush, then went down the canyon road until I was once again seated comfortably on my pony. I retrieved the cow and soon arrived at our summer home.

If I were you I would pray and develop the ability of talking to the Lord and depending upon him to help when his help is necessary. You will find throughout life he will always be there to help you. Without his help, we do not accomplish much. With his help there is nothing we cannot accomplish if we will.

Improvement Era, February 1963.

The Walking Question Mark

DOROTHY D. WARNER

The thin, red-haired boy with the bright blue eyes was busy thinking as he hoed his father's corn. "What a pity farming takes so much time. There are so many other things in the world I would like to learn about."

It was in the colony of Connecticut in 1771; the boy was twelve-year-old Noah Webster. Ever since he could remember, he had asked questions about everything: "Why do cows give milk?" or "Where is that bee going?" His parents had not been able to answer his questions to his satisfaction. They did not know the meaning of many of the words he read.

On Sunday afternoons under the gnarled apple trees, Noah read every book or newspaper he could lay his hands on. Every printed page to him was an exciting and new country to be explored. He had read only a dozen books, but he was sure that, somewhere, there must be many more that would answer all his questions. Already he realized that getting an education was similar to gathering walnuts—one had to crack the outside shell to find the nutmeat inside.

In his bed at night beside his eldest brother, Noah huddled close to a single candle to try to read a bit of the weekly newspaper, but Charles would complain, "Blow out the candle, Noah. How can a working man get enough sleep this way?" Reluctantly, Noah did as he was told, but he did not always go to sleep at once.

Noah liked to think about what he had read—the high taxes on glass, sugar, paper, and tea that the British had now imposed on the colonies. The colonists were angry, and they were calling the British "lobsters" because of their red coats. The American colonists were a spirited people, and Noah had read where they would not long tolerate abuse.

Sometimes Noah lay there and thought about school. He wondered if he would have to quit going to school when he turned fourteen, the age when a working boy became a man. He prayed each night that somehow he might be able to continue learning.

The harvest was over, and the mornings were cold now. Noah got up early to help his father mend harnesses, shoes, and fences, and gather in the frosty pumpkins.

"If you keep up with your work, you may continue your schooling until you finish all the schoolmaster can teach you," his father told him.

So each morning Noah brushed a kiss on his mother's cheek and hurried the four miles to school.

Once he overheard his mother say to his father, "That son of ours is a walking question mark." Her voice was proud when she said it. Noah guessed it pretty well did describe him.

At school, without a word of greeting, the stern schoolmaster, who either taught from the Speller or the Bible, whacked on his desk with a long stick and all the students, large and small, lined up in a row for the spelling lesson.

"Satan!" shouted the schoolmaster, thumping his desk so hard one small girl crouched in fright.

"Satan, S-A-T-A-N!" the pupils loudly chorused. One boy hesitated over the word and received a sharp whack with the stick. The students went on this way, reciting the twenty spelling words they must know each day.

The children were never given any homework because they had no time to study at home. Arithmetic came suddenly out of the schoolmaster's head. They learned of dead kings, vanished cities, and dates of events long past.

Noah wanted to know much more about the world at the present. "Please, sir," he said one day to the schoolmaster, "do you know what makes the King of England so unfair to us?"

The schoolmaster glared at Noah over his spectacles. "That is no part of our lesson," he scowled. "You will have to ask the King himself."

The class tittered, but Noah did not mind.

He tried again, this time to secure a book to read at home. "Can you tell me, sir, where I may borrow books?"

"Too much reading is bad for a boy," his schoolmaster answered. "You should be able to read from the Bible and spell—more than that you will never need."

Noah managed to learn Latin and to borrow books from his young minister. Finally, when Noah was sixteen, after much hard work, his father borrowed money to put him through Yale College. Though he studied law, one of his first jobs was as a schoolmaster.

When Noah wasn't teaching, he worked on a new speller. He called it the *Blue Speller*, and it was a wonderful change from the dull schoolbooks of his day. American parents, children, and teachers loved his new book. It had colorful stories about history, geography, science—subjects never before put into schoolbooks.

There were funny animal fables, each with a moral plainly stated to help a child grow wise. No descriptions of the devil and his ways, but an essay entitled "How to Be a Good Boy." And Noah did not stand over his pupils with a stick and force them to learn.

"A is for apple pie made by a cook. B is for boy who is fond of his book," was the way the alphabet read, and children were eager to pen it each day.

The *Blue Speller* became the backbone of American education of that day. It sold 100 million copies, exceeded only by the Holy Bible.

Noah traveled south to help improve education there, and he made a friend of George Washington when he called at Mount Vernon to show him his speller. Later, when the time came to draw up the Constitution of the United States, Washington remembered Noah Webster's *Sketches of American Policies* and asked him to come to Philadelphia to help.

Noah Webster, the country lad, taught himself twenty-four foreign languages during his lifetime, and he decided he would write a correct and modern dictionary—complete with Greek and Latin sources. So at the age of sixty, he began this great task, which was to take him twenty years to complete. He knew that if this great nation was to grow, it must have up-to-date words and references.

This alone would have been a life's fulfillment for an ordinary man, but Noah Webster also wrote *A Grammar of English Language, A History of the United States,* and *Bible in the Common Language.*

Children's Friend, May 1969.

"Today I Found a Prophet"

ARCH L. MADSEN

I remember being in New York when President David O. McKay returned from Europe. Arrangements had been made for pictures to be taken, but the regular photographer was unable to go, so in desperation the United Press picked their crime photographer—a man accustomed to the toughest type of work in New York. He went to the airport, stayed there two hours, and returned later from the darkroom with a tremendous sheaf of pictures. He was supposed to take only two. His boss immediately chided him. "What in the world are you wasting time and all those photographic supplies for?" The photographer replied curtly, saying he would gladly pay for the extra materials, and they could even dock him for the extra time. Several hours later the vice-president called him to his office, wanting to learn what happened. The crime photographer said, "When I was a little boy, my mother used to read to me out of the Old Testament, and all my life I have wondered what a prophet of God must really look like. Well, today I found one."

"Memories of a Prophet," *Improvement Era*, February 1970.

Frontier Detective

TED McDONALD

"Joe," said the superintendent of the Montezuma Copper Company, "you're to take Kitty and go down the road until you meet the Manuel Gonzalez outfit. They started from Lordsburg six days ago, so you ought to find them about at York's ranch. Just notice particularly where you meet them, and ask them to hurry up. They've got some flour we need."

Joe Armstrong had been looking for this order. Ever since he had begun working for Montezuma he had been sent on these missions. Invariably, three or four days before the end of the month, he and Kitty, the mare, had been sent galloping down the Lordsburg road to meet ox teams delivering supplies and tell them to hurry up.

It was eighty miles to Lordsburg, and all the company's freight had to be carried by ox teams from the railway at that point. The humor of asking that an ox team hurry was not lost on Joe. He knew it took eight or ten days for the plodding cattle to drag the great wagons across the desert and over the hills, and he also knew that there was plenty of flour in the warehouse.

But Joe Armstrong also knew enough to hold his tongue and obey orders. It was not that the mission displeased him;

on the contrary, he was delighted—what healthy boy would not welcome the change from the dull routine of the company's store to a ride on Kitty?

It was sunset when he reached the York ranch, where he stopped for supper. There were three other travelers at the ranchman's table. He knew one of them—Mr. Lampson, who had been a bookkeeper in Montezuma's office and had been discharged for a reason Joe had never learned.

"Going to stop over, Joe?" asked Mr. Lampson, as they stood at the washing trough.

"Why, no, Mr. Lampson," answered the boy. "I've got a bit of business down the road. It's moonlight, and I guess I'll push on my way. Are you going on?"

Mr. Lampson thought not, and he changed the subject; he and his two companions were still at York's when Joe saddled up and started on. Kitty was fresh from her rest and feed of grain, but Joe would not let her gallop. Soon she found her stride, the long, swinging lope of the cow ponies that he knew she could hold for fifty miles if necessary. The brilliant moon almost directly overhead cast a shadow like a purple blanket. Except for the hoof beats, there was no sound.

Joe loved to ride at night. He knew every inch of the way, and each tall, branching cactus that stood out in the moonlight was as good as a milepost to him.

Soon he noted a shadow in the brush by the roadside keeping pace with him. Half a mile farther a companion shadow on the other side of the road drew his attention.

He knew that they were wildcats, obeying the same instinct that makes their tame counterparts follow a man in the city streets in the moonlight. He knew he could send them scurrying away into the brush with a shout, but with the habit of those who live in the wild places of the earth, he had no desire to molest anything that did not molest him. Besides, the leaping shadows were company of a sort, and their presence was a guarantee that no larger savage beast or savage man was near.

Joe lost the companion shadows at the Gila River, when he and Kitty splashed across it.

He had not yet found Manuel Gonzalez' train of ox teams, but he knew it must be comparatively near—probably camped at the spring half a dozen miles farther on. There was nothing to be gained by coming upon it at this time of night. There are certain rules on the frontier, just as in the city, as to breaking a tired man's sleep unnecessarily, so Joe decided to camp near the river and hurry on at daybreak with his message.

He unsaddled Kitty and turned her loose to graze in the river bottom, knowing that she would remain close by. Then, finding a place where the brush was thick enough to screen him from sight of the road, he broke through his leafy wall.

A branch used as a broom sufficed to obliterate the tracks that showed a ride had ended here, and behind his screen of mesquite brush he lay down to sleep, his saddle for a pillow, the soft earth for a bed. He needed no covers, for on that high mesa of the Gila there was no dew.

A city boy might wonder that he took pains to hide himself from the road and to disguise the traces of his camp, but to Joe it was as natural as it is to the town-bred lad to lock his bedroom door at a strange hotel.

Joe said his little prayer, taught to him by the mother whose death had left him to make his way alone two years before, and closed his eyes. A boy is not likely to forget his prayers when the only roof above him is the sky, and every star seems like a bright eye seeing clear through him. Joe did not have to wait for sleep; he was off as soon as his eyes were shut.

Suddenly he was wide awake again. The moon was gone, but the stars were still shining, and by them he knew day was yet far distant. After a moment to collect his wits, he was conscious that somebody was talking on the other side of the bushes. The first words made him all attention.

"Gonzalez' outfit," he heard the voice say, "will come on as soon as it is light, and we had better meet it right here. To meet it tonight might make the bull-driver suspicious; and besides, that boy Joe knows I'm not with the Montezuma company anymore. I want to get the money without having to hurt anybody."

"But say, Lampson," Joe heard another voice, "won't the boy be there just the same in the morning?"

"Not a bit of it," said Lampson. "He'll just give Gonzalez his message and start back. He doesn't know why he is sent. Nobody but the Lordsburg agent and the superintendent is supposed to know there is twenty-five thousand dollars in bills rolled up in a bale of blankets. That much comes every month to pay off the men at the mines. The company is afraid to send it by the stage, because it is held up by rustlers so often. Nobody would ever think of hunting through the freight for the money. The freighter himself hasn't an idea of what he is carrying. They have been doing this for a long time and have never had any trouble, but the boss can't help feeling a little anxious, so he always chases the boy off down the road to make sure where the money train is."

Joe's first impulse had been to shout a greeting, but as the man's words reached him he realized in a flash what they meant. The mystery of his monthly mission that had so puzzled him was a mystery no longer.

"I don't see why we should have a bit of trouble," said Lampson. "I'll just tell Gonzalez that the company is in a hurry for the blankets for some prospecting parties and has sent me on ahead with the buckboard to fetch them. He knows me from seeing me in the office and will probably not ask any questions."

"But," asked one of the others, "suppose the boy has told him you were fired?"

"If I can't convince him the boy lied, we will have to use our guns. Now quit talking. We'd all better get some sleep."

Soon there was silence, broken only by the regular breathing of the three men.

So cautiously that not even a rustling leaf betrayed him, Joe raised his head and peered through the bushes. He saw three men lying asleep—the buckboard standing at the side of the road and the horses unhitched and picketed beside it.

His first thought was to slip the stake ropes and stampede the horses, but he realized that the sleepers might be awakened by the plunging animals, and the thought of what they might do in their anger made Joe feel fearful.

As silently as a fox stalking a wild fowl, Joe skirted the men and buckboard and made for the river bottom. He was soon beside his mare. There was an anxious moment when he was afraid Kitty would greet him with a neigh, but she only raised her head from the tall grass and put out her nose to be petted.

He had ridden her bareback as often as with a saddle, and in a moment he was on her, making his way by a wide detour past the sleeping men. As soon as he was beyond earshot, he gave Kitty her head and sped away. His idea had been that all he had to do was to tell Gonzalez of Lampson's plot. Now he remembered the words of Lampson himself: "Nobody is supposed to know the money is there but the agent of Lordsburg and the superintendent." It was the company's secret, and Joe dared not betray it even to the freighter.

At last a sparkle far ahead showed him the embers of a dying campfire, and soon he was near enough to make out the big white prairie schooners. He had found Gonzalez' outfit.

The voice of timidity whispered that he might discharge his commission with safety to himself. All he had to do was to deliver his message to the freighter as it was given him, turn around, gallop back home, and say nothing of what he had overheard by the river. The company would lose twenty-five thousand dollars, but nobody would blame him.

But another voice—the voice of duty—spoke louder, insisting that taking care of himself was not all he was there for.

"The boss wants you to hurry up; he needs that flour," said Joe to the head freighter, when he had roused him.

Gonzalez grumbled at being wakened for such a message, but he was too sleepy to blame the boy, and finally he told him he had better spend the night with them.

Just then a plan occurred to Joe. "I'll sleep in the wagons if you don't mind," he said.

"Just as you like," yawned the freighter. "There's a big bale of blankets back in the trailer."

So Joe tethered Kitty to the wheel of the trailer and

crawled in on top of the blankets—a rough bale covered with burlap and laced with ropes.

Before dawn he got a sandwich from the camp cook, borrowed a saddle, and with a bundle rolled in his coat and tied on behind, started on his long ride home, while Gonzalez and his crew were yet yoking the oxen to the wagons.

Five miles up the road Joe met Lampson and the two big men rolling along in the buckboard. His heart almost stopped beating until he was past, but the former bookkeeper merely waved him a greeting.

Joe galloped on. He felt safe enough now to chuckle at the scene that would be enacted back there, when the robbers, after carrying off the heavy bale, would open it and find nothing.

The superintendent hailed the boy as he rode up to the office of the copper company. "Did you find Gonzalez?"

"Yes, sir!" shouted Joe. "He said he'd hurry." Then Joe pulled his coat from behind the saddle, handed over the bundle of bank notes, and blurted out his adventures.

"It wasn't much of a trick to untie the bale, sir," he said, "and I tied it up again while Gonzalez thought I was sleeping; but I'm afraid the company has lost the blankets."

"I'm willing to lose them," said the superintendent.

The superintendent talked the matter over with the manager, and at first they thought one of the biggest notes in the package was the proper reward for Joe, whose presence of mind had saved the money. But when the superintendent mentioned it to his wife, she gave him another suggestion, and that is how that, for several years, the item of a boy's schooling appeared on the expense account of the copper company.

If you happen to be interested in the story and ever go out to Arizona, the present superintendent of the Montezuma Copper Company can give you the details of the boy's subsequent career.

The present superintendent's name is Armstrong.

Children's Friend, July 1947.

"I Would Like to Know What You Have Done With My Name"

GEORGE ALBERT SMITH

A number of years ago I was seriously ill; in fact, I think everyone gave up on me but my wife. With my family I went to St. George, Utah, to see if it would improve my health. We went as far as we could by train and then continued the journey in a wagon, in the bottom of which a bed had been made for me.

At St. George we arranged for a tent for my health and comfort, with a built-in floor raised about a foot above the ground; the south side of the tent could be rolled up to make the sunshine and fresh air available. I became so weak as to be scarcely able to move. It was a slow and exhausting effort for me even to turn over in bed.

One day, under these conditions, I lost consciousness of my surroundings and thought I had passed to the other side. I found myself standing with my back to a large and beautiful lake, facing a great forest of trees. There was no one in sight, and there was no boat upon the lake or any other visible means to indicate how I might have arrived there. I realized, or seemed to realize, that I had finished my work in mortality and had gone home. I began to look around to see if I could not find someone. There was no evidence of anyone living there, just those great, beautiful trees in front of me and the wonderful lake behind me.

I began to explore, and soon I found a trail through the woods that seemed to have been used very little and that was almost obscured by grass. I followed this trail, and after I had walked for some time and had traveled a considerable distance through the forest, I saw a man coming toward me. I became aware that he was a very large man, and I hurried my steps to reach him, because I recognized him as my grandfather. In mortality he weighed over three hundred pounds, so you may know he was a large man. I remember how happy I was to see him coming. I had been given his name and had always been proud of it.

When Grandfather came within a few feet of me, he stopped. His stopping was an invitation for me to stop. Then —and this I would like the boys and girls and young people never to forget—he looked at me very earnestly and said, "I would like to know what you have done with my name."

Everything I had ever done passed before me as though it were a moving picture on a screen—everything I had done. Quickly this vivid retrospect came down to the very time I was standing there. My whole life had passed before me. I smiled and looked at my grandfather and said, "I have never done anything with your name of which you need be ashamed."

He stepped forward and took me in his arms, and as he did so, I became conscious again of my earthly surroundings. My pillow was as wet as though water had been poured on it—wet with tears of gratitude that I could answer unashamed.

I have thought of this many times, and I want to tell you that I have been trying, more than ever since that time, to take care of that name. So I say to the boys and girls, to the young men and women, to the youth of the Church and of all the world: Honor your fathers and your mothers. Honor the names that you bear, because some day you will have the privilege and the obligation of reporting to them (as well as to your Father in heaven) what you have done with their name.

George Albert Smith, *Sharing the Gospel with Others* (Deseret Book Co., 1948).

Dawn Boy

THELMA J. HARRISON

S etting Sun, wrinkled and tired, sad and old, sat before the door of his tepee. It was nighttime. The stars twinkled; the moon shed silver-pink beams on a darkened earth; a bird called sleepily; an owl sent forth its weird screech; and from a distance came the wail of a coyote. But Setting Sun neither saw nor heard, so deeply was he wrapped in his own thoughts.

He thought, "No sons have I. No sons! Seven sons were sent to me by the Great Spirit—brave sons they were, handsome as the turkey bird, straight as the water reed, agile as the rainbow fish, fleet as the tawny deer. Good sons they were—gentle like the doe, industrious like the squirrel, courageous as the she cat protecting her young."

As Setting Sun thought, he sighed, but the words went on in his mind: "Seven sons has the great Spirit given me; seven sons have been killed in battle; seven great warriors have gone to the Happy Hunting Grounds.

"Seven sons have I trained that they might be good chiefs; seven sons have I trained so that any one of them would be a fit guide for my people when I, Setting Sun, should die; but now they are all gone even as are all the

101

stalwart young braves of the tribe, for this year there have been many wars. Only the old men are left. If I should pass to the Happy Hunting Grounds, there is no one with wisdom to guide my people; there is no one to read the signs in the heavens; there is no one wise in the secret of herbs. Only the young boys are left. From these youths, I, Setting Sun, must choose one—one who will be a just, wise chief, though very young; one who will guide my people wisely and well. But whom shall I choose? Whom shall I bring to my tepee to train in the ways of a chief?"

For a long time Setting Sun sat, thinking, thinking, trying to decide which boy.

The stars grew pale. The moon disappeared behind a mountain peak. A cool breeze began to creep through Setting Sun's blankets and chill his old bones. Finally, stiff and weary, he arose and went into his tepee. He was very tired but his mind was at rest, for he had made his decision. He had decided that he, Setting Sun, would not himself choose the boy to become chief of his people. He would hold contests, and the boy would show himself.

Next day all the tribe knew of Setting Sun's decision. All the boys were excited and happy. Each boy was thrilled with the idea that perhaps he would become chief of his tribesmen.

For a fortnight contests were to be held—contests in running, in fishing, in hunting. Setting Sun would find who could shoot the surest arrow, who could endure longest in the war dance, who was the swiftest runner. It was also said that by these contests, Setting Sun would know who was fair and just, who was honest and good, for Setting Sun was old and very wise.

And so the contests began. All the young boys assembled with their bows and arrows for hunting, with their spears for fishing; each had resolved in his heart that he would be the one Setting Sun would take to his tepee. Mothers and sisters and little brothers came, all hopeful and confident that the one they loved would outshine the others.

Of them all, one stood forth from the others; one surpassed in all the feats. That one was Dawn Boy, son of

Singing Arrow, who was a great warrior and a friend of Setting Sun.

In the races, Dawn Boy was always the fleetest; in the war dance, Dawn Boy endured the longest; in the shooting contest, not one of his arrows missed the mark. When Setting Sun sent them out to hunt, Dawn Boy was the first to return. With a deer slung over his shoulders and a turkey bird hanging on his belt, he came into camp. When they went to the river to fish, Dawn Boy speared the greatest number in the shortest time. Always joy and strength seemed to radiate from him.

"But," thought Setting Sun, "everything has been easy for Dawn Boy. Nothing has been difficult. Not yet do I know if Dawn Boy is fit to become chief. I must find one more task. I must find something that is difficult for Dawn Boy, something he does not enjoy doing."

So to each of the boys was given one more task. Each one was to make a belt for Setting Sun. The belt was to be made of beads; it was to be beautiful and original in design. One day was given in which the boys should learn the art of beading; then the contest would begin. In three more suns, the belt was to be finished.

So each boy set forth to make a belt. None complained. It was a test given by Setting Sun, wise and beloved chief. It was a final test to find who was worthy to be taught in the ways of wisdom.

Diligently the boys worked. The first day passed, and some progressed rapidly; some, more slowly; Dawn Boy, not at all. Though he tried repeatedly, he could not make a design that was really beautiful.

Dawn Boy's mother watched sympathetically, but she could not help. Setting Sun watched too. He watched when he did not seem to be watching.

"At last," said Setting Sun to himself, "I have found something that is not easy for Dawn Boy—something in which he does not excel. About the belt I do not care. I wish only to see how he acts in time of trouble. I wish only to see if he behaves in a manner fitting a chief."

For half a day Dawn Boy worked. Three designs he started. Three designs lay unfinished. Dawn Boy knew that none of them was good. Finally he arose and, saying no word, disappeared into the nearby woods.

"He's a quitter," thought Setting Sun. "If it's hard for him to do, he's a quitter. A good chief is never a quitter. However, I think I shall follow him and see what he does."

Silently, so that not even a twig crackled, Setting Sun followed Dawn Boy.

On Dawn Boy went, farther into the woods until he came to the winding river. Then he stopped, looked around him to see that he was alone, and, finding himself alone, stretched his arms toward heaven. Looking up, he said, "Great Spirit, ruler of the sun, the moon, and stars, to you I, Dawn Boy, come for assistance. Help me, Great Spirit, to fashion a design for the belt of Setting Sun. Help me, Great Spirit, to work with speed that I may make up the time I have lost. As thou hast helped me before, Great Spirit, I pray thee to help me again that I might dwell in the tepee of Setting Sun; that I might learn to be wise and good as befits a chief." Then Dawn Boy went back to the others.

Setting Sun remained hidden until Dawn Boy was well on his way; then he too went back to camp.

Once again Dawn Boy set to work. Once again it seemed he could make no design; and then a strange thing happened. Crawling up a small twig lying near Dawn Boy's foot was a worm. Dawn Boy reached for the twig to move it lest he step on the worm and crush it, but as he raised the stick, he saw that on the worm's back were many colors. He saw that on the worm's back was a pattern, intricate of design, beautiful in color.

Joy flooded Dawn Boy's face. The Great Spirit, who designed the heavens and the earth, the birds and the animals, had heard his prayer; the Great Spirit had sent one of his own designs to place on the belt of Setting Sun.

Intently Dawn Boy studied the design. Yes, it was the loveliest design he had ever seen. The pattern was repeated over and over again in sections on the worm's back.

Quickly Dawn Boy chose colors from his bowl of beads that corresponded to the colors on the worm's back; then diligently he worked. Occasionally, when it looked as though the worm would crawl from the twig and away, Dawn Boy placed another twig for the worm to crawl on, lest the little creature disappear before he was able to finish the pattern.

At length Dawn Boy finished the first square of his design. He paused to admire it. It was identical to that which was on the worm's back. The pale blue, the deep blue, the black, the white, the orange, and the yellow looked just as beautiful on the bead belt as they did on the worm's back. But not for long did Dawn Boy stop to admire, for he was far behind the others. Back to work he went to repeat the pattern over and over again, just as the Great Spirit had done.

Finally all the belts were finished—all, that is, except Dawn Boy's. Undaunted, he worked on. Not yet had the third sun set. He must finish his task. At last, just as the great, golden sun slipped from view, Dawn Boy finished. He took his belt to the place where Setting Sun and the others were waiting. He hung his belt over the display rod that Setting Sun had prepared. He heard murmurs of admiration as the tribesmen viewed the beautiful belt he had made.

Setting Sun, however, did not look at the belt. He arose and, with an upraised arm, silenced the group. Then he began speaking.

"Seven sons has the Mighty One given me—seven sons, stalwart and handsome, courageous and good. And now, to me he has given an eighth son to dwell in my tepee. He has given me a son like unto the seven; he has given me Dawn Boy, offspring of Singing Arrow.

"Fleet he is like the deer; strong like the pine tree; quick like the winging bird; sure like the arrow. But it is not for these reasons I take him in my tepee. A beautiful belt he has made for me, choice among all others. But it is not for this reason I take him to train in ways of wisdom.

"I take him because of his mighty faith—faith in the power, the goodness, the helpfulness of the Great Spirit. Because of this faith I know that when you, my people, are in trouble—that when he, your chief-to-be, has difficulties—

to the Great Spirit he will appeal for help and guidance. Because of his great faith, I, Setting Sun, have faith in him—faith that when I am gone, he will be a good and mighty chieftain for my people."

When he finished, Setting Sun led Dawn Boy into his tepee.

A great cheer arose from the people—a cheer for Setting Sun, the old chief, good and wise, brave and true, and a cheer for Dawn Boy, the young brave who would follow in the footsteps of Setting Sun.

A Story to Tell (Deseret Book Co., 1971).

"Let's Put a Dollar in Each Shoe"

OSCAR A. KIRKHAM

Two boys, playing along a ditch bank, found a pair of shoes at the edge of a field. One boy said, "Let's fill them with rocks and see what the owner does."

The other boy said, "Let's put a dollar in each shoe and see what happens."

They followed the second suggestion.

The man was watering the field and finally came back to get his shoes, which he had put aside so carefully in order to save them.

When he put his foot into his shoe, he pulled it out again quickly and found the dollar. Then he looked in the other shoe and found another dollar.

Tears came to his eyes, and he kneeled on the ground and thanked his Heavenly Father in a voice filled with emotion that now he could buy some food to take home to his hungry family. The two boys also went home thankful and happy.

Oscar A. Kirkham, *Say the Good Word* (Deseret Book Co., 1958).

The Lost Skates

J. C. NOLAN

One afternoon Jimmie was sitting on the front porch, thinking about his lost skates. He was thinking about them because down the street, near the corner, a little boy was skating back and forth. Watching this boy made Jimmie think about his own skates.

The boy at the corner went slowly and uncertainly back and forth. He seemed to be just learning to skate. Occasionally he tumbled, but most of the time he got along quite well.

As he came close, Jimmie was surprised to see that the boy's skates looked quite new.

"They are very much like mine," thought Jimmie. Just then the boy skated past him.

"They are just like mine," thought Jimmie. Then, when the boy skated past again, Jimmie saw, printed on the straps, the word *Jimmie.*

"Why, they are mine!" shouted Jimmie.

He stepped in front of the boy. "Where did you get my skates?" he demanded.

The little boy stared at him with round, frightened eyes. "They're not your skates," he said. "They're mine. The junkman gave them to me."

"I don't care who gave them to you," said Jimmie, crossly. "They are mine. What's your name?"

"Stephen."

"Well! See! My name is Jimmie, and here it is, right here, where I printed it myself—*Jimmie*. So they are mine!"

The little boy looked worried. "The junkman gave them to me. He found them in the gutter where they had been thrown away."

"They must have rolled down the walk when I took them off," said Jimmie, recalling that day when he had fallen and hurt his cheek. "Well, anyway, I didn't throw them away. And they are mine. Give them to me!"

The little boy sat down and began to tug obediently at the straps. "I guess you're right," he said. "They must be yours."

Jimmie took the skates and ran home. At his own door-step he looked back. The boy was still sitting where Jimmie had left him, but now he was leaning over, his head on his arms, crying.

Jimmie had thought he would be perfectly happy to have his skates back again. He had been so sorry to lose them, and he had hunted high and low for them! But he couldn't help thinking about that little boy. He kept remembering how he had looked, hunched over on the sidewalk with his head down, crying. Jimmie thought so hard about it that he couldn't enjoy his dinner.

As he was getting ready for bed, he suddenly made up his mind. He slipped his bathrobe over his pajamas and went downstairs into the living room where his mother and daddy were.

"I want to talk to you," said Jimmie.

"Why, what is it, son?" asked his mother.

Then Jimmie told them about the boy who had been skating at the corner that afternoon. He told them how the boy had looked—so small and shabby—and how he had put his head down and cried.

"And I think," said Jimmie, at last, "that if you don't mind, Mother, I'll give the skates back to him. He really believed they were his; and somehow it doesn't seem right to take them away, just because the junkman made a mistake and thought they had been thrown away, there in the gutter."

"I think you are right," said his mother. "And I'll tell you something else I think"—and she kissed him—"I think you are a good boy."

And next morning, Jimmie and his mother drove over to the little house by the railroad tracks and gave Stephen the wonderful skates to keep for his very own. Stephen was happy—and so was Jimmie!

A Story to Tell (Deseret Book Co., 1971).

To Run and Not Be Weary

LEO W. SPENCER

I wasn't quite twelve years old, but I worked right alongside my father in the grain harvest over sixty years ago. He cut and I bundled the grain into stooks; it was exhausting labor, day after day.

One Saturday, we began stooking at daylight and stopped about 8:30 that night. I was so tired I wanted to lie down and sleep without even waiting for supper.

My father looked at me and said gently, "Lee, the patch of grain I cut today was very green. If we wait until Monday to stook it, the kernels will be shrunken. We must do it tonight. There's a bright moon outside. Do you think you can help me?"

I fought back the tears and nodded.

My father said, "Okay, we'll have a bite of supper, I'll slop the hogs, and then we'll stook the grain."

We soon finished our bread and milk, but I was still so tired that I could hardly raise my head. As my father went out to feed the pigs, I sat at the table, saying to myself bitterly, "I've never smoked or drank; I've always obeyed the Word of Wisdom. The Doctrine and Covenants says that if you obey the Word of Wisdom you will run and not be

111

weary and walk and not faint. And now I'm so tired I can hardly raise my head." My mouth twitched as I fought to keep back the tears of exhaustion.

It is impossible to describe what happened, but it seemed as though a beautiful shaft of white light entered my body, filling every fiber of my being. I got up when Father came back, and we went out to the fields.

My father was a very fast worker, but he couldn't keep up with me that night, even though he worked as fast as he could. I ran for stray bundles and tossed them, many heavier than I was, from windrow to windrow. I'll never forget the astonishment in my father's eyes.

Ensign, March 1974.

Skating to Danger

MARIE LARSEN

As Wally fastened on his ice skates, his heart beat with hopefulness. The ice-covered meadow was vacant! Joe and the other boys hadn't come skating yet. There was no one to drive him away. This time he'd be able to skate—perhaps even until he learned to keep his legs from going in different directions and from sailing out from under him at the most unexpected times.

"I could skate just as well as anyone in a little while, even if this is the first time I've lived around ice," Wally told himself as he drew the last strap tight. "I've practically memorized the skating manual Mr. Penroy loaned me. I can make my skates work, I know I can! If the boys will only let me try!"

Carefully he stood up. He balanced perfectly and sighed with satisfaction. Then suddenly his feet began slipping along the ice. His body rocked back and forth and his arms made wild circles in the air. His feet slid up off the ice and out from under him. There was a swush! and a splat! and a stinging coldness as he sat down, hard.

"The kid from the city skates kind of fancy," someone chuckled behind him. Wally twisted his aching neck toward

113

the sound of the chuckling. It was Joe! Already he and the boys were here, leaning over the long split poles that fenced the ice-covered meadow from adjoining fields. And they were laughing at him!

Joe straddled the pole fence. He waved an arm. "Go on, beat it, kid!" he said sourly. "We want to skate now. And we don't want you falling under our feet like you did yesterday."

Wally slipped along in a sitting position until he reached a clump of protruding sod near the fence. He stood up and took a deep breath.

"Look, fellows. Mr. Penroy gave me permission to skate in this meadow. I asked him when the river first began freezing and backing up right after we moved here from the city." He gazed at them steadily. "You've sent me away every day, but this time I think I'll stay!"

Joe pushed ahead of the others. "He gave you permission to skate, did he? If you'd skate, it would be different."

Wally thought of the manual. "Maybe I haven't done a lot of skating. But I've a book that tells how—and I'm sure in time I can do it right!"

Joe roared. "Learning to skate from a book! Just like a city kid."

Wally felt a warmness creeping up along his neck. He pressed his lips tight to keep from saying all the things he felt. He stood up again, holding his knees tightly together until he felt confident. Then he pushed one foot slowly forward and at an angle, leaning ahead just a little. When he lifted his other foot a bit he found he didn't wobble as he had done before. He slid it along the ice. His heart leaped. He could keep his feet going. He was skating!

Behind him he heard the sound of skates being dropped to the ice. Joe and the boys were putting on their skates. Perhaps they would leave him alone now that he was showing them he could skate. Slow, yes. But skating just the same!

Soon he heard the swishing of skates behind him, and suddenly the boys were all around him, skating this way and that, zooming very close to him, then twisting away. Wally felt choked. They were not going to leave him alone even today. And now they were trying to confuse him. He could tell, and he tried not to look at them. But when Joe came skating directly toward him, yelling as he came, Wally's ankles wobbled. He tried to remember what he had read about turning. He curved one skate to move out of Joe's way—and then his feet and skates left the ice. Wally hit his head on the hard coldness. There was a swishing sound as Joe curved expertly away, a dull ache in Wally's head as he tried to see him go.

When Wally tried to sit up he felt sick inside. He looked sadly down at his skates and began unbuckling the straps. It was no use. They didn't intend to let him skate. For some reason they didn't like him; they didn't want him to learn at all!

Wally got up and crossed the ice to the pole fence. He sat down and let his skates drop to the sod beside him. He watched the boys cutting fancy figures across the ice-covered meadow, then sailing swiftly toward the icy river to veer expertly away at the very edge of the thinner ice. They had to be good to do that, Wally thought. The ice on the river was dangerous. Mr. Penroy had warned him against trying to skate on the river ice. But Joe and the other boys knew just when to turn back. It looked like a game they were playing. As they circled in the center and whisked away again, he couldn't help wishing he could be good enough to join them.

He watched Joe sailing ahead of the others toward the river again. He was getting mighty close. He should turn now, Wally thought. The other boys turned but Joe kept on. Wally tensed. Surely Joe knew the danger of the river ice—

"Joe!"

Wally didn't know what made him cry out. Somehow he felt a sudden alarm for the boy even before he saw the ice start to split. Joe must have seen it too. He tried to twist away, but his skate caught in the cracking ice. He lost balance and fell flat upon his stomach. Weblike cracks suddenly appeared all about him with the heaviness of his fall. And then Wally saw the ice sink beneth Joe, a huge slab of it, leaving Joe clinging frantically to the edge of a hole.

"Help me! Quick!" Joe screamed.

Some of the boys turned at his cry. They sped toward him, but they stopped at the edge of the weblike cracks.

"We can't get nearer, Joe!" one of them said. "That ice won't hold anybody!"

"You've got to get me out! The ice is giving way!" Joe's face was white. "Hurry!"

Wally had been unable to move before, but he stood up now, clutching the fence poles with trembling fingers. They must help Joe! If the ice he was clinging to gave way he would go under! But what? He had read something— There was something he should remember—

His shoulder brushed against the split poles as he moved. He felt its rough flat surface where it had been split for fence making. His heart leaped. The *poles!* If one of them was long enough to stretch across the weblike cracks—across the caved-in ice to good ice—Joe might be able to cling on until they could help him!

Wally gave a shout for help and began tearing at the top pole. Some of the boys heard him, realized his intentions, and skated swiftly to help. The pole creaked with the effort of their pulling. Then it came free, and they slid in along the ice to the edge of the weblike cracks. Together they pushed it, flat side down, across the hole. Wally took a deep breath. It reached! He felt a deep relief when he saw Joe reach for the rail and cling to it with trembling hands, but he held his breath until he was sure the ice was going to hold.

"Can you make it now, Joe?" someone asked.

Joe turned a white face toward them. His lips were blue, and his teeth chattered. He tried to pull himself up, then said helplessly, "I'm too cold."

Wally said quickly, "I'm the smallest. I'll go out along the pole and help him. Someone go build a fire by the fence. Mr. Penroy won't care if you use one of the poles, I know. The rest of you be ready to drag the pole across the ice if it starts to give way."

He crawled slowly out along the pole toward Joe. He felt Joe's icy fingers clutch his and he pulled hard. He closed his eyes and hoped with all his heart that the pole would hold up. Then he felt Joe free of the hole. He felt him sliding along behind him as they started inching back toward the others.

Helping hands pulled Joe up and carried him toward the fire someone had started. Wally followed along behind them and stood off away from the excitement-stirred circle. Presently he turned to pick up his skates. Joe would be all right when they got him dry and warm.

As he turned away he heard Joe ask, "Where's Wally?"

"You mean the city kid?" someone wondered.

"I mean Wally," Joe said, flatly. "When you call him a city kid it should be with respect. He thought of using the pole, didn't he?"

The circle split. Wally saw Joe sitting by the fire, wrapped in coats.

"Come here, Wally," Joe motioned. "I want to thank you for getting me out." As Wally walked nearer, he went on, "You know, Wally, I've been acting smart. I was even trying to be smart when I went out on the river ice. But I think I'm through being smart. If you still want to learn to skate, we'll leave you alone from now on."

Joe looked around at the other boys. Wally followed his gaze. Some of the boys dropped their eyes and chopped at the ice with the sharp points of their skates. Wally grinned and straightened his shoulders.

"I'll see you tomorrow then," he said.

"Wally—" someone spoke up as he turned again. "Wally, that book on ice skating—the one you have been reading—I think some of us need to read a little of it. How about bringing it along?"

The boy meant it, Wally could tell. And a feeling started to grow inside him that made him want to shout. He thought of several things he could say—things they probably expected him to say to get even. But he grinned instead.

"I'll bring it," he promised.

Children's Friend, January 1948.

"I Don't Need to Be Afraid of a Praying Indian"

SUSANNAH WHITE

The first sawmill in Escalante, Utah, was situated in North Creek Canyon, about fourteen miles from town. This mill was built and managed by Henry J. White.

One Sunday it became necessary for Mr. White to leave his young wife, Susannah, alone at the sawmill until the next day. He disliked doing this because Indians were camped close by, and one was known to be the meanest Indian in the country.

About two hours after Mr. White left, this very Indian came to the mill. He rode up to the cabin and asked, "Where is your Mormon?" Susannah pretended that she wasn't frightened, and she told the Indian that Mr. White had gone to town. The Indian said he wanted to hunt above the mill, and Susannah gave her permission. He rode away, but reappeared in the late afternoon with two deer tied on his horse, and again he asked, "Where is your Mormon?" She told him he was still in town. The Indian then asked if he could stay all night. She told him he could stay; he could put his horse in the corral and feed it.

The deer were hung in a nearby tree and the horse cared

for before the Indian came to the cabin. Susannah had supper ready when he came in, and after eating, they sat by the fireplace. He tried to tell her the town news and passed her a dirty little sack of pine nuts.

While sitting there the Indian asked, "You 'fraid?"

"No, I'm not afraid," replied Susannah. "I can shoot as good as any Indian."

The reply amused the Indian, and laughingly he replied, "You no shoot Indian."

When the time came to retire, Susannah gave him some matches and said, "My Mormon always makes the fire in the morning." She then gave him a quilt and some rugs to make himself a bed by the fire.

Susannah, thinking she would have to remain awake all night and watch him, slipped off only her shoes and climbed into bed. When she looked around, she was amazed to see the Indian kneeling in prayer by the side of his bed.

Susannah had been terribly frightened all evening, but seeing the Indian now, she said to herself, "I don't need to be afraid of a praying Indian." Soon after, she went to sleep and slept until daylight the next morning, when she was awakened by the Indian, who was building the fire. He insisted on helping milk the cows, but she explained that the cows would be afraid of him; he could cut her an armful of wood, though, which he gladly did. He cut a large pile instead of an armful.

After they had eaten breakfast, the Indian left. But before going, he cut two hindquarters off one of the deer and left them hanging in the tree for her.

Children's Friend, September 1943.

The Joy of Giving

NEWELL K. WHITNEY

Once there was a pioneer mother whose husband died and left her to care for several small children. The oldest boy's name was Newell. This little family was very poor; often the children left the table hungry. There was always something in the house to eat, but not a thing to spare. One day the mother was taken sick and had to stay in bed. The care of the home and the little ones was left to Newell.

The boy took the few vegetables he could find and made a soup. It looked as if there would be just enough for the family, and he felt happy. When all was cooked, he carefully took some in a bowl to his mother's bedside. It smelled and tasted good to her.

After the first spoonful, she said, "Newell, take a bowl of this over to Sister Brown."

"But Mother," he said, "why do you give it away when we are so poor and need it ourselves?"

The mother answered, "My boy, if you wait to give until you feel you can afford it, you will never know the joy of giving."

A Story to Tell (Deseret Book Co., 1971).

A Most Important Boy

ROSALIE W. DOSS

"Good morning, Señor Martinez! How are you this fine morning?" said Juan. He smiled at the old man, who was leaning over his workbench.

"Fine!" replied Señor Martinez, looking up from his work.

"Come, Juan, look at this belt I am working on. Does the bird design look right?"

"Oh, yes, Señor Martinez," said Juan, examining the beautiful piece of leatherwork. "The bird is so real it looks as if it could fly right off the belt."

Señor Martinez smiled happily. "Thank you, Juan. You are a big help."

Juan went on down the village street. He was on his way to get a jug of goat's milk from Señor Morales, who lived at the other end of the village. The milk was for Juan's baby brother, Pepe. Juan went after the milk every morning. And every morning he stopped along the way and greeted his friends and neighbors.

This morning, under his bright smile, Juan felt just a little sad. He said, "If only I could make beautiful things out of leather the way Señor Martinez does. Then I would feel

121

important. Señor Martinez must be just about the most important man in our village."

But Juan did not stay sad for long. When he saw Señora Garcia coming out of her neat, whitewashed little adobe house, Juan sang out, "Good morning, Señora Garcia."

"Ah, it is you, Juan," cried Señora Garcia happily. "I was waiting for you to come by. Today is my market day. Could you give me a hand with these baskets? I want to sling them across Benito's back."

"I would be glad to help, Señora Garcia," said Juan.

Benito, the little brown burro, stood very still as Juan helped Señora Garcia place the baskets on his back. The baskets had to be balanced just right so that they would not be burdensome for the little animal to carry. In the baskets were ears of corn, squash, sticks of sugarcane, and strings of ornamental gourds.

Señora Garcia not only took her own produce to market, but she also transported some of the things her neighbors grew. Señora Garcia was the only person in the village who owned a burro.

When they had finished loading Benito, Señora Garcia gave Juan a stick of sugarcane. *"Graciás!"* she said. "I never would have been able to load Benito without your help, Juan."

Juan went off down the street nibbling on the sweet, delicious sugarcane. How he wished he owned a burro! Then he could go to market for his neighbors the way Señora Garcia did. Then he would surely feel very important.

The sad feeling began to come back again, but it did not last long. All along the street Juan met people he knew, and always Juan's bright smile flashed as he greeted them.

At Señor Morales' house there was much shouting and confusion.

"What is it, Señor Morales?" asked Juan. But he already had an idea of what had happened.

"My goats are loose again. The rascals broke out of their pen," cried Señor Morales.

"I will help you catch them," said Juan, setting down his jug. Almost every morning Juan helped Señnor Morales catch his troublemaking goats, who liked nothing better than breaking out of their pen.

With Juan's help, it did not take long to get the goats back into their pen.

After Señor Morales had thanked Juan and filled his jug with milk, Juan started back home. But all the way he kept thinking how wonderful it would be to have a fine herd of goats, even if they were mischievous. He could supply the other villagers with milk the way Señor Morales did. Then he would really be important.

Juan gave the jug of milk to his mother and went back out into the yard. He kept thinking, "Everyone in this village is more important than I am."

At that moment it happened! Juan's thoughts were so far away and so sad that he did not notice the big rock. Flip! Flop! Crash! Bang! Juan tripped over the rock and fell to the ground very hard. A sharp pain started at his ankle and shot right up his leg.

"Are you hurt, Juan?" cried his mother.

"I think I hurt my ankle," moaned Juan.

His mother carefully felt Juan's foot and ankle. Then she breathed a deep sigh of relief. "It is only a sprain. Stay off it a few days, and your ankle will be as good as new."

The next morning the sun was already high in the sky when Juan asked from his chair near the window, "Who will go after Pepe's milk today?"

"I will go as soon as I finish my household chores," said Juan's mother.

But Juan's mother did not have to go. There was a shout outside. It was Señor Morales. He said, "When Juan did not show up for the milk, I brought it myself. I was worried. What happened to Juan?"

Before Juan or his mother could answer, old Señor Martinez hobbled into view. "Where is Juan? I missed him this morning."

"So did I," spoke up another voice. It was Señora Garcia.

Then Juan and his mother explained about the sprained ankle and how Juan would have to rest his foot for a few days.

By this time a crowd had gathered outside Juan's window. They all told Juan how sorry they were about his accident.

Juan smiled at his many friends and neighbors and said, "I did not think anyone would miss me. I did not think I was important!"

"How could I handle my stubborn goats if you didn't give me a hand?" asked Señor Morales, grinning broadly.

"How could I get to market without your help?" said Señora Garcia. "Benito and I both look for you every morning."

"And how could I ever begin my day without your cheery greeting?" said old Señor Martinez. "Your kindness and merry smile make you the most important boy in our village."

Juan's smile now became bigger than ever. There was not so much as even a little twinge of sadness left in his heart. Of course, Juan did not really think he was the most important boy in the village, but it was a warm, happy feeling to know that his friends and neighbors thought so much of him. It made him feel useful and wanted. And what can be more important than that!

Children's Friend, March 1968.

"I Can't Do It, Coach"

CREED HAYMOND

To Harvard Stadium in Cambridge, Massachusetts, in May 1919, the great American colleges had sent their best men, seventeen hundred in all, to compete at the annual meet of the Intercollegiate Association of Amateur Athletics of America. Creed Haymond, a Mormon boy, was captain of the Pennsylvania team. The night before the meet, Coach Lawson Robertson came to his room. He was in good spirits. In the tryouts Penn had qualified seventeen men. Cornell, Penn's most feared rival that year, had qualified only ten. As the scoring for the first five places in each event was five, four, three, two, and one, naturally the number of men each team had in the finals greatly influenced its chance to win.

"Creed," Robertson said, "if we do our best tomorrow, we will run away with it."

"We're going to do our best, Robby."

The coach hesitated. "Creed, I'm having the boys take a little sherry wine tonight. I want you to have a little."

"I can't do it, Coach."

"But, Creed, I'm not trying to get you to drink. I know what you Mormons believe. I'm giving you this as a tonic, just to put all of you on your mettle."

125

"It wouldn't do me any good, Robby; I can't take it."

"Remember, Creed, you're the captain of our team and our best point winner. Fourteen thousand students are looking to you personally to win this meet. If you fail us, we'll lose. I ought to know what is good for you."

Creed Haymond believed he had the best coach in the world (and with reason, for Lawson Robertson was to be chosen head coach of the Olympic teams of 1920, 1924, and 1928). Creed knew too that other coaches felt a little wine to be useful when men have trained muscle and nerve to the snapping point. He also knew that his team needed his best efforts. He intensely wished to give them, but he looked Robertson in the eye and said, "I won't take it, Coach."

Robertson smiled a little. On his grim Scottish face there was a curious expression. "You're an odd fellow, Creed. You have ideas of your own. Well, I'm going to let you do as you please."

He went away and left the captain of his team in a state of extreme anxiety. Supposing, Creed thought, he made a poor showing tomorrow; what could he say to Robertson? He was to go against the fastest man in the world. Nothing less than his best would do. His stubbornness might lose the meet for Penn. His teammates were doing as they were told. They believed in their coach. What right had he to disobey? Only one right, one reason, this teaching he had been following and believing all his life, the Word of Wisdom! He knelt down and earnestly, very earnestly, asked the Lord to give him a testimony as to the source of this revelation which he had believed and obeyed literally. Then he went to bed and slept the sound slumber of healthy youth.

Next morning Coach Robertson came to his room and asked anxiously, "How are you feeling, Creed?"

"Fine," the captain answered cheerfully.

"The other fellows are vomiting. I don't know what's the matter with them," he said seriously.

"Maybe it's the tonic you gave them," Creed volunteered.

"Maybe so," Robertson answered.

Two o'clock found twenty thousand spectators in their seats.

As the events got under way, it became plain that something was wrong with the wonderful Penn team. In that beautiful race, the quarter mile, the grinding test of speed and endurance, Pennsylvania's man was figured to take second place and win four precious points. The startled Penn supporters watched the field run away from him; he came in last. In the half-mile event the intercollegiate champion of the year before was Penn's entrant—this time he finished fifth. Two Pennsylvania men were entered in the pole vault and were expected to take first and second places and win nine points. At a height below their own records, they tied for third place and won between them five points. The man entered for the high jump, confidently counted on as a point winner, did not place. The one who should have taken third in the low hurdles did not run.

The 100-yard dash was announced. The six fastest men in the colleges of America took their marks. This and the 220-yard dash to be run later were Creed Haymond's races.

"Take your marks!" The six sprinters crouched. Each put his fingers on the ground at the line and his feet into the hole he had kicked for the start.

"Set!" Every nerve and muscle strained.

The pistol shot—and every man sprang forward into the air and touched earth at a run, that is, all except Creed Haymond. A tall runner had used that second lane in a previous race, and he had kicked holes for his toe an inch or two behind the holes Creed had chosen for his. Under the tremendous thrust Creed gave, the narrow wedge of earth broke through, and he came down on his knees.

In a flash, Creed Haymond was up and running. At sixty yards, the last in the race—then, seeming to fly, he passed the fifth man—the fourth—the third—the second. Only the leader was between him and victory. With his heart almost bursting with the strain, Creed swept in a whirlwind past the leader to victory.

Through some mistake in arrangement, the semifinals of the 220-yard race were not completed until almost time to close the meet. With the same bad break that had followed the Penn team all day, Creed Haymond was placed in the last heat. Five minutes after winning the heat he was called for the finals of the 220, the last event of the day. One of the other men who had run in an earlier heat rushed up to him.

"Tell the starter, Haymond, that you demand a rest before running again. You're entitled to it under the rules. I've hardly caught my breath yet, and I ran in the heat before yours."

Creed went panting to the starter and begged for more time. Just then the telephone rang, and the starter was ordered to begin the race. Regretfully, he called the men to their marks. Under ordinary conditions Creed would have had no fear of this race. He was probably the fastest 220-yard dash runner in the world, but he had already run three races during the afternoon.

At a high point in the grandstand, Coach Lawson Robertson of Pennsylvania and Coach Tom Keene of Syracuse sat with their stopwatches in hand.

With surprise they saw the starter order the breathless men to their marks and, standing behind them, raise his pistol; then the white puff of smoke. This time the Penn captain literally shot from his marks—he was sprinting away from the field. Running his race alone, unpressed by competition, the little Penn captain drove himself to the tape in a burst of speed, eight yards ahead of the nearest man. As he crossed the finish line, both coaches, directly above him, snapped their stopwatches; they looked at the runners and then at each other, almost with awe. Both watches registered exactly twenty-one seconds.

Penn had lost the meet; to everybody's amazement, Pennsylvania, out of seventeen entrants, had only one intercollegiate champion, Captain Creed Haymond.

Later, Robertson laid his hand on the shoulder of the captain of his team and said, "You just ran those 220 yards in the fastest time ever run by any human being."

A *Story to Tell* (Deseret Book Co., 1945).

No Two Diamonds Are Alike

DARYL V. HOOLE

Ella struggled to hold back her tears as she ran along the stone walk to Aunt Susan's apartment at the rear of her home. As Ella rushed up to her aunt, the tears, which had been too near the surface too much of the time lately, spilled over. "Oh, Aunt Susan," sobbed Ella, "nobody likes me. I'm just no good. I wish I weren't such a dumb—" More sobs blotted out the rest of her words.

Aunt Susan laid her knitting aside and waited for her young niece to go on with her problem. "Why do you feel that no one likes you? What makes you think you're dumb and no good?" she encouraged.

"It's just terrible, Aunt Susan, to live with Bevie and Ruth. They make me feel awful. Bevie is so friendly with everyone and can always find so much to talk about. Everybody just loves her. Almost every phone call at our house is for her. She gets invited to all the parties and has all the fun. Whenever I'm in a group of people, I either say the wrong thing or—or else I can't think of anything to say at all. Bevie isn't afraid to talk to anyone, and she's so clever and full of fun. Oh, I wish I could be like Bevie.

"And Ruth makes me feel so dumb and stupid. She can

do anything. Mother and Daddy are forever bragging about her accomplishments. I never do anything worth mentioning. It seems all I hear around our house is talk about her scholarship from the university, or how the new three-piece suit she just made is so beautiful, or something else she has done. Even the bishop said the other day that when Ruth goes away to school he doesn't know what he'll do for a Sunday School organist. She's always in demand for her piano playing. Everyone says things like 'There's just no one quite like Ruth,' or 'She's the most talented and capable girl I've ever seen.' It goes on and on, and the more she does, the dumber I feel."

Aunt Susan thought for a long time before responding to Ella. Finally she said, "I can understand how you feel, Ella. It would be difficult to live with two very popular, talented older sisters. It could make you feel quite inferior. I would like to make three suggestions to you. You might like to write them down and read them often—even memorize them—so that you'll remember them for the rest of your life.

"First, you're comparing yourself with someone else. This is unfair. You're much younger than your sisters. Bevie has had several years more practice talking with people and learning to express herself well and saying clever things. I feel sure you'll gain in confidence and will feel you have more to contribute to conversations as you grow older. Time has done a lot for Ruth, too. As I think back to her piano playing when she was your age, it sounded just the way yours does. Who's to say what accomplishments will be yours by the time you graduate from high school? You've been busy laying your foundation for life these past thirteen years. It's just about now that you can start to build on that foundation and really do things. It's all wrong to compare yourself with others, Ella. The only real basis for comparison is within yourself. Don't feel bad if your piano playing—or anything else—isn't as good as Ruth's. Just make certain that you play better now than you did a year ago. It's wonderful to have people such as Ruth inspire you to do better and reach loftier goals, but compete with yourself—not someone else!

"Now, the second thing I want you to remember always

is this: What someone else does needn't detract from what you do. Just because Bevie has lots of friends doesn't mean that you have any fewer friends of your own. Just because someone has beautiful eyes doesn't mean that your eyes are ugly. Nothing Ruth knows or does or has need detract from what you know or do or have.

"And third and most important, Ella, our Father in heaven has taken great care to create each one of us individually. Don't try to make yourself like someone else. Be grateful for your own talents and gifts and do your best to cultivate them. Why, it was just last week at Relief Society that I heard several mothers discussing baby-sitters. They mentioned your name and said how confident they feel when you are with their children and how much their children enjoy you. Sister Astin said that because of your conscientiousness toward responsiblity and your ability to handle children exceptionally well, you make an ideal baby-sitter.

"Have you ever realized, Ella, that when someone is ill, you know just what to do to bring the most comfort? I recall my bout with rheumatism last winter—it was you who took the time to run my errands, keep fresh flowers at my bedside, and cheer me. You have a fine mind, Ella. I've observed that you have a quest for knowledge. You love school and do very well there. I could go on, Ella, for you have many gifts and talents that make you special just the way you are.

"I read something last week I want to share with you. I hope it will impress you as it did me. Did you know that no two diamonds are, or ever have been, alike? This diamond I am wearing on my finger is unlike any other diamond on earth. That's one of the reasons the diamond has become, since ancient times, the gem of kings and emperors and holds the greatest value of all worldly possessions. No two diamonds are alike, but they are all jewels. Never forget that you are a jewel, Ella."

Ella's heart felt lighter than ever before.

Daryl V. Hoole and Donette V. Ockey, *With Sugar and Spice* (Deseret Book Co., 1966).

The Magic Running Shell

ADDIE ADAM

Jeff ran down the beach, his bare feet raising little spurs of sand behind him. A sandpiper, hunting for fish in the surf, ran away on long stick legs. A gull feeding on a bit of popcorn flew away with an angry squawk.

But still Jeff ran on until, breathless, he flopped down on a sand dune beside a man who wore dark sunglasses and a pink checkered shirt.

"Hi," the man said. "Are you training for the Olympics?"

"No," Jeff giggled, "I'm not old enough." Then he said, "My Sunday School class is having a picnic here in the pavilion this afternoon, and we're going to run a race. I'd like to win the prize. It's a model sailboat."

"Well, you seem to run well," the man observed.

Jeff shook his head. "No. You see, I'm younger than most of the kids, and I have short legs—" He looked out at the ocean where waves curled, showing their white ruffled edges. "I can't run as fast as they do."

Neither spoke for a few minutes, the man absentmindedly rubbing a shell in his hand.

"That's a jingle shell," Jeff said. One of his hobbies were collecting shells.

132

"Yes, but this one is special. It's a magic thinking-shell."

"Really?" Jeff asked.

"Well, did you ever see a jingle shell with a streak on it that looks like paint?"

They examined the thin shell closely, and Jeff admitted he had never seen one like that.

"Well, there you are!" the man said happily. Suddenly, he snapped his fingers. "I have just what you need! A magic running-shell!" He fumbled in his pocket and produced another jingle shell, laying it on the sand beside the other.

"They look alike to me," Jeff observed.

"Oh, no," the man answered. "Did you ever see a jingle shell with tiny marks like bird tracks?"

Jeff examined the shell and admitted he hadn't.

The man picked up the shells and wrapped each in a leaf from a sea grape shrub nearby.

"You keep this running-shell in your pocket when you run, and I'm sure you'll run better than you ever have."

And Jeff did! For a moment in the race he was afraid he wouldn't win, but the little wrapped shell in his pocket gave him confidence, and he won the race.

The next morning Jeff found his friend on the beach. This time the man was wearing a bright yellow shirt with green palm trees on it.

The man looked up. "Don't say anything until I apologize," he said when Jeff reached him. "I accidentally gave you the wrong shell. I'm sorry."

"But I won!" Jeff said. "See, here is my sailboat!"

"That's wonderful!"

After they examined the little carved boat complete with sails, the man and the boy pulled the shells from their pockets. Sure enough, the man had the running-shell and Jeff had the thinking-shell.

"I guess it just proves that the magic wasn't in the shell," the man sighed. "It was inside you. You know, even with the running-shell, I could never run fast enough to win a sailboat."

Children's Friend, July 1970.

The Best Is None Too Good for the Lord

DAVID O. McKAY

What does it mean to obey the law of sacrifice? Nature's law demands us to do everything with self in view. The first law of mortal life, self-preservation, would claim the most luscious fruit, the most tender meat, the softest down on which to lie.

Selfishness, the law of nature, would say, "I want the best; that is mine." But God said: "... bring ... the firstlings of your herds and of your flocks." (Deuteronomy 12:6.)

The best shall be given to God; the next you may have. Thus should God become the center of our very being.

With this thought in view, I thank my earthly father for the lesson he gave to two boys in a hayfield at a time when tithes were paid in kind. We had driven out to the field to get the tenth load of hay and then had gone over to a part of the meadow where we had taken the ninth load, where there was "wire grass" and "slough grass." As we started to load the hay Father called out, "No, boys, drive over to the higher ground." There was timothy and redtop there. But one of the boys (it was I) called back, "No, let us take the hay as it comes!"

"No, David, that is the *tenth* load, and the best is none too good for God."

That is the most effective sermon on tithing I have ever heard in my life, and, I found later in life, it touches this very principle of the law of sacrifice. You cannot develop character without obeying that law. Temptation is going to come to you in this life. You sacrifice your appetites; you sacrifice your passions for the glory of God; and you gain the blessing of an upright character and spirituality. That is a fundamental truth.

Clare Middlemiss, comp., *Cherished Experiences* (Deseret Book Co., 1955).

Baby's New Mother

SHIRLEY CHRISTENSEN

My story, as told me by my Grandfather Christensen, happened about seven miles south and east of Grace, Idaho, in 1882 or 1883.

In the fall of the year, a family by the name of Vaughn lived about two blocks east of our home. The Williams family lived where we live now. Mr. and Mrs. Vaughn had a small baby boy that had just learned to walk fairly well. In the late afternoon the baby wandered outside and was gone only a few minutes when the mother stepped out to get him. She looked all around but could not see him anywhere. There was a deep gully that came down from the canyon past the house. Thinking he might have fallen in it, she looked, but he was not in sight. Getting very excited, she ran over to the Williams' home to get some of them to help hunt for the baby. They and others in the community came. Everyone hunted without success until it was too dark to see.

Early the next morning they renewed their search. After some time they discovered bear tracks leading past the house and up toward the canyon. Being frantic with fear, they followed the tracks. Every few steps they saw the print of a baby's hand, as if it had been put down or dragged.

136

When they had gone about a mile and a half up the canyon, they came to a pile of leaves. Under it the baby lay sleeping soundly, exhausted from crying and hunger. There was not a single scratch on the child anywhere. I think the mother bear must have wanted to adopt a new baby.

_____

Children's Friend, July 1941.

The Hothead

MURRAY T. PRINGLE

A lexander Selkirk appeared to be a pleasantly average boy, neither better nor worse than any other. That is, with one exception.

Alexander Selkirk had a fiery temper that would erupt at the slightest excuse!

Alex was a likable lad when he wasn't angry. His friends tried to teach him to control his temper, because they knew that sooner or later it would get him into trouble. Alex tried, but it was never very long before it broke loose again and he would be doing or saying things that would have been better left undone or unsaid.

Unknown to either Alex or his friends, the day was fast approaching when the fiery Scottish lad was going to land in some very hot water because of this. It was going to make him a prisoner for four long years and cut him off from home, friends, and everything else he loved, and on more than one occasion, it almost cost him his life. Yet, strangely enough, it was also going to change his name and make him famous! This is what happened:

Two teenage lads stood on a wharf and stared excitedly at the variety of ships that sailed in and out, or rode at anchor, in the harbor of the British seaport town of Plymouth in 1695.

"Ah, 'tis a lovely sight, is it not, Dampier?" breathed Alex, his eager eyes noting the bustling activity aboard the ships.

"It is, indeed," Dampier nodded. "And we'll soon be a part of it. Wonder which ship is ours?"

"There it is!" cried Alex, pointing down the quay. "The *Betsy.* Aye, what a bonnie ship! The most beautiful one in all England, I'll wager!"

Dampier followed the direction of his friend's outstretched arm and saw a trim, sleek sailing vessel riding at anchor a scant hundred yards distant. Every line of her bespoke speed and efficiency.

"Come on!" cried Alex, striding in the direction of the ship. "Let's report aboard!"

"Whoa!" Dampier grabbed his friend's arm. "Not so fast. You'll be needing that, I fancy." He pointed to Alex's bulging duffle bag.

Alex blushed. "Don't know what I'd do without you, Dampier," he said, shouldering his heavy bag.

"Probably forget your head," Dampier grinned. But the grin was soon replaced by a worried frown. Searching his friend's face anxiously, Dampier said, "Now, remember, Alex, you've made me a bargain. Whatever you do, hold onto that frightful temper of yours!"

"G'wan with ye!" Alex chuckled, giving his friend a playful shove. "I promised ye, did I not? Come, let's be off to tell the captain he has two new crew members!"

Thus it was that on a pleasant day in June 1695 the two boys boarded the ship and set sail on a voyage that was to prove anything but dull for a lad named Alexander Selkirk.

During the first few weeks of the voyage, things went splendidly. Alex, under the ever-watchful eye of his friend, seemed to have conquered the habit of losing his temper. And then it happened. One day while Dampier was aloft in the rigging, Alex got into an argument with the captain, no less! The argument grew hotter and hotter and finally the captain, who had done his best to reason with the impetuous lad, shouted, "One more word out of you, me bucko, and I'll set you down on yonder isle!" He waved angrily at the deserted island of San Juan Fernando, which lay starboard of the sailing ship.

Alex, boiling mad, shouted, "Go ahead! See if I care. I'd rather be on a deserted island than to keep on sailing with the likes o' ye!"

"By thunder," roared the captain, "that's done it!" He ordered several anxious crewmen standing nearby to lower a boat and take the hotheaded youngster to the island.

As Alex climbed over the rail, Dampier, who had hurried to his friend, whispered, "I'll get another boat and come back for you, Alex. Don't worry." Stowing aboard a few necessities, the sailors rowed to the island, put the Scottish boy ashore, and returned to the ship.

Alex stood on the beach glaring at the ship, but his defiant attitude collapsed as he watched the vessel slowly disappear from sight. Suddenly the terrible realization dawned on him that he was alone on an island near which no trade ship ever came. He was cut off from the world—perhaps forever!

For four long years Alexander Selkirk lived on that lonely island, striving desperately to stay alive. He had many adventures during that time, and by the end of the fourth year he was convinced that he was doomed to spend the rest of his life there. Then one day he saw something his eyes could not believe—a ship! It stopped close to the island and dropped anchor.

Half running, half stumbling, Alex dashed across the beach, wildly waving his tattered shirt. A small boat set out from the ship and when it nosed onto the beach Alex gasped in astonishment. The first person to step ashore was Dampier! His friend had not forgotten and had finally managed to have a ship pick him up.

But it wasn't till the rescue ship returned to England that the strangest part of the castaway's story began. For it was there that a man who wrote adventure stories came to see Alex. He asked Alex to tell him all that had happened during his four years on the island and said he would make it into a story. Then, if he sold it, he would give half the money to Alex.

The young adventurer agreed, and day after day Alex unfolded his story while the writer made notes. At last it was finished, the writer left, and Alex visited old friends and soon forgot about the man.

Alex's friends were amazed at the change in him. Gone was his fiery temper; no matter what anyone did or said, he wasn't angered the least bit. And though his friends were greatly surprised, they were also very glad to see such a change.

Then, some months later, Alex had a visitor. It was the writer, who had come to give him his share of the money received for the story of Alex's life on the island.

And that's how Alexander Selkirk became famous. Even though a name other than his own was used in the story, everyone knew it was the story of the impetuous Scottish lad who lost his temper once too often.

To be sure, the story was "dressed up" a little, but it was mostly true. Why the writer, Daniel Defoe, chose to give Alexander Selkirk a different name in the story is not known for certain, but maybe he had the right idea, after all. For the name he chose was "Robinson Crusoe"!

Children's Friend, April 1955.

Christmas

ARDETH G. KAPP

The late harvest that year was followed by an early frost, and many of the crops were under a blanket of snow.

As Christmas approached, we children played the wishing game in the Eaton's catalog until the toy section was well marked by the curled edges of the pages. We tried hard to limit our long list of wants to a few special items, knowing that we must be selective since Mom and Dad had to pay Santa for his Christmas treasures. But after a family council to consider a serious matter, our choices were easily made.

Brian, our twelve-year-old crippled cousin who had just been ordained a deacon, was more anxious than ever to walk, and if enough money could be raised, it was possible that the Mayo Clinic could help him. This would require a great sacrifice, but the choice was ours. We could each make our own decision and, if we chose, we could request that the money for our Christmas be given to Brian in hopes of providing medical attention that would allow him to abandon the wheelchair that we had all taken turns pushing so often.

I remember that the Eaton's catalog got lost somewhere in the shuffle as we each talked with great anticipation of our part in helping Brian.

142

Christmas Eve came and with it the children's part at the church. I remember being a little disappointed that Santa wore his shabby old suit to our party, but Mom explained that he kept his good one to wear when he came that night to make his official visit, and that seemed like a good idea to me.

Christmas Eve found cousins, aunts, and uncles all at Mamma Leavitt's big two-story house (she was such a special grandmother that we all called her Mamma Leavitt) and there in her home twenty-one children were tucked into beds of some sort—after hanging up twenty-one stockings, of course.

Even as a child I remember that the air was filled with gaiety and smiles radiated from the faces of young and old.

The next morning our socks were bulging with goodies. Old dolls had beautiful new wardrobes that Santa had skillfully prepared, and old toys had new paint, and Brian was going to the Mayo Clinic.

It didn't take long to tidy things up since there were very few wrappings, but that was good, because we had exciting things planned with our dads while our moms were busy getting ready for the big dinner. The second best turkey in Dad's flock was roasting in the oven and filling the air with that Christmas dinner smell while the very finest turkey had been selected to go into the big box along with homemade pies, jams, jellies, fruits, and vegetables. On top was a handmade apron carefully wrapped in a piece of soft white tissue paper that was tied with a bit of ribbon that had served that same purpose many times before.

Each of us, all bundled up, was lifted onto the big wagon along with the box of goodies and away we went through the deep snow, listening to the steady rhythm of the horses' hooves until we reached the river about three miles away, where Mr. and Mrs. Opstall lived in their little log house.

The Opstalls were an elderly couple from Belgium who had once been wealthy but who had sold all their earthly possessions to flee to freedom in Canada. As we jumped off the wagon into the crunchy snow, we each waited eagerly to be given one of the items from the big box. My brother got to carry the turkey and I carried one of Mamma Leavitt's delicious mincemeat pies. It was quite a job trudging through the deep snow, trying to follow in our dad's big steps with our arms loaded.

Inside the home, the bare floors were warmed by a glowing fire, and the long slab table in the middle of the one-room house was gradually piled higher and higher as we each presented our expression of love.

The Opstalls couldn't speak a word of English, but I remember thinking that I knew exactly what they were telling us. It didn't seem as if the words really made any difference, but I was puzzled by their tears when they seemed too happy, and I recall Mom trying to explain this to me later. It didn't make much sense, but as long as they were happy, I guessed it was OK if they wanted to cry.

I'll never forget sitting down to the big dinner with a special place for everyone, including Brian in his wheelchair at the corner of the table because it seemed to fit better there. And down at the far end Papa Leavitt bowed his head and gave a prayer that lasted ever so long.

That night we all got to stay up late and we just sat around in the big living room with our moms and dads and talked about things.

After our family prayer that night, when I was tucked into bed, indelibly imprinted on my mind was the lesson that Christmas is an excited good feeling inside, and how I wished every Christmas might be like this one!

Once You Get to Know a Fellow

BERNADINE BEATIE

Bud Hale lifted the corral gate, swung it into position, then straightened and shook the rain from his hat. His sight of Sam Roberts, sitting dry and comfortable in the shed, brought a flush of anger to Bud's face. If Sam hadn't put the hinges on backwards, they would be back at the ranch by now!

"Why didn't you saddle the horses?" Bud called out angrily.

Sam rose lazily. "You'd find fault with the way I saddled them," he said, "like you do with everything."

"Humph!" said Bud, walking toward the shed where his quarterhorse, Starface, and the gentle little pinto Sam rode were tied. No use expecting Sam to do anything. He had known that ever since he drew Sam's name from Jake Johnson's hat.

"Oh, boy!" Bud had groaned. "I'm stuck with Sam Roberts!"

"Sam's not so bad, Bud," Jake had said. "He's a city boy, but he can learn."

"Ha! ha!" Mike Davis spoke up. He had been Sam's buddy the one week Sam had spent at the T Bar M last summer.

145

"Give Sam a chance, boys," Jake had drawled. "Once you get to know a fellow, you'll usually end up liking him. Anyway, that's been my experience."

"Not Sam Roberts!" Clem Waters had said, leaning back in his bunk. "All he does is brag about how rich and important his family is."

"That's enough!" Jake had said, unwinding his lanky six-foot frame from a chair at one end of the bunkhouse. "You know the rules!"

Bud had nodded gloomily. Jake was a stickler for rules, and any boy who broke them usually found himself confined to the bunkhouse over the weekend. This was the worst possible punishment, especially for Bud, for it was then that the regular ranch hands took time off to teach the boys trick riding.

The T Bar M wasn't like most summer dude camps. It was a real working ranch, and part of the fun was in helping with the regular ranch chores. Jake Johnson, the ranch foreman, "rode herd" on the boys and had worked out what he called a buddy system. The boys who came each summer drew names of newcomers and were responsible for teaching their new buddy the ropes. If the two hit it off, they could remain partners; otherwise they changed buddies every two weeks.

Bud approved of the system—it was safe and practical—but he was glad this was the last day he'd be saddled with Sam Roberts. It had been a long two weeks. Looking up from cinching the saddle, he noticed that though Sam's new western hat was set at a jaunty angle, there was a lost, lonely look in his eyes. Bud felt a brief twinge in his heart, remembering his first day with Sam. Sam had looked lonely then, too, and he had asked, "Bud, why don't the fellows like me?"

Maybe he should have told Sam to quit bragging about his family, Bud thought, but that was something you hesitate to tell a fellow. Besides, there were other reasons. Sam just didn't know how to do anything. Sam had tried the first few days, but he did everything wrong. Today he had even put the hinges on the wrong side of the corral gate near the line shack Bud was repairing.

"Can't you do anything right?" Bud had exploded.

"Do it yourself!" Sam had replied. "You know everything!"

Now, because of the delay, they'd be out after dark. Bud finished saddling the pinto and motioned to Sam. "I'll just bet we'll be stuck in the bunkhouse over the weekend," he grumbled.

"Who cares?" said Sam.

"I do! The hands are going to round up some calves so we can practice calf roping." Bud looked at the clearing sky. "You know, Sam, we could make it by dark if we cut across country," he said.

Sam's eyes widened. "Isn't that against the rules? We'd have to cross Satan's Wash."

"Yes," said Bud, "but nobody'll know. It'll be safe enough. It takes a real gully-washer to flood the wash."

"It's okay by me," Sam said.

When the boys reached Satan's Wash, they were surprised to see that it was running a foot deep in water. Bud pulled Starface to a stop.

"It must have rained harder up in the hills," he said. "It's okay, though, we can make it."

"I—I'm not a very good swimmer," Sam said, looking uncertain.

"You ride Starface. He isn't afraid of water." Bud swung to the ground as he spoke. "You lead the way, Sam, and I'll be right behind. Head toward that big boulder across the wash. Starface will do the rest."

As soon as he swung up on the pinto's back, Bud knew he was going to have a fight on his hands. The pinto's eyes rolled wildly, and he balked at the water's edge. Starface was already halfway across before Bud was able to force the frightened pinto into the water.

"Easy, boy," Bud murmured soothingly, when he noticed that the water was higher now, and flowing faster. He was relieved to see Starface scramble up the bank to safety. Suddenly a great roaring filled Bud's ears. He glanced upstream and suddenly his eyes widened in horror: a wall of water was cascading down the wash!

The pinto gave a high, shrill cry of terror, lost his footing, and was swept down and under as the water hit. Bud lost the reins as the floodwater closed over his head. He was strangling, but he had presence of mind to kick free of the stirrups. When he surfaced, gasping and sputtering, he saw a huge, uprooted tree bearing swiftly down upon him. Scraggly roots, like the arms of a giant sea creature, towered high above his head. Bud grabbed, and his fingers closed about a root. He clung on frantically and glanced fearfully upward. If the tree rolled, it would carry him under, and he might even get tangled up in the roots. But the tree wasn't moving. Bud gave a gasp of relief when the tree swung a bit and he could see that the branches were caught between two large boulders upstream.

"Bud! Bud! You okay?"

Bud looked toward the bank and saw that Sam had run downstream and now stood opposite him, knee deep in water, holding a lasso awkwardly in his hands.

"I'm okay, Sam! Toss!" Bud yelled.

Sam whirled the noose over his head and threw. The loop landed only a few feet in front of him. Bud groaned as time after time Sam made the same poor throw. The tree lurched. Bud caught his breath in fear.

Strangely he found himself remembering the first day he and Sam had worked together. "How about teaching me to use a lasso, Bud?" Sam had asked. "Wait until you learn which end of a calf to rope!" Bud had replied. "Fat chance I have of learning anything around here!" Sam had grumbled, and had never mentioned it again.

Clinging there, drenched to the skin and shaking with fright, Bud realized suddenly that if he had done his part—if he had tried to teach Sam instead of criticizing him—Sam could have learned many things. He was the one who had been a poor buddy, not Sam!

Sam yelled something then, but Bud couldn't hear. His heart sank when he saw Sam step back onto the bank and hurry toward Starface. Sam must have decided to ride for help. There was a hollow feeling in the pit of Bud's stomach. He tried to pull himself onto a higher root, then clung desperately as the tree swung slowly around. It swayed in the current. Bud couldn't see the bank at all now, but he could see upstream, and the tree had broken free of the boulders.

"Bud! Bud!" a voice sounded over Bud's head. Bud's eyes flew open and he saw Sam's frightened face peering down through the gnarled roots. He gave a cry of relief as Sam had an end of the rope knotted about his waist and dropped it down. Bud grabbed the rope: then Sam's hands were on his, hauling him up.

In a flash Bud saw how Sam had reached him. When the tree had swung around, the top branches had reached the bank and Sam had knotted the lasso about his waist and worked his way through the branches and down the trunk of the tree. Bud gave a sigh of relief when he saw that the other end of the rope was fastened to the pommel of Starface's saddle. Sam had thought of everything!

Miraculously, the tree held as the boys scrambled to the bank and sank gratefully to the ground, breathing deeply.

"The pinto's okay," Sam said finally. "He came out downstream and headed for home."

"Good!" Bud said, looking gratefully at Sam and searching for words. Many things were clear to him now. No wonder Sam had bragged about his family. He had been lonely and ill-at-ease in new surroundings, and nobody had made any effort to get to know him. But Sam was okay—he had proved that! Jake was also right about liking a fellow once you got to know him. Suddenly Bud felt shy.

"Sam," he said, "you're a real buddy, and if you'll give me a chance, I'd sure like to show you I can be a good one, too."

"You—you still want to be my buddy?" Sam asked, his eyes bright. "I—I can't even toss a rope."

"I'll probably have plenty of time to teach you," Bud said, smiling. "I'm going to tell Jake every single thing that's happened. He'll be proud of you and he'll be plenty mad at me. He'll say you also knew the rules and then confine you to the bunkhouse right along with me. I'm sorry."

"That's all right!" smiled Sam.

Children's Friend, August 1968.

The Special Shoes

LUCILE C. READING

John's shoes needed repairing. He had worn them out running up and down on Steensbakken (Steens Hill), where he lived with his mother, Anna Widtsoe, and his two-year-old brother, Osborne. After the death of their father when Osborne was only two months old, the family had moved from Froya, the outermost island off the coast of Norway, to the mainland. They lived in a small apartment in Trondheim, the town known as the Cathedral City. The two little boys and their mother often looked out over the beautiful old capital city to the harbor.

When John showed Mother how his shoes had worn, she asked a neighbor to recommend someone who could repair them. He knew just the right person, he said, and soon a boy came to their door. He was a shoemaker's son who picked up and delivered shoes for his father. A few days later the boy brought back John's shoes neatly mended. A strange little pamphlet was tucked into the toe of each shoe.

John's father had been a schoolmaster. Before he died he had taught his young son to read, but there were so many unfamiliar words in the pamphlet that the boy could not understand what was written.

The next day his mother wrapped another pair of shoes that needed repairing into a parcel, tucked them under her arm, and set out on the half-hour walk to the shoemaker's shop. She seemed more quiet than usual when she returned, and during the next few days she was thoughtful and restless.

When the shoemaker's son delivered the second pair of shoes, new pamphlets were tucked into the toe of each one. John knew that his mother spent many hours carefully studying them. The next Sunday she arranged for someone to be with the boys while she went to a meeting at the shoemaker's sturdy log house.

It was not until some years later that she told John what the shoemaker had said when she went to his shop that first time to ask him why he had put a pamphlet into each of John's shoes.

"You may be surprised," he had answered, "to hear me say that I can give you something of far more value than soles for your child's shoes."

The pamphlets were Mormon missionary tracts. Because of them John, his mother, and his brother became members of The Church of Jesus Christ of Latter-day Saints.

Two years later the Widtsoe family left Oslo, Norway, with twenty other Norwegian Saints to begin the long journey to America.

John was called to be an apostle in 1921, when he was forty-nine. At that time he was president of the University of Utah and had been president of Utah State University at Logan.

The shoemaker in Trondheim, Norway, who had repaired John's shoes truly did give to John's mother and her family something of far more value than soles for a worn pair of shoes. He was also instrumental in giving to the Church a great writer, educator, leader, and friend!

The Friend, September 1971.

Thirsty Oxen

AMY BROWN LYMAN

The following is a true incident in the life of Alma Platte Spillsbury. It was early August, 1850. The weather was hot and dry. The Saints were traveling west from the Missouri River along the plains of Nebraska, and they had become short of water. They were being urged by the captain of the company to travel as fast as possible to get to the Platte River, and had stopped the caravan scarcely long enough for Fanny Smith Spillsbury to give birth to a child. A blanket stretched over the bows of the wagon shielded the mother and baby from the intense heat of the August sun, while the father walked along beside the wagon, prodding the lean, gaunt, thirsty oxen.

Suddenly the oxen raised their heads and began to sniff the air. They were nearing the Platte River and could smell the water. They needed no prodding now. Quickly they left the road and took a short cut to the river at quite a reckless speed. The young father tried desperately to get them back on the road but did not succeed, and he was scarcely able to keep up with the wagon and its precious cargo. Other men in the caravan, seeing his predicament, rushed to help him, but it was useless. They sped on till they reached the river, then dashed over the bank. The oxen went down sideways, and the wagon was overturned in the water.

The running men soon reached the spot and snatched the mother out of the stream. "Oh, where is my baby?" she cried.

"Right here," answered Bishop Edward Hunter, fishing the little bundle out of the water where it had been thrown. "But I'm afraid there is not much life left in him," he added.

"We must bless him and name him at once," said the father. He called the men around him and they took the child in their arms to give it a name before it breathed its last. "What shall we name him, Fanny?" asked the father.

"Alma, for the Book of Mormon prophet, and Platte for the great river from which we have been rescued," she answered.

By the time the prayer was finished, the baby was crying lustily, and they all knelt in prayer to thank their Heavenly Father that the life of this little child had been saved so miraculously.

"On the River Platte," *Relief Society Magazine,* February 1947.

Bailey the Bench-Warmer

M. H. AUSTIN

Robbie Bailey tugged his blue baseball cap low on his forehead as he started through the gate at the baseball park. It was going to be hot in the dugout today.

"Hey, Robbie," someone called.

Robbie turned to see Johnny Warner from his class at school. "Hi, Johnny. Did you come to see the Bluejays beat the Hornets?" he asked with a grin.

"I sure did," Johnny replied amiably. "Now that my team is out of the running, I'd like to see you Bluejays win the championship."

"With Ken Davis, we can't lose," Robbie declared with pride. "He's the leading hitter in the league."

Robbie was confident that the Bluejays could win today. And if his team won, they would earn the right to go to Capitol City for the state play-off. Every member of the team would get to make the trip, even the "scrubs."

"By the way, Robbie," Johnny asked, "what position do you play?"

"Me?" Robbie exclaimed in surprise. "I don't play at all! 'Bailey the Bench-warmer'—that's me!"

"Well, good luck anyway," Johnny said.

"Thanks," Robbie replied as he hurried across the field to join his team.

After the pre-game warm-up, Robbie went to the dugout with the other younger boys who were substitutes on the team. Some of the scrubs were restless, hoping that they would get to play today. But Robbie knew he wasn't good enough to play with the first team. He would only strike out or cause his team someway to lose the game. He didn't mind being a bench-warmer at all. He took his usual place at the far end of the bench and settled back to watch the game.

By the last inning, the Bluejays led the Hornets by two runs. With two outs, the Bluejay pitcher took his time pitching to the next batter. He whiffed in two fast strikes. One more strike, and the championship would belong to the Bluejays.

Then, without warning, the Hornet batter slammed a hit past the shortstop into left field. Ken Davis, the left fielder, ran over to cover the play. As he scooped up the ball to make his throw to the infield, he pulled back his right hand with a cry of pain. He barely managed to make the throw.

Robbie jumped to his feet in alarm. Ken was hurt! Coach Reynolds ran onto the field to examine Ken's hand. He began to lead him from the field.

Ken was rubbing his hand and grimacing in pain by the time he reached the dugout. "It's a badly jammed finger," Coach Reynolds explained. "He can't possibly play any more." He turned toward the bench, searching among the substitutes for someone to take Ken's place.

Robbie shrank down against the bench, hoping he would not be noticed. As Coach Reynolds' gaze settled upon him, his heart began to pound. Surely Coach wasn't thinking of sending *him* into the game.

"Robbie," called Coach Reynolds, "out to left field."

Robbie's legs were rubbery when he tried to stand up. His shoes felt as if their soles were made of lead. He could never take Ken's place!

"Hurry up, Rob," Coach Reynolds instructed.

Robbie stumbled to left field in a daze. His knees were trembling as the Bluejay pitcher began his windup. If only this Hornet batter could be put out so that the game would be over!

Then he heard the crack of the bat. A fly ball flew straight toward him. He ran forward and floated under the ball, trying to keep it in sight while he waited to make his catch. He felt the ball plop into his glove—and then fall to the ground. He had dropped it!

He scrambled after the ball and threw it to the shortstop as quickly as he could, but he was too late. Two Hornet runs scored. The game was tied.

Although the next Hornet batter made the third out, Robbie blinked back tears as he left the field. It was all his fault that the game was tied now. Sick at heart, he climbed into the dugout in disgrace. He slid onto the bench and sat with bowed head, his hands clenched between his knees. He couldn't bring himself to face his teammates, especially Ken Davis.

Then to his astonishment, he heard Coach Reynolds calling him. "Hurry up, Robbie. You're first at bat."

Robbie couldn't believe Coach meant to leave him in the game. "I'll only strike out," he murmured.

He felt a hand clap his shoulder. He looked up to see Ken Davis giving him an encouraging smile. "Just do the best you can," Ken said. "That's all anybody can do." Ken shoved him out of the dugout. Someone handed him a bat and a helmet.

Robbie stepped into the batter's box. Out on the mound the Hornet pitcher seemed to tower over him. The first pitch came in so fast that Robbie's bat never left his shoulder. Strike one!

As soon as the next pitch started toward him, Robbie began to swing with all his strength. Strike two!

Three more pitches whipped across the plate. Dimly Robbie heard the umpire's count: three balls and two strikes.

"Look sharp, Robbie," Coach Reynolds warned.

In desperation, Robbie faced the pitcher for the last pitch. The Hornet pitcher threw the ball so fast that he barely saw it. At the last second, though, he thought the ball dipped low, and he held up on his swing. "Ball four; take your base!" the umpire called.

On first base Robbie tried to remember all the things Coach had taught them in practice. Where to stand, when to run. The next two Bluejay batters were thrown out at first base, but their sacrifice hits moved Robbie to third base. The next Bluejay hitter slammed a grounder toward second base.

"Home, Robbie, home!" Coach Reynolds called out.

Robbie darted for home plate as fast as he could. He slid across the plate just under the catcher's glove. The umpire's arms spread wide as he gave the call: "Safe!"

The game was over. The Bluejays had won on Robbie's scored run.

Robbie felt himself being pounded on the back by his happy teammates. "But I didn't do anything at all," he protested. "It was the other fellows who kept hitting the ball to bring me in."

"Yes, but you had to get on base first," Ken said.

"That's right, Robbie" said Coach Reynolds. "Baseball is a team effort. As long as each player does the best he can, it all adds up."

Johnny Warner was waiting for Robbie outside the ball park. "Congratulations on winning the championship," he said. "But I thought you said you didn't play."

"I don't usually," Robbie explained.

"Well, you did all right today," Johnny said.

"I did the best I could," Robbie replied with a grin. As Ken Davis had said, "That's all anybody can do."

Children's Friend, May 1970.

Judge Men and Women by the Spirit They Have

HEBER J. GRANT

There stand out in my life many incidents in my youth, of wonderful inspiration and power through men preaching the gospel in the spirit of testimony and prayer. I call to mind one such incident when I was a young man, probably seventeen or eighteen years of age. I heard the late Bishop Millen Atwood preach a sermon in the Thirteenth Ward. I was studying grammar at the time, and he made some grammatical errors in his talk.

I wrote down his first sentence, smiled to myself, and said, "I am going to get here tonight, during the thirty minutes that Brother Atwood speaks, enough material to last me for the entire winter in my night school grammar class." For each lesson we had to take to class two sentences, or four sentences a week, that were not grammatically correct, together with our corrections.

I contemplated making my corrections and listening to Bishop Atwood's sermon at the same time, but I did not write anything more after the first sentence—not a word; and when Millen Atwood stopped preaching, tears were rolling down my cheeks, tears of gratitude and thanksgiving

158

that welled up in my eyes because of the marvelous testimony that he bore of the divine mission of Joseph Smith, the prophet of God, and of the wonderful inspiration that attended the Prophet in all his labors.

Although it is now more than sixty-five years since I listened to that sermon, it is just as vivid today, and the sensations and feelings that I had are just as fixed with me as they were the day I heard it. I would no more have thought of using those sentences in which he had made grammatical mistakes than I would think of standing up in a class and profaning the name of God. That testimony made the first profound impression that was ever made upon my heart and soul of the divine mission of the Prophet. I had heard many testimonies that had pleased me and made their impression, but this was the first testimony that had melted me to tears under the inspiration of the Spirit of God.

During all the years that have passed since then, I have never been shocked or annoyed by grammatical errors or mispronounced words on the part of those preaching the gospel. I have realized that to judge the spirit of a man by the clothing of his language was like judging him by the clothes he wore. From that day to this the one thing above all others that has impressed me has been the Spirit, the inspiration of the living God, that an individual had when proclaiming the gospel, and not the language; because after all is said and done there are a great many who have never had the opportunity to become educated so far as speaking correctly is concerned. Likewise there are many who have never had an opportunity in the financial battle of life to accumulate the means whereby they could be clothed in an attractive manner.

I have endeavored, from that day to this, and have been successful in my endeavor, to judge men and women by the spirit they have, for I have learned absolutely that it is the Spirit that giveth life and understanding, and not the letter. The letter killeth.

"The Spirit and the Letter," *Improvement Era*, April 1939.

Roger's River Ride

LUCILE C. READING

R oger danced up and down in excitement. "Please come, Deanne," he begged, "so I can go, too."

An invitation for a boat ride had just been given to seven-year-old Roger and his sister by Mr. Honeycutt, who had a brand new outboard motorboat. Deanne had planned to go swimming, but Roger's enthusiasm changed her mind, and in a few minutes the trio boarded the little boat and started their ride on the Niagara River near Horseshoe Falls. It was a beautiful Saturday morning in 1960.

The children put on the bright orange life jackets Mr. Honeycutt gave them and settled down to a happy morning on the water. Soon the kind gentleman offered to let Roger handle the tiller, and Deanne, completely relaxed, gaily waved to the cars passing far overhead as the little boat passed under the Grand Island Bridge, gateway to the American side of the falls.

Gradually the broad, friendly river became an angry, whirling one, and the thundering sound of the falls pounded close. Roger gave the tiller back to Mr. Honeycutt and stumbled toward Deanne, sobbing, "I'm scared. We're going to drown."

"Hang on!" shouted Mr. Honeycutt. These were the last words anyone ever heard him say, for there was nothing to hang onto. With a lurch the boat tipped over and all were thrown into the churning water. The rapids wrenched Roger and spun him furiously around before lifting and tossing him over the edge of the falls. Just then some tourists spotted Deanne in her orange life jacket and pulled her out of the turbulent water before the fury of the current could carry her after Roger. As she lay on the ground she gasped, "My brother! Save my brother!" Those who had seen Roger's perilous ride had no hope of his survival. One of them softly said, "Say a prayer for your brother." And Deanne did!

A short time later a commercial boat that regularly cruises the river below Horseshoe Falls was almost to its turning-around point when its captain, drenched with spray, spotted a bobbing orange object. Up until this time, only four persons of the many who had tried to go over the falls had ever survived. All of them had been carefully protected in steel drums or padded barrels. Unbelievably, Roger, wholly unprotected, was alive!

A life preserver was thrown toward him again and again and yet again. On the third try, it came close enough for Roger to crawl up onto it.

"Your brother was saved, and he's going to be okay," Deanne was told just as she was wheeled into the hospital where, despite her terrifying experience, she was found to be unharmed.

Before the half-conscious girl closed her eyes in exhaustion, she whispered gratefully, "Thank you, God."

Children's Friend, January 1969.

The Winner

FRANK H. TOOKER

Charlie picked up his fountain pen from the kitchen table. He examined its clip, which, from day-to-day use, had become so badly bent it wouldn't hold the pen securely in his pocket anymore. He noticed that the gold letters of his name were about worn off.

"Oh, well," he said to himself as he slipped the pen into his shirt pocket, "I won't have to use this pen again if I win first prize in the composition contest today—and I *will* win if George Gregson has not written a composition better than mine. What a beauty that prize pen is! I can feel it in my hand right now."

Charlie took a moment to scan through the composition he had written in pencil the night before. All he had to do when he reached school this morning was copy it in ink in his composition book. Because the first prize was a pen, all entries had to be written in ink to be eligible.

"It's the best I've ever done," Charlie decided, tucking the papers into his pocket. He took his books from the table, nestled them under his arm, and darted out the door.

Charlie whistled a tune as he took his usual long strides down Monroe Avenue, then started across Chesnut toward

162

the school. He was about to step onto the curb when something caught his eye. There, lying in the gutter, was a composition book, its pages flipping idly in the breeze.

"Oh-oh," Charlie said to himself. "That must have slipped from under someone's arm."

Then his eye caught a name on one of the fluttering pages—*George Gregson!*

Charlie whistled softly. He snatched up the book. His fingers couldn't move fast enough as he flicked over the pages. Yes, here it was—George's entry in the contest, neatly written in ink, all ready to be turned in.

Charlie's eye's raced over the lines, his hopes sinking lower and lower the further he read into George's composition. Then he snapped the cover closed. He tucked the book between those under his arm.

"Why should I just hand this over to George and let him walk away with the prize?" he asked himself. "If he had not been careless, he wouldn't have dropped it." That didn't sound very convincing. Charlie himself had dropped things more than once on his way to school. "Well, anyway," Charlie argued, "it serves him right if he doesn't have it to turn in. Besides, I'll give it back to him as soon as the contest is over."

The class was just coming to order as Charlie slipped into his seat. Glancing quickly around the room, he noticed that George Gregson's seat was empty.

"He's probably still searching for his composition," Charlie guessed, taking out his composition book and opening it to a blank page. Then he grinned. "Well, he won't find it! It serves him right for being so careless."

The class quieted down. Everyone was either busy writing in his composition book or getting ready to write. Charlie smoothed out the penciled version of his composition, then reached into his shirt pocket for his pen. His fingers closed on nothing but air. He darted his fingers down to the bottom of the pocket. It was empty. His pen wasn't there!

He searched frantically through his trousers pockets, then back to his shirt pocket. "I remember putting it right in this pocket," he insisted to himself. "There's no use looking anywhere else." Then a sudden thought surged into his brain. "That broken clip! It must have dropped out of my pocket when I bent over to pick up George's composition book!"

George! Charlie's eyes swept across the room. George's seat was still empty. Good old George! He wouldn't mind if Charlie borrowed *his* pen. But wait—George had copied his composition at home last night, so he must have taken his pen with him. Probably he had it in his pocket right now. There would be no sense in looking through his desk.

Desperately now, Charlie scanned one after another of his classmates. All were writing. Not one of them would be able to lend him a pen.

Hopeless! That's what it was. Hopeless! Even if the teacher were to give him permission to go to look for the pen, he couldn't possibly go all the way back to Monroe Avenue and Chestnut, then return to the school and copy his composition before the deadline. Frustrated, Charlie dropped his head into his hands.

Suddenly there was a clatter of running feet in the hall. Charlie raised his head just as the door burst open, and George Gregson, red-faced and breathing heavily, sailed into the room. Without slowing his pace, George headed toward Charlie's desk, his hand extended.

"Here, Charlie," he gasped. "... your pen ... found it while looking for my book ... knew you wouldn't have your composition ready ... ran all the way back ... at least, *you* will be in the contest ..."

Charlie's mouth dropped open. For a moment he sat speechless. Then, as conflicting emotions billowed over him, he dug into his desk, pulled out George's composition book, and handed it to him. "I found it on my way to school—" Charlie began.

The teacher rapped for order. George scurried to his desk.

"What a good friend George is!" Charlie thought, over and over. "Imagine him running back with my pen! For all he knows, my composition might be better than his, but that didn't stop him. Well, from now on, that's the way I'm going to be. And who knows? Maybe—just maybe, I might win after all!"

Charlie uncapped his pen and began to write furiously.

Children's Friend, November 1955.

Madeline's Dream

LUCILE C. READING

Madeline, her clothes under her arms, ran down the stairs and into the kitchen where her mother was preparing breakfast. Mother looked up to say good morning to her little girl, but when she saw how pale and breathless Madeline was, she asked, "What's the matter? Are you sick?"

"No," answered Madeline, but at the moment she could say no more. She sank down onto a stool near the fireplace and stared into the flame. She wondered how she could ever put into words the strange dream she had just had.

It had seemed in her dream that she was a young lady sitting on a small strip of meadow close to the vineyard, and that as she watched to make sure the goats didn't tramp on the vines and eat them, she glanced down at a Sunday School book in her lap. As she looked up again, she was startled to see three strange men.

At the remembrance, Madeline shivered in fright, just as she had shivered in her dream. But almost at once there came the feeling of peace that had flooded over her when one of the men said, "Don't be frightened. We have come from a place far from here to tell you about the true and everlasting gospel."

Then the men told her that an angel had directed a boy to find an important book of gold hidden in the earth. They said that someday she, Madeline, would be able to read this book, and then, because of it, she would gladly leave her home, cross the great ocean, and go to America to live.

In the warm, sweet-smelling kitchen Madeline relived her dream. It seemed so real to her that she turned pale again and began to tremble. Father came in from milking the goats and asked, just as her mother had done, "What's the matter? Are you sick?"

Madeline could only shake her head. Father gently stooped down beside her, picked up a stocking, and without another word began to help her dress. Afterward he lifted her onto his lap and quietly asked, "Do you want to tell me about it?"

Madeline nodded. It was hard to get the words started but then they seemed to tumble over each other in their eagerness to be spoken. Mother left her preparations for their simple breakfast of figs, potatoes, and goat milk so she could hear every amazing detail of the dream. Father listened intently, occasionally nodding his head as if he understood more than was being said.

That night when the family gathered around the fireplace for the evening prayer, Father told again the story of why they lived in a small village high in the north Italian Alps. Their grandparents many generations back had had homes in the lovely valleys at the foot of these lofty mountains. There the people lived simple, happy lives, basing all they did on the teachings of the apostles who had lived at the time of Christ. The Vaudois (meaning people who live in the valleys of the Alps) even sent forth missionaries two by two to teach. Many people from other lands were converted to their faith.

News of their success reached Rome, and word went to the Vaudois valleys that they must give up their own church and abide by the dictates of the larger ruling church in Rome. This they refused to do. In fact, the Vaudois clung with even greater faith to the authority and teachings of the New Testament as handed down to them.

Angered, Pope Innocent VIII proclaimed a general crusade for the extermination of every member of the Vaudois church. Soon the peaceful valleys where they lived were filled with tragedy and destruction. There was hardly a rock that did not mark a scene of death. Those who survived were driven from their homes. They retreated higher and ever higher up the steep mountains.

The many years of unbelievable suffering resulted in the deaths of all but three hundred members of the Vaudois church. These people settled high in the Piedmont valleys of the Alps, their villages seeming to cling to the mountainsides. They were surrounded on all sides by inaccessible crags and cliffs.

It was hard to eke out a living. Each spring the women and children went down the steep mountains and, using baskets, carried back up to their terraced fields and gardens the soil that had been washed down in the winter storms. But in these craggy mountains they were quite isolated, and here they raised their hands to the sky and solemnly swore to defend their homes and their religion to the death, as their fathers had done before them.

Madeline's family had heard this story many times, but they never tired of it. Even the youngest children thrilled to hear of the courage of their tall, strong grandparents. The older children often expressed gratitude for their home and for their church with its motto "The Light Shining in Darkness."

Long after everyone else was asleep that night, Madeline could hear the murmur of her parents' voices. The last thing she remembered before she went to sleep was hearing her mother insist, "But we already have the true gospel, so there couldn't be any real meaning to that story Madeline told us."

Madeline did not hear her father's answer, but occasionally as the years went by, he would question her concerning her dream. Even though some of the details became vague to her, they never did to him.

About eight years after Madeline's dream, the king of Sardinia, pressured by England and other countries to stop persecuting the Piedmont Protestants, granted his Vaudois subjects freedom of religion. The tragic 800-year war ended in February 1848.

The very next year Lorenzo Snow, who later became the fifth President of the Church, was called to open a mission in Italy, but he and his two companions could not find anyone interested in their message. Discouraged, he wrote, "I see no possible means of accomplishing our object. All is darkness."

On September 18, 1850, Lorenzo Snow and his two companions climbed a high mountain in northern Italy and, on a large projecting rock, offered a fervent prayer for guidance. They were then inspired to dedicate the land for the preaching of the gospel, and they named the rock upon which they stood "The Rock of Prophecy."

Before leaving the mountain, the missionaries sang "The Hymn of the Vaudois Mountaineers in Times of Persecution." The strains of this song had floated down into the valleys many times from high caves and fissures in the rocks where the persecuted had been hiding. It had been a rallying cry as the Vaudois took up arms to fortify their mountain passes. It had been sung in thanksgiving in their church services. Now the three missionaries, standing on The Rock of Prophecy, sang the stirring words:

"For the strength of the hills we bless thee,
Our God, our fathers' God;
Thou hast made thy children mighty
By the touch of the mountain sod."

Shortly afterward, on a Saturday afternoon, Madeline's father went home early from his work of building a chimney for a neighbor. He told his family that three strangers were coming to bring an important message. "I must dress in my best clothes and go to welcome them," he said.

On Sunday morning he found the men he was looking for and invited them to go home with him. As they walked up over the winding paths and through the dangerously narrow mountain passes, Madeline's father told them of the dream his daughter had had many years before.

When they reached his small rock home, they found Madeline sitting on a little strip of meadow close to the vineyard. She looked up from the Sunday School book she was reading into the faces of three men. They told her they had come to give her people the message contained in a wonderful book of gold that had been taken out of the earth and that she could now read this book.

That evening Madeline's neighbors came to meet the strangers and hear their message. Some of the men found it so unusual and exciting that they stayed up all night to learn more about the newly revealed truths that had been brought to them by these missionaries of The Church of Jesus Christ of Latter-day Saints.

Some baptisms were held in October 1850. Twenty families eventually accepted the gospel, and as Madeline's dream became a reality, the Vaudois area truly became "A Light Shining in Darkness."

The Friend, November 1971.

A Mountain Lion

MYRTLE S. NORDE

When the last bell rang, Phillip Fenner put his books away and walked slowly down the steps of the schoolhouse. "That trip to the Lakeheart Museum is practically in the bag," he thought to himself. "Nobody else knows about that cave with all the Indian pottery pieces in it. Why, I'll have the best collection in school." He started across the playground, pleased with himself. "Yes, sir, that first prize is practically mine."

Phil was in no hurry; he would only have to wait for his father at the library to get a ride home anyway. He wandered over to where some of his classmates were gathered.

Howard Cranny spoke first. "Hey, Phil, you haven't met the new boy we have in school. His name is Leo Balluster. This is Phil Fenner."

Phil smiled. "Hi, Leo. How do you like our school?"

The new boy looked Phil up and down. "Oh, it's all right," he said. "How come you were not here yesterday?"

"I had to stay at home. Dad is having trouble with mountain lions and I had to help take care of some of the sheep. Night before last the lions killed six and mauled twelve others. Somebody had to stay with them, so I did."

171

The new boy laughed. "So, you're the sheepherder's kid, huh?"

Phil felt his face growing hot. He gritted his teeth until he could control his voice. "My dad is a sheep rancher." Phil put the emphasis on the last word. "And that is nothing to be ashamed of."

"Well," Leo said, "you don't have to get huffy about it."

"I'm not huffy," Phil said stiffly. "But we make an honest living on the ranch, and if it weren't for people like us, you would not have such fancy wool pants to wear, either."

"Oh, pardon me!" Leo said scornfully, fluttering his eyelashes. "I didn't know you were so touchy!"

"If this weren't on the school grounds, I think I'd pop you!"

"Well," Leo shrugged, "go ahead. What's stopping you?"

"I don't want us to get suspended from school," Phil said. "That's one reason. Another reason is that I like to get along with other fellows if they will let me." Phil turned then, and walked away. He was almost to the sidewalk when the hated taunt reached his ears. It was the new boy, shouting over and over,

"The sheepherder's kid is a sissy! The sheepherder's kid is a sissy!"

Phil swallowed the resentment that almost choked him, and quickened his pace toward the library. Dad would be waiting. Already he had fooled away too much time. He started running, biting back the bitter indignation that surged through him. "One of these days," Phil thought to himself, "Leo Balluster is going to get over being so smart!"

Riding home in the car next to his father, Phil talked about the free trip to Lakeheart Museum, and soon he had forgotten the incident with Leo Balluster. "Just imagine," he told his father, "all that for having the best collection of pottery specimens. And there are just loads of them up in the old Indian cave on the mountain ridge."

"Maybe somebody else knows about them, too," Mr. Fenner said as he turned through the gate to the big ranch.

"I don't think so, Dad," Phil told him. "Anyway, it is too far out from town for the kids to hike to."

"So you think you can win first prize in the contest."

"I'm sure I can. It's all broken, but we're studying about Indian arts, and the teacher said any kind would do. Just so it's real. I want to go up the first thing Saturday morning so I will have time to label each piece."

"Better put it off until afternoon, Phil," his father said. "In the morning I want you to help fix those feed stalls."

It was just after lunch that Phil left the ranch. He had saddled Charlie and hand-strapped on everything he would need—a gunny sack for specimens, a digging trowel, a torch and a flashlight. Carefully he checked his supplies. Then he set out for the cave.

The pony picked its way gingerly through the already browning sage and the pointed clusters of rocks that poked their way through the earth. The trees were thin along the lower slope, but as the mountain began rising sharply to the summit, they became more dense, and Phil guided the pony along the edge of them, going up the easiest way.

It was always exciting to go up to the old cave, but this time there was real adventure. He hoped his memory had not fooled him about the specimens. He had set his heart on the first prize and the trip to the Lakeheart Museum. Phil had never been to a museum. He urged the pony faster, clicking his tongue. "Come on, Charlie, we haven't got all day."

But Charlie took his time, his ears pricked straight up, listening to the many sounds of the forest. Once he stopped short, his head turned into the wind, his nostrils flaring as if he sensed danger.

"Listen, Charlie," Phil tried to explain, "there isn't anything up here that will hurt you. Let's go!"

He kicked his heels lightly into the pony's flanks, and they moved off again.

At the mouth of the cave Phil reined up and tied Charlie to a large branch of a tree. He flung the gunnysack over his shoulder and checked the matches in his pocket. He was ready to start. His heart pounded under his shirt as he went into the mouth of the cave. The big black hole gaped in the mountainside, and the click of his boots on the rough gravel echoed back to him. He would wait until he could no longer see before flicking on the flashlight. It would save on batteries. He would not use the torch until he found the cache of Indian pottery specimens.

It was almost too dark to see when a shaft of light pierced the blackness far ahead, creeping along the walls of the cave. "Who's there?" Phil called.

The shaft of light leaped through the darkness and settled on his face. The voice at the other end of the cave reverberated back to him. "So it's the sheepherder's kid! Come to make a haul of pottery specimens and win the first prize, eh?"

The voice belonged to Leo Balluster.

Phil winced. It was like being robbed of his personal property. But he knew he had no right to claim the pottery specimens. Leo Balluster had come first. The collection was already his. The first prize was gone. Phil flicked on his light and hurried back to where Leo was squatting, disappointed because he had come too late. "How did you know about this cave?" Phil asked quietly.

"Huh!" Leo snorted. "I know about all the places like this around here. My dad is an archaeologist."

"What's an archaeologist?"

"Boy, are you dumb! That's somebody who searches old ruins to learn how early mankind lived. My dad knows all about this country. He told me about this cave."

Phil's heart sank. He had wanted so much to win that first prize, but now his hopes were shattered. The new boy had found the treasure first. He stared at the ground, wondering what to say next.

Leo smirked. "What's the matter? Can't you take it?"

Phil was trying hard to be a good sport. He wanted to congratulate Leo, but Leo was being rude, making sarcastic remarks, wearing Phil's patience thin. His pride had been insulted. He turned flashing eyes on Leo. "Why, I ought to—" He clenched his teeth. A pebble dropped from the roof of the cave and landed at his feet. Phil's breath caught in his throat. A sudden fear gripped him.

Leo had stood up. "Well?" he taunted.

Phil had instinctively focused the beam of his flashlight along the roof of the cave. There was a ledge along the ceiling. The shaft of light caught a glistening sheen in its path, then the frightening glare of yellow eyes. Horror crept up Phil's spine. The animal lay crouched on the ledge, its tail lashing, its muscles quivering in the pale light. It was a mountain lion, ready to spring. Fear gripped him. He felt the tightening in his throat, but he knew he would have to yell now or it would be too late. The lion was poised to strike.

He screamed. "Run, Leo, run! There's a lion!" It was a relief to shout. Phil leaped and was out of the way just in time, because the lion landed between them. Leo ran to the back of the cave.

Quickly the lion turned on Leo, its swishing tail snapping savagely. Phil collected his wits. There was no time to lose. He was sure of one thing, and that was what he had to do.

Leo was shrieking, "Help! Help me!"

Phil pulled the matches from his pocket, his fingers shaking. Already the lion was crouched to leap again, his glistening eyes narrowing on Leo. Phil lighted the torch he still held in his hand. The flame shot up and the cave was ablaze with light. Daringly he threw the match at the lion. The animal snarled deep in his throat as the lighted match hit the ground. He wheeled and slapped the match out.

Instantly Phil thrust the torch close to the lion's angry face, waving it back and forth. The lion swung, confronted with the burning thing, and roared. Phil's hair stood on end. Chills ran over his body. The piercing screech of the mountain lion resounded along the walls of the cave. Phil glanced ahead. Leo stood against one side as though he were petrified.

"Listen, Leo," Phil swallowed. His breath was quick. "Climb up on that ledge in the roof. I'll force the lion back into the cave. Then you can jump down."

There was no answer. Only the sharp sound of Leo's heels scraping on the rock could be heard, and the heavy breathing of the two boys. The mountain lion was warily moving to and fro across the cave, its lithe body rippling with every step.

Leo was on the ledge now; Phil was sure of that. "Now stay there, Leo, and don't fall off. Just don't fall off."

"Don't worry, I won't."

Phil began advancing. Slowly. One step at a time. Waving the torch before him, closer and closer to the lion. The lion snarled, snapped at the flaming torch, and began moving backward. Phil was close to him now, forcing him farther and farther back into the cave. He was under Leo now, then past him.

"Jump, now! Jump, Leo!" he called back.

There was a thud as Leo landed on the ground. "What shall we do now?" he asked.

Phil knew what they had to do. "We'll back out and build a fire in the mouth of the cave. One of us will keep the fire going and the other will go for help," Phil told him.

Slowly they began backing out of the cave, with the lion advancing with them. When they reached the opening, Phil sent Leo to gather wood for the fire. They piled wood across the entrance, and Phil lighted the half circle with his burning torch.

"Well," Phil asked, "who is going for help?"

"Can't we just leave him?"

"I should say not! This is the fellow that has been killing all my dad's sheep," Phil said sharply. "Do you want to stay or do you want to go?"

Terror leaped into Leo's eyes. "Where will I go?"

"After my dad."

"But I don't know how to get there."

Disgust burned in Phil. "Listen," he said. "You stay. And don't let that fire get too big and smoke too much or else that lion will leap over it. Then you will be in a spot. Just keep him inside that fire line, and he won't hurt you."

Leo swallowed hard. "All right. I'll try it."

Phil could hardly wait to get back with his father. He just hoped that Leo would still be there when they got back.

He was. He was faithfully tending the fire when Phil and Mr. Fenner rode up.

"Nice work, fellow," Mr. Fenner said as he dismounted. "Is the lion still in there?"

"You bet he is!" Leo told him.

Phil interrupted. "This is my father, Leo."

"I am glad to meet you, Mr. Fenner," Leo smiled.

"Same here!" Mr. Fenner said. "You boys can stay out here and hold the horses so they don't run away. I'm going in after the lion." He kicked some of the firewood to one side and disappeared into the cave, the lighted torch making a path through the darkness.

As soon as Mr. Fenner was out of sight Leo turned to Phil. "Phil," he said slowly, "I want to tell you how sorry I am for the way I acted and the things I said. I was just being smart, I guess. I had a lot of time to think it over and I am really sorry."

Phil fumbled with the reins. "I am sorry for the way I acted, too. I should not have been so ready to fight just because you teased me. I'm too quick tempered," he said. "And I do hope you win that trip to Lakeheart. That will be a swell trip."

Leo smiled then. He dug his hands into his pockets. "I don't think I will be winning that trip. They really are your specimens, Phil. You deserve the first prize."

"No," Phil said. "You found them first."

"Say, I wouldn't even be alive now if it had not been for you," Leo replied. "Anyway, I want you to come to see my father's collection of specimens. Not broken ones, either. We can help you label your collection with real scientific names and everything. Please, Phil, won't you?"

"Thanks, I'd like to."

Leo shoved his hand out. "Then shake, pal."

"Shake is right," Phil said, as he took his new friend's hand. A glow of satisfaction swept over him. You just have to get to know some people, he decided, before you can really like them.

"And, say," he added, "how about coming out tomorrow and helping me collect specimens. Then we can go over to our house and I'll show you a real sheep ranch."

Children's Friend, March 1946.

"Brethren, I Feel Impressed . . ."

VIRGINIA BUDD JACOBSEN

It happened in 1921, while President McKay and Elder Hugh Cannon were making a tour of the missions of the world. After a day of inspiring conference meetings in Hilo, Hawaii, a night trip to the Kilauea volcano was arranged for the visiting brethren and some of the missionaries. About nine o'clock that evening, two carloads, about ten of us, took off for the then very active volcano.

We stood on the rim of that fiery pit watching Pele in her satanic antics, our backs chilled by the cold winds sweeping down from snowcapped Mauna Loa and our faces almost blistered by the heat of the molten lava. Tiring of the cold, one of the elders discovered a volcanic balcony about four feet down inside the crater where observers could watch the display without being chilled by the wind. It seemed perfectly sound, and the "railing" on the open side of it formed a fine protection from the intense heat, making it an excellent place to view the spectacular display.

After first testing its safety, Brother McKay and three of the elders climbed down into the hanging balcony. As they stood there warm and comfortable, they teased the others of us more timid ones who had hesitated to take advantage of

178

the protection they had found. For quite some time we all watched the ever-changing sight as we alternately chilled and roasted.

After being down there in their protected spot for some time, suddenly Brother McKay said to those with him, "Brethren, I feel impressed that we should get out of here."

With that he assisted the elders to climb out, and then they in turn helped him up to the wind-swept rim. It seems incredible, but almost immediately the whole balcony crumbled and fell with a roar into the molten lava a hundred feet or so below.

It is easy to visualize the feelings of those who witnessed this terrifying experience. Not a word was said—the whole thing was too awful, with all that word means. The only sound was the hiss and roar of Pele, the fire goddess of old Hawaii, screaming her disappointment.

None of us who were witnesses to this experience could ever doubt the reality of "revelation in our day"! Some might say it was merely inspiration, but to us it was a direct revelation given to a worthy man.

———————

Clare Middlemiss, comp., *Cherished Experiences* (Deseret Book Co., 1955).

A Practical Joke

ORA PATE STEWART

It was during the war; tensions were high, and the arms plants were running full blast. Noise was incessant. It was before the innovation of "the break," and the men at the Local Arms sometimes took out their mischief in what they thought was innocent horseplay—scuffling, jousting, practical jokes.

One man especially came in for a sizable share of jostling. He was just a little different. He dressed oddly. His clothes were ill-fitting. He was thinner than the rest, and too many of his teeth were missing. He was slow of speech and awkward of movement. We shall call him Andrews.

On this particular day, after a playful bout, Andrews came up with a torn sleeve. Not bad at first; but each man gave it another little tug, and soon a sizable strip, ribbonlike, trailed behind him. As he passed too near a moving belt, this strip was sucked into the machinery; and in a split second the sleeve, the shirt—Andrews was in trouble, dragged into a position of grave danger to life and limb.

Alarms were sounded, switches pulled, buttons pushed; and, because the foreman happened to be close at hand, he and the man managed to get the machinery stopped before he had lost more than his shirt. But the call had been so close that all the men were shaken and unnerved.

It was eleven-thirty, early for a noon recess, but the foreman did not restart the machines. In the deathly quiet he summoned the men of the division to come closer. He had a story to tell.

"In my younger days I worked in a small factory," he began. "I remember Mike Travis—he was big and witty, always making jokes, playing little pranks. Mike was a leader. Then there was Pete Lumas. He always went along with Mike. He was a follower. And then I remember Jake, who was a little older than the rest of us—quiet, harmless, apart. He ate his lunch by himself. He wore the same patched trousers for three years straight. He never entered into the games we played at noon, wrestling, horseshoes, and such. He was different.

"Jake was a natural target for practical jokes. He might find a live frog in his dinner pail or a dead rodent in his hat. But he always took it in good part.

"Then one fall when things were slack, Mike took a few days off to go deer hunting. Pete went along, of course, and they promised all of us that if they got anything they'd bring us each a piece. So we were all quite excited when we heard that they'd got back, and that Mike had got a really nice big buck.

"We heard more than that. Pete never could keep anything to himself, and it leaked out that they had a real whopper to play on Jake. Mike had cut up the critter and had made a nice package for each of us. And, for the laughs, for the joke of it, he had saved the ears, the tail, and the hoofs—it would be so funny when Jake unwrapped them.

"Mike distributed his packages during the noon hour. We each got a nice piece, opened it, and thanked him.

"The biggest package of all he saved until last. It was for Jake. Pete was all but bursting, and Mike looked very smug, deadpan. Like always, Jake sat by himself; he was on the far side of the big table. Mike pushed the package over to where he could reach it, and we all sat and waited.

"Jake was never one to say much. You might never know that he was around, for all the talking he did. In three years he'd never said a hundred words. So we were all quite hypnotized with what happened next.

"He took the package firmly in his grip and rose slowly to his feet. He smiled broadly at Mike—and it was then we noticed that his eyes were glistening. His Adam's apple bobbed up and down for a moment and then he got control of himself.

" 'I know I haven't seemed too chummy with you men, but I never meant to be rude. You see, I've got nine kids at home—a wife that's been an invalid—bedfast now for four years. She ain't ever going to get any better. And sometimes when she's real bad off I have to sit up all night to take care of her. And most of my wages have had to go for doctors and medicine. The kids do all they can to help out, but at times it's been hard to keep food in their mouths.

" 'Maybe you think it's funny that I go off by myself to eat my dinner. Well, I guess I've been a little bit ashamed, because I don't always have anything between my sandwich. Or like today—maybe there's only a raw turnip in my dinner bucket.

" 'But I want you to know that this meat really means a lot to me. Maybe more than to anybody here, because tonight my kids'—he wiped the moisture from his eyes with the back of his hand—'tonight my kids will have a real—' He tugged at the string.

"We'd been watching Jake so intently we hadn't paid much notice to Mike and Pete. But we all noticed them now, because they both dove at once to try to grab the package. Nearly cracked their heads when they hit.

"But they were too late. Jake had broken the wrapper and was already surveying his present. He examined each hoof, each ear, and then he held up the tail. It wiggled limply.

"It should have been so funny. But nobody laughed. Nobody at all.

"But the hardest part was when Jake looked up. He tried to smile."

Ora Pate Stewart, *From Where I Stood* (Deseret Book Co., 1960).

A Sleigh Ride Surprise

LUCILE C. READING

Snow lay deep over Salt Lake Valley. When the children became tired of playing in it, they would dare each other to wait for a sleigh to come by so they might catch a ride on its runners.

The most beautiful sleigh in all the valley was one owned by Brigham Young. Nearly every afternoon he would go for a ride in it while his coachman guided a fine team of horses over the frozen ground.

Six-year-old Heber often watched this sleigh and dreamed of someday riding on its runners. They stuck out so far behind the rest of the carriage that he thought them a perfect place on which to stand and ride. One day as he watched the sleigh, it slowed down to go around a corner. Heber was so close to it, he was able to jump onto the runners before it began to speed again.

At first it was exciting fun to ride throuh the crisp air as the horses tossed their heads and the sleigh bells tinkled merrily. Heber thought he would go only a few blocks and then when the horses slowed down, he would hop off and hurry home. But the animals did not slacken their speed. They ran swiftly through the town and beyond it into the country. Heber was nearly breathless as the bitter wind and snow whirled around him. His teeth chattered with cold and fear as he prayed that he might get back home safely. He shivered at the thought of what Brigham Young might say and do if he found a boy riding on the runners of his sleigh.

When the horses had gone more than five miles, they came to a frozen stream and slowed down at last to make their way across it. Heber jumped off and started racing back toward town. He had gone only a short way when he heard a kind voice call, "Stop! Stop, little boy. You are almost frozen. Come, get warm under my buffalo robe and then we'll take you home."

This moment was one Heber J. Grant never forgot. It was his first meeting with Brigham Young, the second President of The Church of Jesus Christ of Latter-day Saints. Heber became its seventh President!

Children's Friend, February 1963.

The Savior Stood Right Here

LeROI C. SNOW

One evening while I was visiting Grandpa Snow in his room in the Salt Lake Temple, I remained until the door keepers had gone and the nightwatchmen had not yet come in, so Grandpa said he would take me to the main front entrance and let me out that way. He got his bunch of keys from his dresser. After we left his room, and while we were still in the large corridor leading into the celestial room, I was walking several steps ahead of Grandpa when he stopped and said, "Wait a moment, Allie, I want to tell you something. It was right here that the Lord Jesus Christ appeared to me at the time of the death of President Woodruff. He instructed me to go right ahead and reorganize the First Presidency of the Church at once and not wait as had been done after the death of the previous Presidents, and that I was to succeed President Woodruff."

Then Grandpa told me what a glorious personage the Savior is, and he described his hands, feet, countenance, and beautiful white robes, all of which were of such glory of whiteness and brightness that he could hardly gaze upon him.

Then he came another step nearer and put his right hand

185

on my head and said, "Now granddaughter, I want you to remember that this is the testimony of your grandfather, that he told you with his own lips that he actually saw the Savior, here in the temple, and talked with him face to face."

"An Experience of My Father's," *Improvement Era*, September 1933.

Prudence, the Pioneer

CLARENCE MANSFIELD LINDSAY

Prudence, we're going to ride over to Goodman Hale's and bring back the kettle he said he'd sell us. Do you think you can keep house till we get home again? We won't be very long."

Prudence Knight looked up into her father's face and nodded brightly. "Yes, indeed, Father! I can do it!"

"Since you're the eldest, you'll have to look after Thankful and Deziah," said Mistress Knight, smiling down at the three children. "Remember that, Prudence!"

"Yes, Mother! I'm sure everything will be all right—if no Indians come prowling around while you're gone."

"I don't think they will. It's been weeks now since we saw any of them about the settlement. But if they *do*, probably they'll be the friendly Sokokis."

The Knight cabin stood in the wilds of Maine near the New York border, and in those pioneer days of the early eighteenth century the Mohawks sometimes made trouble for the settlers.

Prudence watched as her parents started off along the trail, her father guiding the horse that bore them, with Mistress Knight mounted behind him on the pillion. Just before

187

they disappeared from view, she waved a hand in farewell; then, turning, she went back into the cabin where Thankful and Deziah had already started building a little house with blocks from the woodbox.

"I'm going to build a barn, too!" said Deziah, happily.

"But we haven't any cow to put in it," laughed Thankful.

At that moment there came to the ears of all three the distant tinkle of the bell that was attached to Moo-Moo, one of the two cows owned by the family. The cows were allowed to browse in a small pasture some distance from the cabin. It was a friendly sort of sound, and Prudence always liked to listen to it.

Like all young folk of those early days, Prudence had plenty of work to do, and now she sat down at the spinning wheel and began to spin flax. Whir-whir went the wheel, the while Prudence sang a little song to herself:

"Spin, spin the spinning wheel!
Around and around it goes!
While I keep time with tapping heel
A-thinking of the clothes
Which I shall wear when—"

Suddenly she broke off singing and allowed the wheel to slow down to a dead stop. What had she heard?

A cowbell, once more; and if Prudence hadn't been a pioneer girl she would have paid no attention to it this time at all, but would have gone right ahead spinning and singing. But she had a very keen ear, and she didn't at all like the sound of the bell now! She knew that sometimes the crafty Indians would remove the bell, drive off the cows, and then ring the bell by hand so that the owners of the cows, hearing the continued sound, would not guess anything was wrong.

The bell tinkled again—and again. It seemed to be drawing nearer the cabin.

Jumping up, Prudence ran to the door, but she didn't open it. Peering out through the narrow opening at one side (called a "lookout") she saw two painted savages. Muskets in hand, they were creeping toward the cabin! That they were Mohawks, and not the friendly Sokokis, she was certain.

Thankful and Deziah were still at their play, building

their little house on the floor and talking and laughing merrily. Prudence looked at them and wondered how she was to save them—and herself! It was too late to creep out at the back of the cabin and escape into the forest.

If only her parents hadn't gone after that kettle! Even as she thought of that, her anxious glance fell upon the two brass kettles over by the hearth. Why not hide beneath them? There wasn't a second to lose!

She told Thankful and Deziah that Indians were near the cabin, and that the only thing for them to do was to hide under the kettles. As she spoke, she lifted the edge of one, and the two little girls crept into their strange shelter. "Remember," Prudence warned them in a whisper as she let the edge down once more level with the floor, "you mustn't say a word, or even *move!*"

Next, she hastily tossed the blocks of the unfinished toy house back into the woodbox—something Thankful and Deziah wouldn't have liked. But the Indians must not know that anyone was in the cabin. Finally, she managed to creep under the remaining kettle. Mighty lucky for her that she was strong and sturdy!

Everything had been done as swiftly and silently as possible, and not a whit too soon; for no sooner was she safely curled up in her queer hiding place than the unwelcome visitors reached the door, which Prudence had purposely left unbarred but shut. They knocked sharply; then, hearing nothing, tried the door, pushed it open, and strode into the cabin.

"White man not here," grunted one. "Squaw gone, too."

"Never mind!" said the other. "We'll hide somewhere along the trail and get 'em on their way home."

Prudence couldn't help shuddering when she heard that; and she felt sure that the speaker was no Indian, but a renegade white, who had decked himself out as a Mohawk.

"Maybe someone here," said the Indian. "Me take look."

Prudence waited fearfully while the searcher poked about in both rooms of the cabin. Listening to every movement, she knew he had looked in the big cupboard and beneath the square bed and in every place where he thought one might hide, and every moment she expected him to overturn the kettles.

But neither the Mohawk nor the renegade seemed to think it worthwhile to do that. Finally they sat down—one on the kettle beneath which Prudence cowered, and the other on the kettle that sheltered her sisters!

While they rested they talked, and though their talk was brief, Prudence, listening to every word, learned that these two were merely scouts, and that a large band of armed Mohawks would soon follow, bent on destroying the entire settlement.

At last they rose and, after helping themselves to some food, went out of the cabin. Just as soon as she dared, Prudence pushed her way from under the kettle. Then, having satisfied herself that the intruders were well out of sight and hearing, she released Thankful and Deziah, who were both too frightened to even notice that their nearly finished house of blocks wasn't there anymore.

Prudence was very thankful that she had saved her little sisters and herself, but how could she save her dear parents?

Quickly she resolved she would take a shortcut through the forest and reach the trail in time to warn them of their danger. With a word to Thankful and Deziah, she hurried to the door at the back, swung it wide, and stepped out into the open. But she had not gone more than a few yards across the clearing before she met her parents returning. They had come by way of the woodland. She greeted them joyfully and briefly told them what had happened in their absence. They explained that they, too, had heard the mysterious cowbell and, suspecting it was a decoy, had left the trail and returned to the cabin through the woods.

When the horse had been stabled and the family was in the cabin, Prudence related all that she had overheard while hiding under the kettle. Her parents decided that the others in the settlement must be warned immediately. So Goodman Knight and his little family left the cabin and, making their way quietly through the forest, saw to it that every settler had the news.

Thus it was that when the Mohawks appeared, hoping for

an easy victory, every man, woman, and child was safely sheltered in the big garrison-house; and under the heavy fire of the defenders' muskets, the chagrined savages finally gave up the fight and left the neighborhood. They had little time for pillaging and burning of cabins, since some of the bolder men pursued and harried them in their retreat.

Not a life was lost among the whites, and to this very day people in that part of Maine repeat to their children the story of the brave girl whose resourcefulness and pluck saved a whole settlement.

Children's Friend, November 1948.

"I Can Sleep in a Storm"

OSCAR A. KIRKHAM

This story is about a boy. It happened some years ago in a land far across the sea, where most of the people were farmers. And once a year the farmers and the young men and women who worked for them went to a fair—they called it a hiring fair—and struck a bargain for the next year, what work they would do and how much they would be paid. It was the only holiday away from home they had all year 'round—this hiring fair—so you can imagine how they looked forward to it.

Now it happened that Farmer White was very much dissatisfied with a man who worked for him on his farm, so he set out for the fair to hire another man. And when he came to the fair he saw the gay tents, booths, flags—and the strong young farm workers walking up and down, so he began to look around. As he walked about, he saw a young, awkward, gawky young man, and he stopped him.

"Well, young fellow," said Farmer White, "what is your name?"

"John, sir."

"And what do you do?"

"I work on a farm, sir."

"Do you know anything at all about farming?"

192

"Yes, sir."

"What do you know?"

"If you please, sir, I know how to sleep on a windy night."

"You what?"

"I know how to sleep on a windy night, sir."

"Well, that's no great recommendation," said Farmer White. "Most of my men can do that only too well now."

So Farmer White walked around the fair and talked to this one and that, but he found no farm helper that suited him. Then he met John again, asked him the same question, and got the same strange answer. There was something in the boy's honest eyes he liked, something behind what he said that interested him. But he wasn't willing to hire a boy whose only boast was that he could sleep on a windy night, so he made the rounds of the fair again. Late in the afternoon he saw John still waiting to be hired. He quickly made up his mind, walked over to the youth, and said, "You are certainly a curious kind of farmhand, but come along to my farm, and we'll see what you can do."

John worked for several weeks, not much noticed—and that isn't a bad sign, either. When anything is working well, it isn't much noticed. And then one night the wind woke up Farmer White. It hammered against buildings, tore at the haystacks, and howled down the chimneys, and when Farmer White heard it, he sat straight up in bed. He knew that wind. Many a time it had wrenched doors off his barns, scattered his hay, and bowled over his chicken coops. So he jumped out of bed and shouted for John.

Now, John was sleeping in the attic. "John!" the farmer called, but he didn't receive an answer. "John!" he shouted louder than the wind, but no word came from John. So the farmer bounded up to the attic and shook John hard. "Now, John, my lad, get up; the wind's taking everything." But John lay like a log—he never moved.

Farmer White rushed out into the windy night, expecting to see everything tumbled about. But he found the stable doors safely fastened, the horses safely tethered, the windows firmly locked, and the cattle all snug in their stalls. He found the stackyard intact—the stacks well roped and the ropes well pegged. He found the pig-sty secure and the chicken coops firm—and the wind tearing fiercely around them all the time. Then Farmer White laughed out loud. Suddenly he realized what John had meant when he said, "I can sleep in a storm."

Oscar A. Kirkham, *Say the Good Word* (Deseret Book Co., 1958).

"The Indians Overtook Me"

JOSEPH F. SMITH

One bright morning in company with my companions—namely, Alden Burdick, almost a young man grown and a very sober, steady boy; Thomas Burdick, about my own age, but a little older; and Isaac Blocksome, a little younger than myself—I started out with my cattle, comprising the cows, young stock, and several yoke of oxen that were unemployed that day, to go to the herd grounds about one and a half or two miles from Winter Quarters.

We had two horses, both belonging to the Burdicks, and a young pet jack belonging to me. Alden proposed to take it afoot through the hazel and some small woods by a side road and gather some hazelnuts for the crowd while we took out the cattle, and we would meet at the spring on the herd ground. This arrangement just suited us, for we felt when Alden was away we were free from all restraint; his presence, he being the oldest, restrained us, for he was very sedate and operated as an extinguisher upon our exuberance of youthful feelings.

I was riding Alden's bay mare; Thomas, his father's black pony; and Isaac, my jack. On the way we had some sport with "Ike" and the jack, which plagued "Ike" so badly that he left us in disgust, turning the jack loose and with the bridle on. And he went home.

When Thomas and I arrived at the spring we set down our dinner pails, mounted our horses, and amused ourselves by running short races and jumping the horses across ditches, Alden not having arrived as yet. While we were thus amusing ourselves, our cattle were feeding along down the little spring creek toward a rolling point about half a mile distant. The leaders of the herd had stretched out about halfway to this point when all of a sudden a gang of Indians, stripped to the breechclout, painted and daubed, and on horseback, came charging at full speed from behind this point toward us.

Thomas Burdick immediately started for home, crying "Indians! Indians!" Before he reached the top of the hill, however, for some cause he abandoned his pony, turning it loose with bridle and rope, or lariat, attached. My first impulse was to save the cattle from being driven off, for in a most incredibly short time I thought of going to the valley; of our dependence upon our cattle; and of the sorrow of being compelled to remain at Winter Quarters. I suited the action to the thought and at full speed dashed out to head the cattle and, if possible, turn them toward home.

I reached the van of the herd just as the greater number of Indians did. Two Indians had passed me, in pursuit of Thomas. I wheeled my horse in almost one bound and shouted at the cattle, which, mingled with the whoops of the Indians and the sudden rush of a dozen horses, frightened the cattle and started them on the keen run toward the head of the spring, in the direction of home.

As I wheeled I saw the first Indian I met, whom I shall never forget. He was a tall, thin man, riding a light roan horse, very fleet; he had his hair daubed up with stiff white clay. He leaped from his horse and caught Thomas Burdick's, then he jumped on his horse again and started back in the direction he had come. While this was going on the whole gang surrounded me, trying to head me off, but they did not succeed until I reached the head of the spring, with the whole herd under full stampede ahead of me, taking the lower road to town, the road that Alden had taken in the morning. Here my horse was turned around at the head of the spring, and down the stream I went at full speed till I reached a point opposite the hill, where other Indians had concentrated and I was met at this point by this number of Indians who had crossed the stream to head me off. This turned my horse, and once more I got the lead in the direction of home.

I could outrun them, but my horse was getting tired or out of wind and the Indians kept doubling on me, coming in ahead of me and checking my speed, till finally, reaching the head of the spring again, I met, or overtook, a platoon which kept their horses so close together, and veering to right and left as I endeavored to dodge them, that I could not force my horse through. I was thus compelled to slacken speed and the Indians behind overtook me.

One Indian rode upon the left side and one on the right side of me, and each took me by an arm and leg and lifted me from my horse; they then slackened their speed until my horse ran from under me, then they chucked me down with great violence to the ground. Several horses from behind jumped over me but did not hurt me. My horse was secured by the Indians, and without slacking speed they rode on in the direction from whence they had come.

About this moment a number of men with pitchforks in hand appeared on the hill. Thomas had alarmed them with the cry of "Indians!" These men were on their way to the hay field, and at this juncture, as the men appeared on the hill, an Indian who had been trying to catch the jack with corn made a desperate lunge to catch the animal and was kicked over, spilling his corn, which, in his great haste to get away before the men could catch him, he left on the ground. The jack coolly turned and ate the corn, to the amusement of the men on the hill as well as my own.

At this point I thought I had better start after Thomas, and as I reached the top of the hill I saw him just going down into the town. The Indians having departed, the men returned with the pitchforks to their wagons and I continued on to the town. When I arrived, a large assembly was counseling in the bowery, Thomas having told them of our trouble. My folks were glad to see me, you may be sure. A company was formed and on horses started in pursuit of the Indians, and a second company on foot with Thomas and myself to pilot them, in pursuit of the cattle. We took the road we had traveled in the morning and went to the spring.

In the meantime Alden had arrived at the spring, had found nobody there, dinner pails standing as we had left them, and, alarmed, took the herd by the lower road and drove them home. We who did not know this hunted most of the day, and, not finding our cattle, we returned home disheartened. I was filled with fears that we would not now be able to journey to the valley.

When we returned home we learned that Alden had found the cattle and they were all home, safely cared for, and so this trouble was soon forgotten. Thomas's horse was recovered, but the one I was riding was not found. It cost the Indians too much for them ever to part with it. I was at this time about nine years of age.

Joseph Fielding Smith, *Life of Joseph F. Smith* (Deseret Book Co., 1938).

From Bones to Brawn

CLARE MISELES

Theodore Roosevelt sat back in bed and closed his eyes. It was better to keep his eyes shut than to look out of the window and see a pretty, sunny day. Not that he didn't like sunshine, but he was seldom outside to play in it. He was always in bed with a cold!

His father came into the room and sat down beside his bed. "It is a pretty day, isn't it!"

He pulled the curtain aside and saw two boys running down the street. Then he slowly let the curtain fall and turned to his son. "How would you like to play and run like those two young lads down there?"

Theodore winced. He wished his father wouldn't talk that way. It wasn't his fault if he caught colds all the time.

"Well, I think you can!"

"But—father—" Theodore began to explain how poorly he felt.

"But you must try to get strong and well. God has big plans for you, Theodore!" He patted the sneezing head and sat down to talk about those plans.

"I think that God expects you to try and get strong—"

"But—but how—" Theodore asked tentatively.

"And I'm going to help you, too!"

Theodore's head began to ache even more. Whatever did his father mean? He didn't understand; he wasn't sure he could understand.

But he soon learned. Shortly after this talk, his wealthy father brought men and strange–looking bars and equipment to the house. What for? To build a gymnasium!

"Here, in our house?" cried Theodore's mother.

"Why not?" exclaimed his father. "If our Theodore can't go to a gymnasium, then we'll bring one to him!"

So the construction of the gym began. In the meantime, Theodore was both excited and afraid. What—what if he couldn't exercise? Maybe he was too weak!

His father hurried the workmen. He was anxious for Theodore to get started on what he called a "physical fitness" program.

The first day he started, Theodore could barely lift a dumbbell; and when he tried to chin himself, he fell to the floor and hurt his ankle. But soon—and it didn't take long— he lifted the dumbbells with very little effort and chinned himself again and again.

The time even came when Theodore could turn one somersault after another—and found it fun! Cartwheels were also fun. And when it came to lifting weights, then his heart really swelled with pride and thanks.

That wasn't all. He began to eat as he had never eaten before. He was always hungry. Exercise and the good nourishing food he ate built him exactly as his father said they would—strong and well.

Then there were camp-outs. He and his father camped together. They had great fun and he learned to ride like a cowboy. He also liked to hike. What could be more satisfying than to walk through God's woodlands or climb his scalloping green hill? And the stars that covered the dark sky when they camped out at night! Wasn't it good to sit below and look up into God's sparkling wonders?

One night, just before he and his father called it a good camping day and turned in to sleep, Theodore flexed his arm and smiled.

"From bones to brawn." His father smiled, with thanks in his eyes.

Theodore felt his arm. His father was right; he did have muscle, good muscle. He smiled and repeated, "From bones to brawn." It was a phrase he could never forget. It set in his heart with thanks to God and his father. It set so well that in years to come when he fulfilled the great plans God had for him, he did everything in his power to help everyone become good and strong and well.

Children's Friend, September 1969.

Pen Pal Convert

HELEN PATTEN

Helen Patten was in the fifth grade when she began writing to a pen pal by the name of Charlotte Alvoet in Dundee, Scotland. Helen told her what she did in Primary, later Mutual, and sent pictures of the Church's temples and other buildings, and places of interest in Utah.

Last year an elder from Helen's ward, Bruce Draper, was called on a mission to Scotland. Since Helen secretly wished that he might teach the gospel to Charlotte, she wrote a letter to Elder Draper, telling him about Charlotte and giving her address in case he should be assigned to work in Dundee.

About a week later Charlotte wrote to Helen telling her of the visit of two "Yanks." It so happened that Charlotte had gone to a concert, so she was not home when they first called. The elders waited about two hours for her return but finally they had to leave. They left word with her grandmother that they wanted to call again the following Saturday. Charlotte returned home about fifteen minutes after they left. When she heard of the visit, she was so anxious to see these young men that she wrote to Helen that she could hardly wait for the next Saturday to come.

The next letter Helen received began, "Guess who was baptized yesterday! Guess who will be confirmed tomorrow! Guess who is the happiest girl in the world! ME ME ME!" She went on to write that both she and her mother had been converted in only two weeks.

Subsequent letters told of her interest in church activities, her new friends, and her part in the branch's roadshow.

On August 21, she wrote the following:

"I just had to write this to you. I absolutely had to. I guess if I did not I would burst. Oh, the marvelous happening all because of being a Mormon. I must tell you from the beginning or I'll get too mixed up.

"You see, in Scotland we have no LDS schools, so when I was baptized I stayed at the school I had been attending previously, the Harris Academy. This is a Presbyterian school, where pupils of all Protestant faiths attend (Methodists, Episcopalian, and all that). In school we have one period each week for instruction in religion, and this is in the Presbyterian faith. Well, when I was baptized, there was little change since all we did was read the Bible. But this year our teacher decided that our religion period should be informal and should be a period for debate, so he said he would ask us to write one question that he would try to answer and that the class would discuss.

"I didn't ask one question—I asked six! I knew all the answers, but I wanted to explain our teachings and doctrine to him.

"I asked: (1) the interpretation of Revelation 14:6; (2) the meaning of 1 Corinthians 15:29 (baptism for the dead); (3) which is the true church of Jesus Christ; (4) the nature of the Godhead (if they were three in one or three separate beings); (5) the correct method of baptism; (6) the reason for baptism.

"None of my friends had questions, so mine were all copied. Well, a fortnight later (yesterday) the teacher decided that we would discuss the question concerning the personality of our Father in heaven. He blithered on for a wee while about heathens and atheists. Then we got down to business. I brought up the belief of some that our Father,

Jesus Christ, and the Holy Ghost are three in one. Since we don't believe that, I told him so. He asked me for proof, and was he surprised when I rattled off a list of scriptures! You see, I had sat up the night before reading the books I was given when the elders were teaching me. I read scriptures concerning our Father being separate from Jesus Christ and the Holy Ghost. After I had proved my point that they were not three in one, my master went on to another subject, saying, 'Of course, we all know God is a spirit,' and I read more scriptures about our Father in heaven having a body, hair, eyes, and back parts. It was marvelous. One thing led to another, and soon I was deep in telling the class the Joseph Smith story. I was inspired, and I know I had the Holy Ghost and the Spirit of the Lord within me as I talked. At the end I took over the class and was answering questions. Now twenty-one people know about Joseph Smith and heard my testimony as I bore it to them. They also saw the Book of Mormon.

"May God bless you always,
Love,
Charlotte"

Improvement Era, April 1962.

"Let Me See That Brown Velvet, Please"

LUCILE C. READING

A queer-looking bed wagon, with a woman comfortably settled in it, stopped at the toll bridge. The keeper smiled in amusement. Then he saw the anxious look on the face of the boy who was driving, and he hid his smile. The boy explained that his father had helped him make a special wagon for his ailing mother. "Any boy who is that good to his mother can drive over the bridge without paying," said the tollman. He bowed and waved the wagon on.

The boy was Brigham Young, who had been born in Whittingham, Vermont. His family moved to Smyrna, New York, a few years afterward, but today, 170 years later, he is still remembered in Whittingham. Opposite a store on Route 8, many visitors stop to see the marker that has been placed there in his honor. It reads:

"Brigham Young's birthplace. Founder of Utah born here. Southward up the steep hill was the birthplace of Brigham Young, June 1, 1801. Three years later the family moved to New York state where he became a Mormon. He led the people from Illinois to Utah and founded Salt Lake City in 1847."

Brigham was the ninth child of the family. His mother was not well, and all the children learned to work in the home as well as on the farm. Later in his life Brigham said that as a boy he had "no opportunity for letter," but "I had the privilege of picking up brush, chopping down trees, rolling logs and working among the roots, getting my shins, feet and toes bruised. I learned how to make bread, wash the dishes, milk cows and make butter. . . . Those are about all the advantages I gained in my youth. I learned how to economize, for my father had to do it."

When Brigham was fourteen, a great sorrow came to him. His mother, for whom he had felt a special love and closeness, died. It brought sadness in another way too, for Brigham was "farmed out" among the neighbors, and he missed being at home almost as much as he missed his mother.

The story of Brigham Young's conversion to Mormonism in 1832 and how he became President of the Church after Joseph Smith's martyrdom are well known to Church members. Many other people, however, acknowledge his greatness in leading thousands of pioneers across the plains to Utah and are familiar with his words, "This is the place," which he spoke when the first party arrived in the Salt Lake Valley. Children throughout the Church have come to know Brigham Young as a prophet and a colonizer but less known are stories that reveal him as a kind and loving man.

Clarissa Smith had two best friends. Both of them were daughters of Brigham Young. One day when the girls were together, shortly after Salt Lake Valley was settled in 1847, Josephine and Maimie Young were called from their play and told to meet their father. Clarissa was given permission to go with them. This was an exciting experience for Clarissa, because the meeting place was ZCMI, the biggest store in the little pioneer city. She could hardly wait to look at the beautiful piece goods she had heard about. She had often dreamed of a new dress or coat she might someday be able to have.

Brigham Young warmly greeted his two daughters and their friend. He ushered them through the store until they reached the counter where fabrics were sold.

"Let me see that brown velvet, please," he said to the storekeeper. The bolt of cloth was lifted down from the shelf and the material was spread out on the counter.

"Please measure off a piece long enough to make cloaks for Maimie and Josephine," their father directed the storekeeper. Then he looked down at the other little girl, whose eyes reflected her longing to at least touch the beautiful cloth.

"And cut off another length for Clarissa," he said. Brigham Young smiled down at the girl, whose face shone with surprise and delight. "And please make it a very generous one," he added.

The Friend, June 1971.

"I Don't Want to Live With a Thief"

AUTHOR UNKNOWN

He was a bank errand boy, and in his home he had an invalid mother and a little sister who could not walk. The doctor had been to the home recently and had told John that unless the mother could get into the country where there was plenty of fresh air, she was going to grow worse and perhaps would be gone in the fall. So John had tried to find some way by which he could send the two away, but there seemed none at all, and his heart seemed almost ready to break as day after day his mother grew less and less strong.

One day when John was sweeping under the table in the bank, he found a roll of bills—a big roll with some treasury certificates in the pile. He picked them up and started to go to the office of the president, but he stopped. "Just think what those bills will do," he thought. "They will send mother and Millie away for the whole summer, and then they will be well. No one knows I have them, and they don't belong to the bank. They were in the waste paper. I'm going to keep them. Finding is keeping, and they are mine." So into his pocket they went, and he finished his sweeping and started for home. But somehow the roll did not feel good. He put it

208

into his inner pocket, and then shifted it to his coat pocket. He felt sure that everyone must see it.

About an hour after John had gone home, he came back to the bank, knocked for admittance, and went to the office of the president. He threw the bills on the desk, saying, "I found them when I swept," and then with a cry of pain, he ran from the bank.

Next morning John was there at his work, and after the bank had opened he was called to the president's room. "John," said the president, "I wish you would tell me why you brought those bills back last night. I know why you wanted them, and what they would have done at home. We didn't know you had them. Why did you bring them back?" Away over the desk leaned John, and looking straight into the eyes of the man he said, "Sir, as long as I live, I have to live with myself, and I don't want to live with a thief." A few days later the mother and Millie went to the country. But they did not go alone; John went with them for the whole summer, as a gift of appreciation of the bank for his nobility.

A Story to Tell (Deseret Book Co., 1971).

"Throw It Here, Sissy"

HEBER J. GRANT

As I was an only child, my mother reared me very carefully. Indeed, I grew up more or less under the principles of a hothouse plant, a growth which is long and lengthy but not substantial. I learned to sweep and to wash and wipe dishes but did little stone throwing and little indulgence in works which are interesting to boys, which develop their physical frames.

Therefore, when I joined the baseball club, the boys of my own age and a little older played in the first nine, those younger than I played in the second, and those still younger, in the third, and I played with them. One of the reasons for this was that I could not throw the ball from one base to another, and another reason was that I lacked the strength to run or bat the ball. When I picked up the ball, the boys would generally shout, "Throw it here, sissy!"

So much fun was engendered on my account by my youthful companions that I solemnly vowed that I would play baseball in the nine that would win the championship in the territory of Utah. My mother was keeping boarders for a living at the time, and I shined their boots until I saved a dollar, which I invested in a baseball, and spent hours throwing the ball at Bishop Edwin D. Woolley's barn, which caused him to refer to me as the laziest boy in the Thirteenth Ward.

Often my arm would ache so that I could scarcely go to sleep at night, but I kept on practicing and finally succeeded in getting into the second nine of our club. Subsequently, I joined a better club and eventually played in the nine that won the championship in California, Colorado, and Wyoming, and thus made good my promise to myself and retired from the baseball arena.

(When Heber could not sleep because his arm ached as a result of throwing the ball, his mother would wrap it with bandages dipped in cold water to relieve the pain.)

Bryant S. Hinckley, *Highlights in the Life of a Great Leader* (Deseret Book Co., 1951).

The Present Mother Kept

RUTH F. CHANDLER

The day before Mother's Day, Susan found a quarter. She picked it up and wiped it with her handkerchief, then skipped through three puddles and on down the hill with her red raincape flying out behind.

To find a quarter any day was lucky. Of course it wasn't much money, but it would buy a little present for her mother. In school Susan had made a card with a verse and a pink carnation on it, but a card wasn't a real present. If she asked for money, it would not be a real surprise.

She ran lickety-clip to the shopping center.

In the florist's shop she saw some red roses, so she opened the door and went in.

"How much is that rose?" she asked, pointing to the smallest one.

"Fifty cents," said the man.

"I'm sorry. I only have a quarter," Susan told him.

She went to the drugstore and looked at the boxes of candy, bright with flowers and pretty ribbons.

"Have you any little boxes that cost a quarter?" she asked the clerk.

No, his candy cost much more than that. She looked at

212

the cards. One had a carnation that opened like a real flower, but it was marked thirty-five cents. Susan shook her head and walked out.

The next store was the market where they sold frankfurters and rolls and boxes of cereal. On the candy counter she saw a sign "Special today only—giant size chocolate bars—25 cents."

Her mother liked chocolate bars, so Susan chose one with almonds in it. As she waited in line to pay for her things, she planned how she would wrap it in pretty paper, tie it with a red ribbon, and hide it until tomorrow.

She wished the woman in front of her would hurry, but she didn't. Instead, she took everything out of her pocketbook and began to feel around inside.

"That's funny," she said, "I know I had some change." Then she stuck two fingers through the bottom of the bag.

"Look at that," she said to the clerk. "The seam has ripped. I've been all over town this morning. I wonder how much money I have lost." Then she took a bill from another place, paid for her groceries, and left the store.

On her way home, Susan did some thinking. Maybe that woman lost her money on the hill. Susan walked along slowly, looking on the sidewalk, in the street, and even in the puddles.

She kicked at something in the mud. It was another quarter! Soon she found a penny, and another penny, a nickel, and two dimes. She was so excited she could hardly breathe. Now she could buy the rose or the card that was so much prettier than the one she had made in school. She turned back toward the stores.

But instead of feeling happy, with a pocketful of money, she felt kind of sick inside. Her mother would surely ask, "Where did you get the money for these nice presents?" And it wasn't honest "Finders Keepers" when you knew a lady had lost it.

Slowly she walked back, past the florist's shop and past the drugstore. She pushed open the door of the market and went to the clerk.

"I found the money that woman lost," she said, laying it

on the counter. Then, with a sigh, she took the chocolate bar from the paper bag.

"Can I have my quarter?" she asked.

The clerk looked at her. "What goes on here?" he asked.

"You know the lady. Her pocketbook was ripped," Susan explained.

"Yes. But what's the matter with the candy?"

"Nothing. I bought it with a quarter I found, before I knew the money was hers."

"Oh." He took a quarter from the cash register and laid it with the other money. "It's a wonder you didn't eat the candy."

"It wasn't for me. It was for tomorrow, a present for my mother."

The clerk made a clicking noise with his tongue. "What's your name?" he asked.

"Susan Bradley."

Customers were waiting in line, so Susan hurried out. She walked slowly past the money place and on up the hill. Her mother met her at the door.

"You were gone so long I was worried," she said, "then that nice Mrs. Swanson telephoned." She put the groceries away while Susan took off her raincape and boots.

"Who is Mrs. Swanson?" she asked.

"Darling, she's the woman who lost the money." Mother put her arms around Susan. "And you found it and gave it to the clerk. Oh, Susan, I'm so proud of my little girl."

"She telephoned?" Susan asked.

"Yes. The clerk saw her in the parking lot and gave her the money. Then she found Bradley in the telephone book and called to thank you."

Susan told her mother the whole story. "I didn't want to give back the candy bar. It had lots of nuts in it."

"I know, dear, but it's all right. I don't want any present."

Susan remembered the card she had made in school and ran to get it. It was better than nothing.

Her mother looked at the carnation Susan had colored so carefully and the words she had printed neatly inside.

"I will try in all I do to show how much I love you."

"Susan," she said, "you couldn't have bought anything in a store so precious as this. Flowers die, and we'd soon eat the candy. But this card I shall keep forever and ever."

Children's Friend, May 1963.

Remember the Bee

ELIZABETH J. BUCKISCH

In a sunny kitchen of the parsonage in Alsace, four-year-old Albert looked up from play as his minister-father came in from the garden.

"Papa, could I go with you today?" he begged as he noticed his father getting ready to go out to his beehives. "I have never seen you take the honey from the bees."

Albert knew quite well what this trip meant. For supper the family would have good fresh honey on delicious homemade bread.

"You're too young, Albert. If you move around or make a sound I cannot take the honey from the bees."

"But I'll sit very, very still. I promise, Papa. You will see."

"Very well then, little son, you may come. But remember, you must not get near the bees."

Picking up a dishpan, heavy gloves, and a helmet-type hat with a mosquito-net veil to protect his face, the tall young minister and his eager son set out.

While his father put on the gloves and helmet and moved cautiously over to the beehives, Albert sat on an old stool some distance away and watched with interest. He would sit, oh! so still, just as he had promised.

In a few minutes a long procession of bees swarmed out of the hive, evidently furious that anyone should dare disturb them and their honey. Working gently and speaking softly to the bees, his father loosened a square filled with honey and placed it in the dishpan. After a while, tired of watching. Albert laughed gleefully as he admired a little creature that had lighted on his own small fist.

Suddenly he felt a short, sharp, stabbing pain in his hand and let out a shriek. "Papa! Papa!" he screamed. His father dropped everything and ran over to the boy. The household, hearing the loud screams from the far end of the garden, came running out also. His mother, Maria the maid, his older sister, and a younger brother all stood or knelt around him, trying to comfort him. Maria kissed the bee-stung hand, his father and mother petted him, and Albert felt a great wave of satisfaction come over him.

As suddenly as it had come, the pain stopped. Albert's conscience began to give him little twinges. "That's enough attention now," it seemed to say. "You are not in pain any more." But this was too good an opportunity to waste, so Albert howled right on and got some more petting. But for the rest of the day he felt uncomfortable and couldn't enjoy his play—not from the bee-sting, for that had long since stopped hurting, but from that still small voice inside him. He felt he was a fraud. He had done something dishonorable. The day that had started so happily was ruined.

This little boy grew up to become one of the most famous medical missionaries in the world, Dr. Albert Schweitzer, who devoted his life to a jungle hospital deep in the African Congo. He won great renown for his work with the natives, and he was honored at royal courts by kings and queens and by many other heads of government.

But whenever Dr. Schweitzer felt he was trading on people's sympathies, whenever he was tempted to exaggerate or to get undeserved praise, he said to himself, "Remember the bee!"

Children's Friend, August 1963.

President Smith Took Him by the Hand

LUCILE C. READING

Eleven-year-old John Roothoof lived in Rotterdam, Holland. He had once been happy going to school and church, playing with his friends, and doing all the things a boy enjoys. Then without warning, a painful eye disease caused him to lose his sight. No longer could he go to school or read. He could not even see well enough to play with his friends. Each day was filled with darkness and suffering.

Word reached the Latter-day Saints in Holland that President Joseph F. Smith would visit them. John thought about this for a long time, and then he said to his mother, "The prophet has the most power of any missionary on earth. If you'll take me with you to the meeting so he can look into my eyes, I believe I'll be healed."

At the close of the meeting the next Sunday, President Smith went to the back of the small chapel to greet the people and shake hands with each one. Sister Roothoof helped John, his eyes bandaged, go with the others to speak to their beloved leader. President Smith took him by the hand and then with great tenderness lifted the bandages and looked into John's pain-filled eyes. He blessed the boy

218

and promised him he would see again. Arriving home, John's mother took the bandages from his eyes so she could bathe them as the doctors had told her to do. As she did so, John cried out with joy, "Oh Mamma, my eyes are well. I can see fine now—and far too. And I can't feel any pain!"

The Friend, August 1973.

"See What You Have Done for Me"

MATTHEW COWLEY

I was down in the Southwest Indian Mission. When I went into church one day, a fine-looking Navajo woman came in. A missionary said to me, "I want to introduce you to this sister," so he took me up and introduced me to her, and we had a little chat.

After meeting the young missionary came to me and said, "Well, I am glad you met her. A few months ago my companion and I went to the Navajo reservation. We went into a hogan. There lay this woman on her back—on sheepskin. She had been there for six long years. She had never stood up. When we were about to leave, she said to us, 'Isn't there something you people do for people who are sick and afflicted?' I said, 'Yes.' She said, 'Will you please do it for me?' So we got down on our knees; one anointed her with oil, the other one sealed the anointing. After we left—we were only a short distance away—she came running out from the hogan and said, 'Come back and see what you have done for me.' She has been walking ever since."

BYU Speeches of the Year, February 18, 1953.

The Dutchman's Magic Eye

MURRAY T. PRINGLE

One evening back in 1674 a group of townsfolk gathered in the town square of Delft, Holland. "What shall we do," said one, "that we may amuse ourselves?"

"I know," answered another. "Let us go to the city hall and watch the madman who looks at nothing and pretends to see something. Let us go to see Anton Leeuwenhoek."

"Of course!" said the others. "A great idea. Let's go!"

In the basement of the city hall, they gathered around a serious young man, who sat at a rough wooden table peering through a strange device.

"Look you, my friends," laughed a fat merchant. "All night Herr Leeuwenhoek sits and stares at nothing. Here, my foolish fellow, here is a hair from my moustache. Add it to your collection of fly brains and fish scales."

Anton Leeuwenhoek looked up angrily. "Laugh!" he said. "Fools always laugh at that which they do not understand. I have here a glass like no other in the world. With it I can see animals which are invisible to your eyes."

"Then why do you not let us see for ourselves?" demanded the fat merchant. "Why do you always refuse?"

"Because you come only to scoff," replied the young man,

221

"but perhaps it is what you need to be convinced. Very well, you shall see. I shall put this drop of water for you to examine. Now look, and then scoff!"

The fat shopkeeper smiled triumphantly as he sat down and peered into the instrument. "He is right! I see many little animals in that drop of water. They swim! They dance!"

One by one everyone else in the room sat down and looked at the strange sight. Each one got up and apologized to the "madman" for having laughed. Leeuwenhoek then showed them that there were horrid little creatures living on their teeth.

The people were so amazed that they spread the miracle of Anton Leeuwenhoek's "magic eye" far and wide. Finally, it came to the attention of scientists in London, England.

"Your instruments are marvelous, Herr Leeuwenhoek," the scientists told him. "We have none so fine as these in all England. Can you make some for us?"

The Dutchman generously agreed to their request, and the British scientists went away happy. Anton Leeuwenhoek, meanwhile, returned to his study of the strange creatures he had discovered with his microscope.

He spent every moment he could spare from his janitorial duties peering through his glass, seeking answers. And he found them. He discovered, for example, that rainwater was clean and free of the horrid creatures.

"Aha," reasoned the amateur scientist, "then that must mean that they come from dirty pots and unclean fingers."

He conducted further studies and experiments, and then one day he announced his finding to a group of scientists.

"When you boil water, gentlemen," he told them, "the little animals disappear or die. That is strange, is it not?"

It was, indeed! Even Anton Leeuwenhoek did not fully realize the truly great discovery he had made. The little beasts he had discovered were microbes.

Today we realize what a truly tremendous debt we owe to that humble Dutchman of long ago and his "magic eye."

Children's Friend, March 1965.

George Did It!

MURRAY T. PRINGLE

There was nothing special about that day in the early 1860s; it was a lazy, "nothing" sort of day. Passengers aboard the train sprawled lethargically in their seats or dozed.

George didn't doze, but he did stare unseeingly out of the window, thinking of nothing in particular. It was warm, and George, a teenager, certainly had no idea that this would be the day he would embark on a career that would make him rich and world-famous.

Suddenly the train went into a long, clattering halt that jolted all the dozers into wakefulness, and it made George reach out to retain his balance. In answer to the passengers' clamor to know what had happened, the conductor explained that two freight trains had collided head-on up the line. Until the debris was removed, the passenger train would have to wait.

Thankful for something to break the monotony, George left the train and walked up the track to have a look. The rails were a shambles. Both engines were demolished, and most of the freight cars were a mass of twisted metal and splintered wood. Neither engineer had been taken unaware; both had seen the crash coming. Why, then, hadn't they

223

done something about it? They had—everything possible, but that wasn't much.

Each had used his hand brake, but that only controlled his engine. Each had whistled to his crew in the cars behind, a signal to apply brakes to the individual cars. This was standard operating procedure, but it was time-consuming. Long before enough brakes could be set to forestall it, the accident had happened. Engineers and crews had leaped to safety but both engines, a long string of box-cars, and the freight they carried were destroyed.

A real train wreck, even a relatively undramatic one like this, is something every boy would remember. George not only remembered it, but he also worried about the inefficient braking system that had allowed it to happen. Lives *could* have been lost; lives *had* been lost in similar mishaps and would be in the future.

Back at his father's factory in Schenectady, New York, George continued to ponder the problem. There must be some way to stop a speeding train more quickly! But how? George began devoting his lunch hours to the project. For months he considered and discarded one possibility after another. Not enough power. What would provide that power? A mechanical automatic brake? Perhaps. Steam?

Then one day he was idly leafing through a magazine when an article caught his eye. It told of an engineering project in Switzerland. He read the account with growing excitement. A tunnel was being blasted through the Alps. It was an ambitious undertaking. A new type of drill, run by compressed air, was enabling the contractors to make remarkable progress. This could be it, George thought excitedly. Compressed air could supply the motive power for his brake.

But when he finally had it worked out, no one would accept his idea. Railroad men listened incredulously as he propounded his idea of stopping a train with *air*. Then they laughingly dismissed him as a teenage dreamer. Even his own father, an inventor, smiled indulgently. But George persisted.

When it finally seemed to George that no one would ever

give him a serious hearing, he found a man who would—and did—listen. The man was Andrew Carnegie, who was then amassing one of the world's great private fortunes. Carnegie and his associates financed the construction of an air brake for one train.

In September 1868, an engine equipped with George's invention and coupled to four cars was ready. On board were Carnegie, his associates, railroad officials, some newspapermen—and the brake's 22-year-old inventor. As the run began at a point a few miles outside of Pittsburgh, George's hands felt clammy and his throat was dry. Suppose something went wrong? Suppose the brakes failed to hold? This was his one and only chance.

If he failed, everyone who had laughingly dismissed his idea would chuckle and say: "Air to stop a train? The kid's a crackpot! He's had that crazy idea for years. Carnegie was a fool to listen to him!" Carnegie! George cast an anxious glance at the millionaire and swallowed hard. Then, as the train gathered speed, he settled down to some long and serious praying.

With a rushing roar, the train bore down on the Steel City, heading into the Union Station. Then the air brake was applied. The train did not exactly slow down to a coasting stop. The moment the control switch was thrust home, every passenger aboard was thrown from his seat!

George ran forward to assist Andrew Carnegie, who was on his hands and knees in the aisle. "Works, doesn't it, boy?" Mr. Carnegie grinned up at him.

George was over the hump; ahead lay clear track. He would go on to found a great company and contribute more than 400 other inventions for the benefit of mankind. No one said, "Let George do it," but he did it anyway. And the railroad industry and the whole world owe a debt of thanks to a persevering young man named George Westinghouse!

Children's Friend, September 1968.

The Black Polish Shoes

LUCILE C. READING

It was nearly sundown, and the boys and men of Willard, Utah, had been busy since early morning clearing the road that Brigham Young's carriage would take to reach the bowery. All day as Evan threw rocks out of the rutted road, he tried to think of something he could do about a coat and some shoes to wear at the choir program which was to be held before the banquet in the bowery.

Evan was only twelve and every other member of the choir was many years older than he. They all called him their "Boy Alto."

Evan's family lived more than sixty miles away. He earned his board and room doing farm work. There was no one he felt he could talk to about his problem, and so as he walked to his room through the early dusk he was deep in thought.

As Evan passed the general store he saw a can of shoe polish in the window and suddenly decided what to do for shoes. After he put on his best pants that evening he turned up the cuffs, then took a can of shoe polish and carefully painted some make-believe shoes on his feet. He couldn't think of anything he could do about a coat, so he started toward the bowery in his shirt sleeves. As he hurried along the road he wiped away the tears that kept filling his eyes. He hoped no one would see them, but a choir member stopped him and asked why he was crying.

"I'm crying because I haven't any shoes and I'm ashamed for Brigham Young to see me barefooted with all the big folks," Evan said simply.

"President Young won't think any the less of you for not having shoes," the lady assured him. "Come, Boy Alto, and sing with us." Evan walked as far as the bowery entrance with her but wouldn't go on.

Just then Brigham Young and his party arrived. Evan wanted to run and hide but as he turned to do so, President Young held out a hand to stop him and asked, "Why are you running away? Why don't you go inside?"

"I-I sing in the choir," Evan stammered, "but I'm not dressed well enough to sing with them tonight." He looked down at his bare feet covered with shoe polish. Brigham Young glanced down; then with understanding he looked deep into Evan's eyes. "Don't feel bad," he said as he patted Evan's shoulder. "We're all friends."

More than sixty years later, after Evan Stephens had become a great musician, the Salt Lake Tabernacle Choir leader, and the composer of 86 LDS hymns, he recalled this shining moment in his life and said, "And ever after that I felt that there was an acquaintance between me and the President."

Children's Friend, January 1967.

"If We Had Skated"

CLARENCE HUFFMAN

Tom Carr walked briskly down a woodland road one Saturday afternoon. A pair of skates swung at one side, while a knapsack was fastened to his back. Two boys, with similar loads, accompanied him, their bright colored sweaters and caps in strong contrast to the black tree trunks and the gray sky.

Tom turned to his companions. "I say," he began, "I believe it's going to snow. It's getting warmer and that sky—"

"Don't look at it," answered Jack Reed, a short, chubby boy who panted as he tried to keep with Tom's sturdy strides. "We didn't come out into the country to look at snow, but to skate on the river."

"Yes," broke in Ralph Bronson, a tall, thin boy, "I hope we do get to skate. You have plenty of chances, Tom, since you live in the country, but it's a treat to us city boys."

"Well," laughed Tom, "I didn't say I was going to make it snow, did I? I only said it might. We're down in the river valley now. There's old Mr. Blake's shack."

Jack and Ralph gave a shout. They ran ahead of Tom in their haste to get to the frozen river.

Tom called to them. "Hold it a minute. I don't see any smoke coming from the cabin."

Tom knocked loudly on the door of the small dwelling. A weak voice invited him to enter. Tom pushed open the door and was followed by his friends.

Over in a corner of the one room stood a crude bed, covered with well-worn but clean covers. The face of an old man peered out from the blankets.

"Why, Mr. Blake," Tom cried, "you're not sick?"

"No, not exactly," quavered the old man, "but I don't feel very well. Been spending most of my time in bed because—" He stopped and looked at the fireplace.

Tom's eyes followed his and saw that no flames danced there.

"No fire!" he exclaimed.

"Yes," replied the old man. "I got too weak to chop any wood, and no one has come this way for many days. All I could do during this cold spell was to stay in bed all the time, eating just a snack. I even ran out of kerosene for my lamp."

Tom turned around to Jack and Ralph. His eyes were sparkling. "Suppose we take time to cut up some wood for Mr. Blake!"

"But what about the skating?" asked Jack.

"Yes," chimed in Ralph. "We can't do both. Can't you send a neighbor out when we get back?"

"Mr. Blake needs a warm fire." replied Tom firmly, looking at the feeble old man. "Besides, it may snow, and then it's not easy to get back here. The pile of poles would be covered then and it would be hard to chop them."

Tom threw off his skates and knapsack. "I'm staying," he announced. "I know where you keep the ax, Mr. Blake."

Jack and Ralph were throwing down their loads by this time. "We'll have a good time after all," said Jack. "Going to cook supper in the cave—"

"And we can come back another Saturday this winter to skate," added Ralph.

Soon the three boys were busy at the pile of poles that the old man had cut down in the fall for his winter fuel. While Tom cut the young trees, Jack placed them in a small shed that adjoined the cabin. Ralph took some pieces into the room where the old man lay, and soon a bright fire was dancing in the fireplace. He placed a small pile of wood in one corner of the room for immediate use and broke up some fallen limbs and dead bushes for kindling.

It was mid-afternoon when the work was done. Mr. Blake thanked the boys but they scarcely waited to hear him, as they were in a hurry to get to the cave. Only Tom lingered for a moment. "Make out an order for any groceries you want to buy, Mr. Blake," he said, "and I'll ask dad to bring them to you the first of the week. Wish I'd known sooner, for he and my mother drove to town this morning."

By this time the sky was getting grayer and a few flakes were sailing lazily to the ground. "Dad may have to take you two back to town in a bob-sled tomorrow morning," said Tom. "Hey! here's the cave."

The three had reached a dark hole at the base of a sandstone cliff. Laying down their skates and knapsacks again, the boys collected a supply of fallen wood, which they dragged into the cave. As they crawled inside with their last load, they noticed that a wind was rising.

"Just in time!" cried Jack. "It's getting colder outside."

The boys built a fire in one corner of the cave. A small hole had been chipped above and a piece of stove-pipe inserted in the opening to let out the smoke.

"It's a dandy place!" exclaimed Jack, looking around at the sandstone walls over which the red light was flickering.

"I thought you two would like it," said Tom. "Now let's eat."

The contents of their knapsacks were spread out upon the sand floor, and soon the smell of frying bacon and eggs filled the air. There were sandwiches, oranges, and roasted potatoes.

Two hours flew by before the boys were ready to leave. By that time the last mouthful of food had been consumed, the last piece of wood had burned to coals.

Ralph gave a shiver. "Seems to me it's getting colder," he said.

"We'll get warm as soon as we begin to walk," Tom replied. "Let's start for home."

When the boys had crawled out, they could hardly believe their eyes. Twilight had come, and the world was full of whirling snow that almost blinded them. The air was freezing. For a moment Tom's heart sank; then he called, "Bad night, fellows, but we'll soon hit the road. Just keep close to me, that's all."

There was no chance to climb up the opposite hill for a shortcut through the woods. The hill was already a deep mass of white.

The boys crept along the base of the cliff. They could hardly see the river below. It was also a flat white expanse.

On they trudged until they came to a pile of fallen trees. Tom stopped short. "We're going the wrong way," he said, trying to speak cheerily. "Right-about face."

They ended at the river. Once more the three turned. "We've got to keep moving," advised Tom.

Up and down through the blinding white they tramped. It was getting colder and colder and darkness had deepened.

Then a light, a little light, was seen shining through the blizzard!

"I know where we are now!" cried Tom joyfully. "There's Mr. Blake's cabin."

"If we had skated—" Jack began.

Tom did not seem to understand. "I'm glad Mr. Blake will be warm tonight," was all he said.

Children's Friend, January 1965.

Christmas at Our House

EMILY SMITH STEWART

We believe in Christmas. To us, the George Albert Smith family, Christmas is one of the most blessed and precious days the year brings. We strive to make each Christmas as loving and living as our parents made them for us.

The first Christmas I remember was spent in the home of my great-grandfather, where the fireplace was so large that Santa Claus actually stepped out of the fireplace, where the Christmas tree was so tall that it touched the ceiling, and where the long banisters, slick and polished, let us ride two stories without getting off. I shall never forget the great crocks of spicy doughnuts and the shelves of fat mince pies in the pantry, nor the beds made all over the floors throughout the huge house where all of us slept, or tried to sleep, until Christmas morning. Even now I see the doll, with its real hair wig, that was mine this first remembered Christmas!

The next Christmas, I remember, we spent in the new house that Father and Mother had built for their family. This Christmas my best present was a new baby sister who had come since Thanksgiving, in time for Mother to be up and around by Christmas. This sister was my extra special gift and always will be because she is the only sister I have.

Preparations for Christmas at our home were always very special. Our plans were extensive and carefully laid, the money budgeted, the gifts painstakingly chosen. Father and Mother always insisted that whatever means we had to use for Christmas must be spread over a wide territory, for they planned that we should learn for ourselves that it's always "more blessed to give than to receive." We began with the wonderful box that Mother always prepared for the Relief Society and into which she put all of the goodies that we planned for ourselves, including mince pies and plum puddings with a wonderful buttery sauce. We assembled the contents of this Relief Society Christmas box for days. After everything was ready, it was loaded on the sled and dragged on top of the crisp, icy snow to the Relief Society room at the 17th Ward. Thus began our custom, one that was always Father's, of providing Christmas for those persons that others forgot. He always considered the fact that where people were well remembered, they might well do without his remembering them in a substantial way, other than to extend his sincere good wishes, while gifts and fancy holiday foods should be taken to those too frequently overlooked.

Christmas Eve at our house began family festivities. We hung our stockings in front of the fireplace in the dining room. Father always hung a great, huge stocking, because he assured us that Santa never could get all the things he wanted in just a regular sock. And then, to add to the gaiety of the occasion, each year he brought his tall rubber boots up from the basement and stood one at either side of the fireplace in the dining room.

After stockings were hung, we spread a table for Santa Claus' supper—a bowl of rich milk and bread and a generous wedge of mince pie. We wrote a note to encourage him on his way and then went to bed, but it seemed morning would never come. The length of Christmas Eve night and the shortness of Christmas day was something we could never understand.

No matter how excited we children were, we never were permitted to go downstairs until we were washed, combed, and fully dressed. Then we had morning prayers and sat down to breakfast, the worst breakfast of the year because it took so much time and seemed to hinder our getting to our stockings. Always there was something very unusual and very special down in the toe. First, we laughed and laughed over the things Santa Claus put in Father's boots—coal and kindling and vegetables; and then we were offended because we thought Santa was not very kind to our father, who is always generous with everyone else. After this first experience with bootsful of jokes on Christmas, we bought something very special for Father the next year to make up for the slight Santa Claus had made.

After we had enjoyed our toys and gifts in the stockings, the folding doors into the parlor were pushed aside and we beheld our twinkling candlelit Christmas tree. Under the colorful, green tree were the packages for friends and the rest of the family. These were distributed and all had a very happy, festive time.

After our own mirth and merriment had partially subsided, Father always took us with him to make the rounds of the forgotten friends that he habitually visited on Christmas. I was a very little girl when I went with Father to see how the other half of the people lived. I remembered going down a long alley in the middle of a city block where there were some very poor houses. We opened the door of one tiny home and there on the bed lay an old woman, very sad and alone. As we came in, tears ran down her cheeks, and she reached over to take hold of Father's hand as we gave her our little remembrances. "I am grateful to you for coming," she said, "because if you hadn't come I would have no Christmas at all. No one else has remembered me." We thoroughly enjoyed this part of our day.

Christmas dinner was another high spot in our Christmas celebration. We always had very wonderful Christmas dinners, usually turkey dinners served on our beautiful blue-lace plates.

One Christmas that I shall never forget is the one when Father was very seriously ill. Expenses had been extremely high and it seemed that we were not going to be able to afford much of a Christmas. Mother longed to provide our usual happy Christmas, but she knew she could not do so and still pay the tithing due before the end of the year, and which had accumulated as a result of Father's illness. She felt that her children were entitled, as are all children, to a happy Christmas. If she bought the usual gifts and dinner for them, however, she couldn't possibly pay her tithing. If she paid her full tithing her children could have no Christmas. It was a difficult decision, but she finally decided that she must pay her tithing before she gave it further thought, as the desire to do something for her children might tempt her too greatly. Hurriedly, she put on her wraps and went to the bishop, where she paid her tithing in full.

On her way home her heart was very heavy. She was convinced that her children could have nothing for Christmas, and she dreaded our disappointment. She was walking through the snow, head down, when Mark Austin, her good neighbor, said, "Just a moment, Sister Smith. I have been thinking that your expenses have been exceedingly heavy during Brother Smith's long illness, so I should like very much to have you take this little gift and buy yourself something very special for Christmas. I am sure you haven't had anything for yourself in a long, long time." Mother, choking with tears, tried to thank him. She took the check, folded it, and went home, her heart fairly pounding with joy and thanksgiving. When she entered the house and turned the light on, she found he had given her one hundred dollars, the exact amount that she had paid in tithing.

When that Christmas morning arrived, Mother said, "This is really your tithing Christmas, children," and she told us the story as the day progressed. Bit by bit the blessing of tithing was thus deeply impressed upon us.

Since that tithing Christmas, we spent Christmases in many different lands. Some were spent in England, some in the United States, and others in many states within the United States. We had plentiful Christmases and meager Christmases, happy Christmases and Christmases that were not so joyous. Irrespective of what our personal sorrows may have been, Father always saw to it that those who needed Christmas, who were not of our particular family, were not forgotten. All of our holiday celebrations at Christmas time were motivated by the thought impressed upon us in early childhood: "It is more blessed to give than to receive." In fact, not only Christmas, but every day of our father's life stressed this philosophy, the practicing of which made a lifelong impression upon our minds. We believe in Christmas!

A Story to Tell (Deseret Book Co., 1971).

The Sheaf of Grain

BERNADINE BEATIE

It was Christmas Eve. Young Mike sat at the window of his home, looking down the highway to the west. He could just see the lights of Old Mike's filling station, glimmering through the swirling snow. In front of every house, on each side of the highway, stood a tall pole to which a sheaf of grain had been attached.

"Ma," young Mike called. "May I go stay with Grandpa?"

"You just want to hear your grandpa's Christmas story again." His mother came and stood beside Mike. "Sometimes I think we all hang up those sheaves of grain more to please your grandpa than for any other reason."

"No," said Mike, "for the birds and for Olaf."

"Humph!" she said. "Everybody but your grandpa knows Olaf's been dead these many years. Nobody could have lived through that storm."

Mike supposed his mother was right, but it was too bad. Grandpa wanted a better ending for his Christmas story—a happy one—and so did Mike.

"Well, run along," his mother said. "But you and your grandpa close up and be home by ten."

Mike reached the filling station just as a large car pulled

237

up. A tall man slid from beneath the wheel. He wore a trim-looking dark blue uniform and a cap with a visor that was covered with gold braid. He looked larger than life, somehow, outlined against the dark, snow-swept prairie. Mike's eyes bulged when he heard his grandpa call the man "Captain." Mike had never seen a sea captain before.

"Tell me," the stranger asked, "why are sheaves of grain hanging before the houses?"

Mike's grandfather perked up. "Do you have time to hear a story?"

"There is always time for a story," said the man from the sea.

"Then come inside, where it is warm."

The stranger shook his head when Mike's grandpa offered him a chair near the small hissing stove. Instead, he pulled his cap low over his eyes and sat in a shadowy corner of the small room. The grandfather took his regular place beside the stove, and Mike sat beside him, hoping no customers would come and disturb the telling of the story.

"Once, many years ago," his grandpa started, "there lived a kind of rancher and his wife who loved children. Years passed, and when no children came to bless their home, they started caring for homeless boys who came their way. And there were many of them, for those were the days of the great depression, when hunger stalked the land. First one boy drifted in, then another, until every room of the rancher's home was filled with homeless boys. They were a rough lot, those lads, rough and wild. The rancher was always getting them out of scrapes at school or in town. Many of the folks around said he was just raising the boys for the jail house. Maybe he was—they were a wild bunch all right!

"Then one spring day, a different kind of lad drifted in. He was tall, with hair the color of sun-ripened wheat, and he gave his name as Olaf Jensen. He came from a land far across the sea, and he was as strong as a winter storm. Yet, there was something strangely gentle and kind about him. Flowers that he planted bloomed more quickly than others, birds sang when he was near, and the orneriest critter on the ranch would settle down at the sound of Olaf's voice."

Young Mike looked up, knowing his grandpa would pause at this point—he always did. Knowing, too, that there would be a far-away look in the old man's eyes, almost as though he were hearing Olaf's voice.

"Yes," the tall stranger prompted softly.

"The boys did not like Olaf," Grandpa continued. "He was different from them. 'Yah,' he said, instead of 'yes,' and sometimes he spoke in a strange foreign tongue. They felt too that the old rancher and his wife had a feeling for Olaf that they did not have for them, and they grew jealous. When the rancher and his wife were not around, the boys would torment Olaf with every meanness they could think of. The ringleader was a lad named Mike. This grieved Olaf, who looked on every living thing with love."

Young Mike hitched his chair a little closer to the stove, struck with wonder that Grandpa had once been that young Mike of the story—wild and rough.

"Why didn't this Olaf fight back?" the stranger spoke from the shadows.

"One day he did. One Christmas Eve—snowy and cold— very much like today. Olaf had attached a sheaf of grain to a pole and stuck it in the ground fifty yards from the house.

" 'For the birds,' he said. 'It is a custom in the country of my people.'

"The boys laughed at him, pulled down the pole and scattered the grain. Olaf replaced the grain and the pole time after time. Finally the boys tired of the sport and left the pole standing. Later, however, Mike saw a bird fluttering around the grain, took a sling shot, and killed the bird. Olaf saw. He ran forward and touched the bird with gentle fingers; then he turned on Mike, his eyes flashing blue fire. He threw Mike to the ground and fell on him.

"The other boys, shocked by the fury of Olaf's rage, pulled at him.

" 'Stop! You'll kill him!' One of the boys cried.

"The madness and anger went from Olaf's eyes. He stood, a deep sadness swept over his face. 'I go now,' he said softly. 'I bring only unhappiness to this place. My heart is sick. When it heals, perhaps I will return.' Olaf buttoned his jacket around his neck and disappeared into the swirling snow.

"The boys were frightened as the storm developed into a blizzard. It was twenty miles to the nearest town. Olaf would surely die! They went to the rancher and told him.

"The rancher stood very straight. 'Where have I failed you, my sons?' And he saddled a horse and rode out into the storm, searching for Olaf.

"Darkness fell and he did not return. The boys saddled horses and formed a line to search, calling to each other so that none would be lost in the storm. After many hours they found the old rancher, fallen from his horse and half-buried in the snow. They wrapped him in their coats and carried him to a line shack that was used during roundup time. But the old man was burning up with fever; without medicine and warm food he would surely die.

"The boys drew lots to see who would go for help. The lot fell to Mike. He rode out, pulling his cap down against the blinding snow. Soon he was lost in a white world of darkness. But he rode on, hoping his horse would take him home. Then his horse shied at an unknown sound and he fell to the ground. He grabbed at his horse's reins, but his horse was gone. Mike stood and stumbled on. He prayed—this Mike who had never prayed before—prayed for strength to find help for his friends, and for the old rancher who had befriended them all. But after a long time, he knew his strength was gone. He stumbled and fell. Then his hands closed upon something—upon a pole standing above the snow. Attached to the top was a sheaf of grain. Olaf's pole! And Olaf's pole saved the life of the old rancher, for Mike found the ranch house and help was sent."

"What happened to those other boys?" the stranger asked.

Grandpa seemed lost in dreams so young Mike took up the story. "They changed after that. They settled down and tried to be good sons to the old rancher. Most of them are still living close by, and many of their children, too."

"That's the reason," Grandfather finished up, "for the sheaves of grain."

"So no trace was ever found of Olaf?" the stranger asked.

"No," young Mike said. "That's the part of the story I don't like—the ending."

The stranger chuckled softly. "How should it end?"

"Olaf should come back!" young Mike said. "He should come back and learn that he did not bring unhappiness, that because of him the boys gave up their wild ways!" Mike sighed. "Christmas stories should have happy endings!"

The stranger stood. He seemed to fill the room as he swept his cap from his head. His hair was snow white, but the unshaded light, hanging from the ceiling, turned it the color of sun-ripened wheat.

Young Mike's eyes were as wide as saucers and the only sound in the room was the soft hissing of the gas stove. Then Grandpa moved forward. His face was like an answered dream as he grasped the sea captain's extended hand.

"Olaf—Olaf!" Grandpa whispered.

Very softly, young Mike crept from the room. It seemed fitting, somehow, that the two old men should finish the telling of the story alone. But he smiled and hugged the happy ending to his heart.

Children's Friend, December 1966.

"I Would Be a Deacon"

BRYANT S. HINCKLEY

In a conversation with Dr. Creed Haymond, James A. Farley, who was Postmaster General under President Franklin Delano Roosevelt, said, "I am a Democrat of some national prominence, and Reed Smoot is a Republican; but I consider him to be the greatest diplomat in the United States Government. He knows more of what is going on, attends more meetings, and is a better authority on all that goes on than anyone else I know. I wish we had more men exactly like him.

"I have been reliably informed that Reed Smoot was offered the nomination for the presidency of the United States on the Republican ticket, if he would deny his faith— his being a Mormon would make it impossible for him to receive any such nomination."

Dr. Haymond continued: "Fifteen years later, Senator Smoot was in my office and during the conversation, I told him what James Farley had told me. He said, 'In two national Republican conventions, I was offered the nomination for President of the United States, if I could turn against my Church.'

"I said to him, 'Wouldn't it be worth it?'

242

"He whirled on me, took me by the arm, and said, 'Young man, maybe you do not know my stand in regard to my church. If I had to take my choice of being a deacon in The Church of Jesus Christ of Latter-day Saints or being the President of the United States, I would be a deacon."

Bryant S. Hinckley, *The Faith of Our Pioneer Fathers* (Deseret Book Co., 1956).

The Countess and the Impossible

RICHARD THURMAN

No one in our Utah town knew where the Countess had come from; her carefully precise English indicated that she was not a native American. From the size of her house and staff we knew that she must be wealthy, but she never entertained and she made it clear that when she was at home she was completely inaccessible. Only when she stepped outdoors did she become at all a public figure—and then chiefly to the small fry of the town, who lived in awe of her.

The countess always carried a cane, not only for support, but as a means of chastising any youngster she thought needed disciplining. And at one time or another most of the kids in our neighborhood seemed to display that need. By running fast and staying alert, I had managed to keep out of her reach.

But one day when I was about thirteen, as I was short-cutting through her hedge, she got close enough to rap my head with her stick.

"Ouch!" I yelled, jumping a couple of feet.

"Young man, I want to talk to you," she said. I was expecting a lecture on the evils of trespassing, but as she looked at me, half smiling, she seemed to change her mind.

244

"Don't you live in that green house with the willow trees in the next block?"

"Yes, ma'am."

"Good. I've lost my gardener. Be at my house Thursday morning at seven, and don't tell me you have something else to do; I've seen you slouching around on Thursdays."

When the Countess gave an order, it was carried out. I didn't dare not come on that next Thursday. I went over the whole lawn three times with a mower before she was satisfied, and then she had me down on all fours looking for weeds until my knees were as green as the grass. She finally called me up to the porch.

"Well, young man, how much do you want for your day's work?"

"I don't know. Fifty cents, maybe."

"Is that what you figure you're worth?"

"Yes'm. About that."

"Very well. Here's the fifty cents you say you're worth, and here's the dollar and a half more that I've earned for you by pushing you. Now I'm going to tell you something about how you and I are going to work together. There are as many ways of mowing a lawn as there are people, and they may be worth anywhere from a penny to five dollars. Let's say that a three-dollar job would be just what you have done today, except that you'd have to be something of a fool to spend that much time on a lawn. A five-dollar lawn is—well, it's impossible, so we'll forget about that. Now then, each week I'm going to pay you according to your own evaluation of your work."

I left with my two dollars, richer than I remembered being in my whole life, and determined that I would get four dollars out of her next week. But I failed to reach even the three–dollar mark. My will began to falter the second time around her yard.

"Two dollars again, eh? That kind of job puts you right on the edge of being dismissed, young man."

"Yes'm. But I'll do better next week."

And somehow I did. The last time around the lawn I was exhausted, but I found I could spur myself on. In the exhila-

ration of that new feeling, I had no hesitation in asking the
Countess for three dollars.

Each Thursday for the next four or five weeks, I varied
between a three- and a three-and-a-half dollar job. The more
I became more acquainted with her lawn, places where the
ground was a little high or a little low, places where it needed to be clipped short or left long on the edges to make a
more satisfying curve along the garden, the more I became
aware of just what a four-dollar lawn would consist of. And
each week I would resolve to do just that kind of a job. But
by the time I had made my three dollar or three-and-a-half
dollar mark I was too tired to remember even having had the
ambition to go beyond that.

"You look like a good consistent $3.50 man," she would
say as she handed me the money.

"I guess so," I would say, too happy at the sight of the
money to remember that I had shot for something higher.

"Well, don't feel too bad," she would comfort me. "After
all, there are only a handful of people in the world who could
do a four-dollar job."

And her words were a comfort at first, but then without
my noticing what was happening, her comfort became an
irritant that made me resolve to do that four-dollar job, even
if it killed me. In the fever of my resolve, I could see myself
expiring on her lawn, with the Countess leaning over me,
handing me the four dollars with a tear in her eye, begging
my forgiveness for having thought I couldn't do it.

It was in the middle of such a fever, one Thursday night
when I was trying to forget the day's defeat and get some
sleep, that the truth hit me so hard that I sat upright, half
choking in my excitement. It was the *five-dollar* job I had
to do, not the four-dollar one! I had to do the job that no one
could do because it was impossible.

I was well acquainted with the difficulties ahead. I had
the problem, for example, of doing something about the
worm mounds in the lawn. The Countess might not even
have noticed them yet, they were so small; but in my bare
feet I knew about them and I had to do something about
them. And I could go on trimming the garden edges with

shears, but I knew that a five-dollar lawn demanded that I line up each edge exactly with a yardstick and then trim it precisely with the edger. And there were other problems that only I and my bare feet knew about.

I started the next Thursday by ironing out the worm mounds with a heavy roller. After two hours of that I was ready to give up for the day. Nine o'clock in the morning, and my will was already gone! It was only by accident that I discovered how to regain it. Sitting under a walnut tree for a few minutes after finishing the rolling, I fell asleep. When I woke up minutes later, the lawn looked so good and felt so good under my feet, I was anxious to get on with the job.

I followed this secret for the rest of the day, dozing for a few minutes every hour to regain my perspective and replenish my strength. Between naps, I mowed four times— two times lengthwise, two times across, until the lawn looked like a green velvet checkerboard. Then I dug around every tree, crumbling the big clods and smoothing the soil with my hands, then finished with the edger, meticulously lining up each stroke so that the effect would be perfectly symmetrical. And I carefully trimmed the grass between the flagstones of the front walk. The shears wore my fingers raw, but the walk never looked better.

Finally about eight o'clock that evening it was all completed. I was so proud I didn't even feel tired when I went up to her door.

"Well, what is it today?" she asked.

"Five dollars," I said, trying for a little calm and sophistication.

"Five dollars? You mean four dollars, don't you? I told you that a five-dollar lawn job isn't possible."

"Yes it is. I just did it."

"Well, young man, the first five-dollar lawn in history certainly deserves some looking around."

We walked about the lawn together in the light of evening, and even I was quite overcome by the impossibility of what I had done.

"Young man," she said, putting her hand on my shoulder, "what on earth made you do such a crazy, wonderful thing?"

I didn't know why, but even if I had, I could not have explained it in the excitement of hearing that I had done it.

"I think I know," she continued, "how you felt, because the same thing happens to almost everyone. They feel this sudden burst in them of wanting to do some great thing. They feel a wonderful happiness, but then it passes because they have said, 'No, I can't do that. It's impossible.' Whenever something in you says, 'It's impossible,' remember to take a careful look and see if it isn't really God asking you to grow an inch, or a foot, or a mile, that you may come to a fuller life! . . ."

Since that time, some 25 years ago, when I have felt myself at an end with nothing before me, suddenly with the appearance of that word, "impossible," I have experienced the unexpected lift, the leap inside me, and known that the only possible way lay through the very middle of impossible.

Quoted in a talk by Vaughn J. Featherstone, *Conference Report,* October 1973. Reprinted by permission from *The Reader's Digest,* June 1958.

A Dog's Best Friend

LUCILE C. READING

A little boy sat on a New York subway one day. In his arms he held a miserable–looking Boston terrier. The dog had been hurt. Clumsy bandages tied around its leg showed that the boy had tried to doctor his pet. It was hard to tell which was the saddest-looking, the boy or the dog.

Across from them sat a big, rough-looking truck driver. He watched the boy and the dog for a few minutes, then turned to a man sitting next to him and asked, "Did you ever see such a sorry sight in your life?"

The man looked across the aisle and shook his head.

The little dog whined in pain, and the boy hugged the animal closer to him while a solitary tear slid down his cheek. This was too much for the truck driver. He leaned across the aisle. "What's the matter, sonny?" he questioned.

"My dog's been hurt," the boy answered. "Pop says I have to take him to the Humane Society because we haven't any money for a vet. And you know what I've heard? If he's hurt too bad, they'll gas him. Boy, have I been praying that he'll be all right."

The truck driver looked again at the dog, then at the people in the subway car. Finally he stood up. "Folks," he

249

called in a loud voice. The noise in the car stopped. The truck driver went on. "This boy has trouble. We're spending billions of dollars to help people all over the world. Let's spend a little to help a boy right here at home take care of his dog." He dropped something in his hat and handed it to the man next to him, who also dropped something into the hat and passed it on.

A few minutes later the hat returned to the truck driver, who squeezed it tight and then put it into the boy's hand. The boy looked at the people in amazement. He could hardly believe the money was all for him. Then be breathed a fervent, "Thank you, mister, and thanks to everybody, too."

The dog whimpered. He almost seemed to understand that now he would have a chance to live.

_____

Children's Friend, May 1964.

"Well, Mary, the Cattle Are Gone"

JOSEPH F. SMITH

We camped one evening in an open prairie on the Missouri River bottoms, by the side of a small spring creek which emptied into the river about three quarters of a mile from us. We were in plain sight of the river and could apparently see over every foot of the little open prairie where we were camped, to the river on the southwest, to the bluffs on the northwest, and to the timber which skirted the prairie on the right and left. Camping nearby, on the other side of the creek, were some men with a herd of beef cattle.

We usually unyoked our oxen and turned them loose to feed during our encampments at night, but this time, on account of the proximity of this herd of cattle, fearing that they might get mixed up and driven off with them, we turned our oxen out to feed in their yokes. Next morning when we came to look them up, to our great disappointment our best yoke of oxen was not to be found. Uncle Joseph Fielding and I spent all the morning, well nigh until noon, hunting for them, but to no avail. The grass was tall, and in the morning was wet with heavy dew. Tramping through this grass and through the woods and over the bluff, we were soaked to the skin, fatigued, disheartened, and almost exhausted.

In this pitiable plight I was the first to return to our wagons, and as I approached I saw my mother kneeling down to prayer. I halted for a moment and then drew gently near enough to hear her pleading with the Lord not to suffer us to be left in this helpless condition, but to lead us to recover our lost team, that we might continue our travels in safety. When she arose from her knees I was standing near-by. The first expression I caught upon her precious face was a lovely smile which, discouraged as I was, gave me renewed hope and an assurance I had not felt before. A few moments later Uncle Joseph Fielding came to the camp, wet with the dews, faint, fatigued, and thoroughly disheartened. His first words were: "Well, Mary, the cattle are gone!"

Mother replied in a voice that fairly rang with cheerfulness, "Never mind; your breakfast has been waiting for hours, and now, while you and Joseph are eating, I will just take a walk out and see if I can find the cattle."

My uncle held up his hands in blank astonishment, and if the Missouri River had suddenly turned to run upstream, neither of us could have been much more surprised. "Why, Mary," he exclaimed, "what do you mean? We have been all over this country, all through the timber and through the herd of cattle, and our oxen are gone—they are not to be found. I believe they have been driven off, and it is useless for you to attempt to do such a thing as to hunt for them."

"Never mind me," said Mother; "get your breakfast and I will see," and she started toward the river, following down spring creek. Before she was out of speaking distance the man in charge of the herd of beef cattle rode up from the opposite side of the creek and called out: "Madam, I saw your oxen over in that direction about daybreak," pointing in the opposite direction from that in which Mother was going.

We heard plainly what he said, but Mother went right on and did not even turn her head to look at him. A moment later the man rode off rapidly toward his herd, which had been gathered in the opening near the edge of the woods, and they were soon under full drive for the road leading toward Savannah and soon disappeared from view.

My mother continued straight down the little stream of water until she stood almost on the bank of the river. And then she beckoned to us. I was watching her every movement and was determined that she should not get out of my sight. Instantly we rose from the "mess-chest" in which our breakfast had been spread and started toward her. And like John, who outran the other disciple to the sepulchre, I outran my uncle and came first to the spot where my mother stood. There I saw our oxen fastened to a clump of willows growing in the bottom of a deep gulch that had been washed out of the sandy bank of the river by the little spring creek, perfectly concealed from view. We were not long in releasing them from bondage and getting back to our camp, where the other cattle had been fastened to the wagon wheels all the morning. And we were soon on our way home rejoicing.

Life of Joseph F. Smith (Deseret Book Co., 1969).

Christmas in Pioneer Times

AUTHOR UNKNOWN

I remember our first Christmas in the Valley. We all worked as usual. The men gathered sagebrush and some even plowed, for though it had snowed, the ground was still soft, and the plows were used the entire day. Christmas came on Saturday. We celebrated the day on the Sabbath, when all gathered around the flagpole in the center of the fort, and there we held a meeting. And what a meeting it was. We sang praise to God, we all joined in the opening prayer, and the speaking that day has always been remembered. There were words of thanksgiving and cheer. Not a pessimistic word was uttered. The people were hopeful and buoyant, because of their faith in the great undertaking. After the meeting, there was handshaking all around. Some wept with joy. The children played in the enclosure, and around the sagebrush fire that night we gathered and sang:

"Come, come, ye saints,
No toil nor labor fear,
But with joy wend your way."

That day we had boiled rabbit and a little bread for our dinner. Father had shot some rabbits, and it was a feast we had. All had enough to eat. In a sense of perfect peace and good will toward all men, I never had a happier Christmas in my life.

The principal thing was to get together enough food for a dinner, for it was very scarce that winter. I think the people met as families and friends in the fort. I went to my mother's house. She lived in a little log room behind where the Bee Hive House now stands. To me that one log room looked like a palace. It was so grand to have a home with a roof over our heads. I remember that we gathered all of the good things we could to make a dinner. Mother made a cake, which was a very unusual thing to have. Little Isaac Perry Decker, about seven years old, ate so much dinner before the cake was cut and served that he looked at it almost crying and said, "Mother, what shall I do? I can't eat it!" His voice was full of regret, for he loved cake and had not had a piece for a long time. Mother said, "Well, you can save it until tomorrow." Little Perry's face brightened up with the thought that he could really eat the cake another time.

The Christmas of 1848 found the Saints with much more of a variety of things for their Christmas dinner. Some had wild duck or prairie chicken and a little cake. Although sugar was scarce, some molasses had been made by squeezing cornstalks and making what they called "cornstalk molasses." Serviceberries and chokecherries had been gathered from the canyons, and pies were made of these. Some gingerbread was mixed and made into various shapes to please the children. They were indeed happy with this cake, and they did not even think of looking for more. The families in the fort generally organized themselves into groups for dinner so that all might have share of the good things.

My first Christmas dinner in Utah was partaken of in 1848 in the old fort, at my Uncle Daniel's table. It was customary for everybody to cook the best they had on such occasions.

Plenty of vegetables had been raised and corn dried in the fall, and I am sure there must have been some kind of dessert. Our fruit consisted of serviceberries and chokecherries, which we gathered in the canyons.

In the early days sugar was scarce, and molasses was

made from sugarcane, watermelons, and frozen squashes, the juices having been boiled down into a syrup.

Our amusements consisted mostly of dancing and having concerts. These exercises were always opened and closed with prayer. We never lacked for music or musicians, for we had both brass and martial bands.

As there was not money to buy presents, suitable mottoes were worked out on cardboard; gloves and mittens were knitted; and crochet work done. Rag dolls were made and dressed for the little girls, and sleds and wagons were made for the boys. The stockings were generally filled with home-made molasses candy, popcorn, sometimes a popcorn ball, a fried cake. These made the children very happy.

Our neighbors were remembered on that day by sending them some of our fare, or inviting them to eat with us. The poor were always remembered in a substantial way. The people raised their own beef and pork, and I think there was never a pig or a beef killed without a piece being sent to the nearest neighbors.

As the years went by, food and money were more easily obtained, and as a result the Christmas celebrations were a little more elaborate. As the menu for Christmas dinner in the various homes differs at the present time, so did it in the early days. Some had chicken or duck, others had pork or rabbit pie. Some had pumpkin pie or squash pie for dessert, others had currant or vinegar pie, while others had plum pudding made with spices, dried currants, and serviceberries.

For years, however, there were many families that did not have stockings to hang up on Christmas Eve, and the presents they received were laid on the mantel or by the plates at the breakfast table. In the families where the children did have stockings, they were hung on the mantel or on a string extending from the mantel to some article of furniture. The presents consisted of dried serviceberries and a little molasses candy, popcorn, etc. In later years the children found a few dried peaches, or apples, or a bow of ribbon. Sometimes the girls received hair ornaments made of velvet ribbon trimmed with beads. Hats made of braided wheat straw, and toys carved out of wood were also among the presents.

The fried cakes that were also important at Christmas time were made of saleratus, sour milk, and flour. The saleratus was obtained by the fathers and brothers from the shores of the Great Salt Lake. This was placed in water so that the sand which was scraped up with it would settle to the bottom. A certain quantity of this water was poured with sour milk and mixed with the flour, and rolled out on a board. The dough was cut in long strips, twisted, the ends fastened together and put in the hot fat to brown. The fat used was carefully saved bit by bit for days and days before Christmas. While the most fortunate Saints were enjoying the Christmas day with their families, they were not forgetting those in poverty or sickness. A bag of flour, a piece of pork, or a bit of cake was sent to the poor. The sick were given extra good food and special attention. The children ran from house to house shouting, 'Christmas gift! Christmas gift!' although they did not expect a single gift to be given. They loved the joy that comes from mingling with each other.

A Story to Tell (Deseret Book Co., 1971).

"In the Death of Your Mamma"

HEBER J. GRANT

My wife Lucy was very sick for nearly three years prior to her death. At one time I was in the hospital with her for six months.

When she was dying, I called my children into the bedroom and told them their mamma was dying. My daughter Lutie said she did not want her mamma to die and insisted that I lay hands upon her and heal her, saying that she had often seen her mother, when sick in the hospital in San Francisco, suffering intensely, go to sleep immediately and have a peaceful night's rest when I had blessed her. I explained to my children that we all had to die some time, and that I felt that their mamma's time had come.

The children went out of the room, and I knelt down by the bed of my dying wife and told the Lord that I acknowledged his hand in life or in death, in joy or in sorrow, in prosperity or adversity; that I did not complain because my wife was dying, but that I lacked the strength to see my wife die and have her death affect the faith of my children in the ordinances of the gospel. I then pleaded with the Lord

258

to give to my daughter Lutie a testimony that it was his will that her mother should die.

Within a few short hours, my wife breathed her last. Then I called the children into the bedroom and announced that their mamma was dead. My little boy Heber commenced weeping bitterly, and Lutie put her arms around him and kissed him, and told him not to cry, that the voice of the Lord had said to her, "In the death of your mamma the will of the Lord will be."

Lutie knew nothing of my prayers, and this manifestation to her was a direct answer to my supplication to the Lord, and for it I have never ceased to be grateful.

Heber J. Grant, "When Great Sorrows Are Our Portion," *Improvement Era*, June 1912.

What Manner of Man Was This Joseph Smith?

LEON R. HARTSHORN

It is a warm day—the date, June 29, 1844. A boat is approaching a horseshoe bend in the Mississippi River. Situated prominently on that bend is a city. A traveler seeks to identify the city from his map, but the map, which was printed a few years previously, shows no such city. Upon inquiry the interested traveler is told that the city is Nauvoo and that the boat would make a brief stop there.

As the boat docks, the traveler becomes curious as to why long lines of people are waiting to enter a large home on the river front. Being in no hurry to reach his destination, he informs the captain that he is going to remain in Nauvoo for a few hours, or perhaps overnight.

As the visitor approaches the end of the line, it becomes apparent that these are grief-stricken people. All of the ladies and many of the men are weeping. The stranger approaches one of the mourners and inquires, "Excuse me, but what are these lines for; what are you waiting to see?"

The mourner looks at him in amazement. "You mean you don't know?"

"I'm a stranger here. I just arrived on the boat," he answers, pointing in the direction of the pier.

"Oh, I see," replies the mourner. "These people and myself are waiting to view the bodies of Lieutenant General Joseph Smith and his brother Hyrum Smith, who were killed two days ago."

"Lieutenant General Smith?" the visitor asks.

"Yes, he was the lieutenant general of a legion of five thousand men, most of them uniformed and equipped."

"How many others were killed with them?" asks the stranger.

"None," replies the mourner. "This is perhaps one of the reasons why Joseph died. He believed that it was his life that was wanted and that if he died, the lust for blood would be satisfied and others would not be killed. He wanted his brother Hyrum to live, but Hyrum insisted that he be by the side of his brother. 'In life they were not divided, and in death they were not separated.'"

The traveler asks, "How did the trouble that led to their deaths begin?"

"The most immediate cause was the destruction of the printing press of the *Nauvoo Expositor*," replies the mourner. "The *Expositor* was owned by the enemies of Joseph Smith, and they published a libelous paper. An order to close the paper was issued by the city council and the mayor, Joseph Smith."

"Joseph Smith was the mayor of this city?"

"Yes, he was," comes the reply.

"This is a very new city, isn't it?" says the stranger. "Why, it isn't even on my map."

"Yes, yes, it is new. Why, just six years ago this was nothing but a swamp."

The traveler says, "It is a beautiful city. I noticed as I came up the river that most of the farms and corrals are outside of town."

"Yes, this is the way Joseph planned the city."

"Joseph planned this city?" repeats the stranger.

"Yes, so that the people, who are mostly farmers, could have the advantages of city life by all living together—so that we might associate together and learn from each other."

The traveler comments on the wide, straight streets and the well–built houses. He also tells the mourner that he has seen a large white building apparently under construction. The building is on the most prominent rise of land in the city. The mourner informs the visitor that the building is the temple and that Joseph Smith had designed it to be the dominant landmark in the city.

"Joseph Smith designed the temple!" the stranger exclaims.

"Yes, Joseph designed it," comes the reply.

The traveler then remembers something. "You were telling me what led to the death of this Joseph Smith."

"Oh, yes, the *Expositor* incident. But the trouble began a long time ago, long before that incident, even before Joseph translated the ancient record."

"He was a translator of ancient languages?" repeats the visitor. "How many languages did he know?"

"I am not certain," replies the mourner, "but he knew Hebrew, German, and Egyptian."

"What happened to this translation of the ancient record?" questions the traveler.

"It has been published and it is called the Book of Mormon."

"Has he published any other books?"

"Oh, yes, as president of the Church."

"President of the Church?"

"Yes, president of The Church of Jesus Christ of Latter-day Saints. Almost everyone here in Nauvoo is a member of the Church. As I was saying," continues the mourner, "as president of the Church, he published the Doctrine and Covenants."

"What kind of book is that?" asks the amazed visitor.

"It is a book of revelations that were given to the Prophet Joseph Smith by the Lord."

"The *Prophet* Joseph Smith!"

"Yes, he was a prophet. God the Father and Jesus Christ appeared to him and conversed with him. In fact, it was after Joseph, full of joy and boyish enthusiasm, told his neighbors that he had seen a vision that the persecution first began. Not only was Joseph persecuted, but also all of his followers. Why, many of the people you see about you here were driven from homes in Missouri. None of us were paid for our losses. Joseph tried in vain to obtain redress, but we were refused. That is the principal reason that Joseph became a candidate for the presidency of the United States."

"A candidate for the presidency of the United States!" the bewildered traveler exclaims.

The mourner continues: "It was four days ago that Joseph bid a reluctant farewell to his family, looked longingly at the temple and then at his farm, and said, 'This is the loveliest place and the best people under the heavens,' as he rode toward the county seat at Carthage to turn himself over to his enemies. He said to those who accompanied him, 'I am going like a lamb to the slaughter, but I am as calm as a summer's morning.' He was promised protection and a fair trial, but two days ago, on June 27th, a band of over one hundred men with blackened faces stormed the Carthage jail. A few moments later they retreated, and Lieutenant General Joseph Smith and his faithful brother, Hyrum, lay dead."

The traveler views the body, his face registering surprise and disbelief. He speaks almost silently, "This is Joseph Smith!" He sees a young man, a handsome man with a prominent nose and a slightly receding forehead. He is stunned; he had expected to see an old man with white hair and a long flowing beard and a face drawn and wrinkled with age. He quietly whispers to the mourner, "How old was he?"

In a subdued tone comes the reply, "He was thirty-eight years of age."

As the traveler looks almost in disbelief, he thinks, "Lieutenant general, linquist, translator, author, mayor, prophet, president, city planner, architect, presidential candidate— *what manner of man was this Joseph Smith?*"

The silence is interrupted as a man in the corner of the room asks for the attention of the group and says, "My dear brothers and sisters, it is five o'clock. We would like to clear the room so that the loved ones of those deceased can view the bodies for the last time."

As the traveler and the mourner make their way out through the open door, the traveler stops to shake the mourner's hand and to thank him. When he reaches the gate he turns and begins walking in the direction of the temple.

As he walks, the same question escapes his lips: "*What manner of man was this Joseph Smith?*"

He continues up the street and is lost from view.

Leon R. Hartshorn, *Joseph Smith, Prophet of the Restoration* (Deseret Book Co., 1970). Note: The historical facts in this story are correct; the author has created a visitor and a mourner to make the information more interesting to the reader.

Index